Cast of

Reginald Fortune. A deceptively amiab

General Duddon. Except that he believes that giants once walked in England, a sensible enough man and Reggie's considerate host.

Seymour. The supercilious chief constable of Durshire.

Cope. A shrewed, genial banker who dressses and thinks like his own grandfather.

Jim Tracy. A hard-drinking, ill-tempered man, owner of the finest estate in the country, whose young son Charles disappeared ten years earlier.

Alison Tracy. His lovely redhaired daughter.

Francis Aston. His once-imposing estate is nearly in ruins and he's in danger of losing everything. There is no love lost between him and Jim Tracy.

Mrs. Aston. His wife, the owner of some very fine diamonds.

Giles Aston. Their son, who is in love with Alison.

William Brown. A newly rich millionaire who with Tracy is trying to buy up all the best land in the county. He and his wife are anxious to see Giles and Alison wed.

Superintendent Bubb. Second in command to Seymour and his successor. He may be brighter than Seymour but is no more effective at his job.

Lomas. Head of Scotland Yard's CID and Reggie's staunch friend and ally.

Miss Brabazon. Proprietress of Ye Catte's Cradle, an antiques shop.

Elijah Hawke. Jim Tracy's surly gamekeeper.

Lord Werne. The local squire.

Inspector Underwood. One of Scotland Yard's finest.

Plus assorted policemen, servants, and villagers.

Black Land, White Land

A Mr. Fortune novel by
H.C. Bailey

Rue Morgue Press
Boulder / Lyons

978-1-60187-029-2

Rue Morgue Press

87 Lone Tree Lane

Lyons CO 80540

www.ruemorguepress.com

800-699-6214

Printed by Johnson Printing

Boulder, Colorado

PRINTED IN THE UNITED STATES OF AMERICA

H.C. Bailey

The first Mr. Fortune stories by H.C. Bailey appeared in book form in the early 1920s at the same time that Arthur Conan Doyle was publishing what would be the final adventures of Sherlock Holmes. Just as Holmes was at his best in the shorter form—with the grand exception of *The Hound of the Baskervilles*—Reggie Fortune was, for the most part, more successful with readers when taken in short doses. Perhaps no other major fictional detective of the Golden Age appeared in as many short stories as the cherubic country doctor turned detective. Starting with *Call Mr. Fortune* in 1920 and ending with *Mr. Fortune Here* in 1940, Bailey published an astonishing twelve collections of Fortune short stories, not counting three omnibus collections of previously published material.

While Bailey was considered one of the five most important British mystery writers of the Golden Age (roughly 1913 to 1953), he is perhaps less well-known today than his contemporaries, no doubt because he made his reputation on the basis of his short stories, a form no longer as popular as in Bailey's lifetime. His American publisher, the Doubleday Crime Club, was certainly one of his biggest fans, referring to his second Fortune novel, *Black Land, White Land*, as "unquestionably the finest mystery story of his career. And as Reggie Fortune is already established as one of the leading fictional detectives of all time, and since the mantle of immortality which has previously cloaked only Sir Conan Doyle and Edgar Allan Poe must also be applied to H.C. Bailey, it can be said that this is possibly one of the outstanding detective stories of our time."

The Pulitzer Prize-winning poet, Stephen Vincent Benet was no less a fan, writing: "Perhaps Mr. Reginald Fortune comes nearest to the dream of all good detective-story readers—the dream of the lamp lit again in Baker Street, the fog settling down outside and Watson smoking his pipe by the fire when the knock comes at the door. Not that Fortune is in any sense an imitation of Holmes—he is a distinct and admirable creation, with his individual mannerisms and methods. When he says, as he sometimes does, 'not a nice murder, Lomas,' one feels the cold and authentic shiver in the spine."

Born in London on February 1, 1878, Henry Christopher Bailey attended

City of London School, a highly regarded day school which produced a very large number of nationally known writers, scholars and scientists (it was the first school in England to offer courses in chemistry). The school also enjoyed a unique relationship with journalism and publishing firms. In his last year, Bailey was named Head of School, responsible for out-of-school discipline and representing the school at official events.

Having won a scholarship to Oxford's Corpus Christi College, he was a classics scholar studying Latin and Greek language, literature and history. Small in stature (his pictures make him look a little like the actor Barry Fitzgerald of *Going My Way* fame), he was ideally suited to coxswain his college's eight-man rowing team. He took a first-class honors degree and went to work as a correspondent for the *Daily Telegraph*, a leading Tory newspaper of the time. He worked there as a drama critic, a war correspondent and as a leader (editorial) writer.

After he retired from journalism in 1946, Bailey and his wife Lydia moved to North Wales and took up residence at Bernina, a house built as a holiday residence by Lydia's father. It was at Bernina that Bailey died on March 24, 1961, at the age of 83, having published his last novel, *Shrouded Death*, eleven years earlier.

For more information on Bailey see Tom and Enid Schantz' introduction to the Rue Morgue Press edition of *Shadow on the Wall*.

CHAPTER I *Evidence of a Giant*

IN THE OPINION of Mr. Fortune this case was his first masterpiece. He will explain, when allowed, that he had not before matured the confidence in his own ability to rearrange the wicked world which is the birthright of the natural man.

If his explanations are permitted to continue, he shows a singular affection for the case, inspired by the primeval, savage force of its sequence of evil. The first cause of it lay far off in the building of the earth. It was the harvest of the warfare of thousands of years of men for the earth's good things. Those who worked out the catastrophe were driven on by an inheritance of immemorial greed and hate and enchained therein. So, given lives to live out in the cheerful peace of the friendliest of twentieth-century countrysides, they achieved their horrors. Mr. Fortune compares them to the tortured souls who agonize in the family histories of which the Greeks made tragedy, creatures of inexorable fate, doomed by a curse of blood. After which he will point out modestly that he was like the god who comes on a machine at the end of the tragedy and clears up the mess, only he came soon enough to be of some use.

When he came, he did not know that there was a tragedy in need of his assistance. Yet the summons which he obeyed had an element of fate, a source remote in the way the earth was built. Not only the malignant poison of the case but the final antidote of his presence are thus ascribed by him to the nature of things. If the coast of Durshire had not been constructed of chalk with sand in it as well as the dark lias, there would have been a different case or none; the cliffs would not crack and split; they would not have made a landslip in that wet Christmastide, and General Duddon would not then have found the bones of his giant.

The other element in the summons was the mind of General Duddon. Nothing of the inevitability of fate can be discovered about that. It is magnificently inconsequent. Soldiers say that he was a brilliant leader of cavalry. He now divides his energies between the working of acres of embroidery and

belief in the desperately incredible. For exercise of the latter hobby he prefers the past. Mr. Fortune was first attracted to him by a row in which his
proof that Noah's flood formed the Atlantic excited chaste and orthodox
men of science to frenzy. Friendship became affectionate when the general
revealed a fine taste in sweets.

Among the articles of General Duddon's faith it is laid down that the world
was once inhabited by giants. For evidence of this he quotes first the authority of the book of Genesis, that the sons of God married the daughters of
men, and "there were giants in the earth in those days." But he draws his
proof from the county of Durshire, where he has set up house. Durshire has
produced impressive remains of the extinct reptiles which poetry calls "dragons of the prime." General Duddon also calls them dragons and considers it
a clear and certain inference that there were giants in Durshire to fight them.
For the final confusion of the dull skeptic he points to the hillside whereon
the turf has been cut away, no one knows when, to leave the white figure of
a "Long Man," obviously a portrait monument of the giants who won the
land from the reptile beasts, and to the pits in the summit of the chalk above
the valley which, everyone knows, are Giants' Graves.

All this had been often heard by Mr. Fortune, who gave it demure encour-
agement to lead his general upon further flights. He was rewarded beyond
hope when, emerging from a family Christmas, he found among the bills of
the end of the year an excited letter and disentangled from it the announce-
ment that in the fall of a landslip beyond the Haunches, General Duddon had
found a giant's bones.

Mr. Fortune whistled "God rest ye merry, gentlemen, let nothing you dis-
may." With the simple purpose of amusing himself, he telegraphed accep-
tance of the general's invitation to come and see the discovery. It is one of
his favorite examples of the rule that you never know what you are doing.

The breakfast car express to Durshire is neither swift nor popular. Mr.
Fortune chose it because of all railway meals he finds breakfast least de-
pressing. But he was in a state of pensive meditation when he rejected the
marmalade and went back to the Colsbury portion of the train. Its compart-
ments were sparsely inhabited. The occupants who looked at him showed
the right English loathing of another traveler. Somebody had done better.
The blinds of one compartment were drawn.

Reggie resisted the impulse to look at the corpse and subsided into his
solitary seat and smoked himself to sleep. When he woke, the landscape of
Durshire was sliding by in slow time under the pale December sunshine.
Plowland glistened dark with an oily sheen, the pasture's winter grass was
rich and full of cattle. Nothing but great trees broke the flat for miles, but the
distance was shut in by bare whaleback hills which loomed gray.

Their round shoulders stood close when the train crossed a river of wide, black mudbanks and sluggish water, swirling like greasy ink, and drew up in Colsbury station.

Reggie had hardly shown his round face at the carriage window when he heard a shrill cry: "Fortune!"

General Duddon was considered by his regiment to look like a pious jockey. He is one of the smallest of men; he has the voice of a sea gull and the gait of an earnest terrier. Making the most of these advantages, he came through the legs of porters and populace—they are very social at Colsbury—and fell upon Reggie and his suitcase, talking nineteen to the dozen.

So good of Reggie to come down—that was the first five hundred words—the most marvelous find ever made—that was working up to the thousand before they reached his car. In the midst of it Reggie's wandering eyes observed that the compartment in which the blinds had been drawn was emitting a man. He had waited till everyone else was on the platform; he turned from the way out and was hidden in a waiting room. Reggie had only a glimpse of a big pink face, but it seemed sorry for itself.

"You want to go over the ground at once," General Duddon told him, making one word of it. "We'll just have a sandwich at the club and drive straight out; lot of old women but not a bad place." He thrust the car, hooting, to its portico.

In the hall of dowdy, musty comfort men were drinking sherry. The little general, leading Reggie through them at the double, was hailed facetiously: "Hallo! Here's Jack the giant killer. What's the price of giants today? Any more on offer? Buyers shy?"

These jests came from a group of three. The general stopped. "Oh no, somebody knows something, but not you, begad. Ever hear of Mr. Reginald Fortune, Seymour?" He glanced up at a bald man who wore the clothes and the manner of the supercilious official. "This is our chief constable, Fortune," he sneered, and trotted on to the dining room without waiting for the how-d'ye-do's. The three were not hospitable to Reggie.

"There, that's the level of intelligence down here," the general fumed, and screamed for sandwiches and sherry. "Snob and a job that fellow Seymour—snob and a job. The fellow who called me 'Jack the giant killer'—did you notice him? He's the county wit, Cope is; quite a sound fellow; banker; his family have had the bank here for a century, and he still dresses like his grandfather and thinks the same way: not an idea beyond money and a horse."

Reggie nodded. Mr. Cope looked it. A plump, dark person, he was picturesque in his double-breasted broadcloth; his bird's-eye cravat with a fox-tooth pin and the leather chin strap to his watch pocket completed the horsy harmony. But neither horsy bankers nor supercilious policemen interested Reggie so much as the ham in the sandwiches. That had character.

His general went on to curse the third of the humorists. That redhaired fellow with the poker face, that was Tracy, nasty, sour mind, always out to hurt. Ah, well, let him go, poor devil, best estate in the county and no pleasure in life for him; he had his own hell.

Reggie let him go without objection, and the general was happy in a fairytale reconstruction of the age of giants in Durshire. This still continued as they drove away from the prim streets of Colsbury to the scene of his discovery. The road led down the valley, through flat, dark fields. Seaward and westward the land rose to chalk hills. Over Reggie's round face came the wondering pleasure of a child at the delusions of the grown-up as the general explained that the fields were made by tropical forests inhabited by huge dragons, while the giants grew up on the hills. He was only hundreds of millions of years out in his facts, and he was beautifully happy, and it became more than ever interesting to speculate where he would get to.

But all of a sudden he came down with a bump on reality. "Black land and white land, d'ye notice?" He pointed from the dark fields to the white glare of a chalk pit. "Now it's a very striking thing, there's a proverb in Durshire, black land and white land, always at strife, and begad you'll find it's the eternal truth of the place. The black land's devilish rich, the best farming you could have, corn or cattle, and the chalk's good for nothing but sheep, so everybody who has come here has fought to get the black land and shove the other fellow out. That's in history; you read about it in all the troubles and civil wars and conquests—Normans and Saxons and Celts—and devil a doubt the Celts fought the stone-age people and the cave men for it. Don't tell me that isn't behind everything, black land and white land."

"I don't. No," Reggie purred. "Greed. Struggle for life. And so man is an advancer. To some divine far-off event."

"Look at that place." The general pointed to a great house which frowned over the black land in ponderous masses of dark stone, long pillared front, towered wings. That was Puxdon Court, Tracy's place. The Tracys came in with the Normans and grabbed the best bit of the valley, and they had been grabbing more ever since, always on the winning side. Then there were the Astons; they traced back to Saxon times. They'd owned a lot of the black land, on and off, but they were pushed out to the edge years ago, and old Aston had hardly a free acre left, poor devil. That brute Tracy laid a bet he couldn't carry on another year.

The road began to climb. "White land now," the general lectured. "You notice the chalk hills come round; they make a ridge all along the coast. Elstow Manor, Aston's place, is just here on the ridge."

Reggie saw a gracious Elizabethan house, the stone of which glowed mellow in a symmetry of curving windows. But dingy blinds blocked most of the glass, and only one wisp of smoke rose from its chimneys. The parkland which sloped from it was bare of timber. Its gatehouse stood empty and ruinous, and the gates lay against it, off their hinges. "Pity, you know; damnable pity," the general squeaked. "A lovely place, past saving now. I don't know how Aston can bear to see it. He ought to have sold years ago, but he's crazy with pride; rather let the whole property crash than part with anything. There it is."

They drove on over the flat top of the ridge to the pale gleam of the sea. In a little while the general stopped the car. "Now then, we'll cut across, Fortune. I'll show you the cliffs above the landslip and you'll see how it went, and then we'll get down to it. That's the way." He scurried on over rough turf. They had come in sight of the foam on the beach and turbid water when he checked. "Why, there's a fellow been at the place. Who is it?" A tall man appeared on the cliff and a woman followed him. They paced slowly along the edge. General Duddon went on faster than ever, and after a minute screamed, "Hallo, Aston, hallo!"

Man and woman started round and stared. Reggie saw again the ravaged good-looks of the shy man of the train and the station. "Ha, Duddon," he called out in a tone of dreary contempt, and touched his hat and took the woman on.

"Have you found anything more?" the general cried.

"What do you take me for?" A peevish laugh came back.

"There you are," the general complained to Reggie. "There's Aston. You see—"

"Yes, I did take him for that," Reggie said.

"Nobody here has a mind to grasp any serious matter," the general went on. "Now look—as we get near the shore you see the whole cliff is unstable." Cracks opened in the turf, some slight, some broad clefts, in the depths of which could be seen the mixed structure of the cliff, chalk with bands and pockets of gravel and something like dark clay at the bottom. The general proceeded to a lecture, and Reggie's patience failed and he summed up curtly:

"Yes. As you say. Quite clear. Chalk and gravels resting on blue lias. Rain soaks through till it gets down to the lias and can't go any farther, so it breaks out of the cliff face, washing the gravels through with it, and makes cavities, and the cliff cracks. That's going on all the time. When you have a long spell of heavy rain, the gravel is rushed out fast and there may be a landslip of some size. Now let's look at the results."

General Duddon's mouth was not to be shut. As they picked their way down a greasy, broken path to the beach he instructed Reggie that those deep gravels were very ancient, laid down close upon the time of the huge reptiles, the dragons, and when there was a great earth movement you couldn't set any limit to what might be revealed.

"Oh no. I wouldn't. I don't," Reggie said, while gulls, startled from the cliff face by their coming, screamed in the same key as his general.

CHAPTER II *Evidence of an Elephant*

THEY CAME TO THE BEACH and the spread of the landslip—a hundred yards of shapeless mounds of chalk and sand falling into mud which made the rising tide a pale yellowish soup.

"What a mess!" Reggie stood still in contemplation. "Glimpse of the awful past. As it was in the beginning. The earth was without form and void and the waters moved on the face of the earth. However. Where did you dig out your giant?"

The general scrambled over the heaps toward the torn cliffside, explaining fast. He had come out as soon as he heard of the slip and searched the whole mass, but especially the stuff next to the cliff, that came from the deepest levels. There, close up there, he had seen the big bone sticking out. Not bad work, was it? Lucky, of course, but, begad, he'd used his luck. He brought a couple of men out quick and had the gravel round dug up and taken to his place.

Reggie wandered about, looking close at the gravel which remained, poked into it, picked up fragments. "Quite old stuff, yes," he murmured. "Forest-bed gravel. Might get very curious things." His round face had a look of bewildered surprise.

General Duddon laughed. "Aha, I knew you'd be keen. I have, begad. Come along now, and I'll show you." He trotted away, but Reggie was slower, examining with intent and wistful eyes a small handful of gravel. When they reached the car he put this into an envelope with care. "Taking a sample of the earth? That's right," the general approved.

"Yes. Exhibit A," Reggie said.

They drove on along the ridge parallel with the sea, and the general was still instructive. Those two lumps of cliff were the Haunches. That ghastly new house in concrete like a white gasometer—Brown, the cheap stores millionaire, put that up; people barred him like the devil for it. He was out to buy the county—an absolute outsider, of course—but you could live with him. He had bought all the land along the coast there and a devilish good thing too; no trouble about getting leave from him to dig in the landslip. If it had been Aston's ground, not a chance—and it used to be Aston's till the mortgagees foreclosed on the farms there and sold, and Aston was like a bear with a sore head about it still.

Deuced funny business, really. Those two old county fellows, Aston and

Tracy, hating like cat and dog. Tracy tried to buy the farms to spite Aston, Bill Brown butted in and snapped them up under his nose, and Tracy was mad with him, and so was old Aston, and both of 'em loathed each other worse than ever, and Brown went on to have a game making up to Aston's son and Tracy's daughter. He had a way with him, the bounder, and he knew how to make money talk.

The winding dark water of the river Cole opened out before them. "This is the end of the chalk, where the river works into the sea," the general continued. "Just up above are the pits of Giants' Graves. All fits in, doesn't it? Now we're looking down from the white land to the black land again. And here we are." He turned the car into a drive between hydrangeas which led to a red-brick villa. "Just a spot, and we'll go to the workshop."

Reggie was taken to a large wooden hut with equipment of quaint variety. On the concrete floor lay a mass of earth. Reggie was bustled round it to a worktable. "There!" General Duddon squeaked in triumph. In enameled iron dishes lay lumps of diverse shapes and sizes and shades of yellowish red. "I had the deuce of a trouble extracting them. They're so fragile with age, they break at a touch. But they are bones, aren't they?—and the fellow must have been gigantic."

"Yes, I think so," Reggie murmured. He took up the largest lump and scraped at the gravel on it. "No probable possible shadow of doubt. Real old bone. Owner on a large scale."

"Enormous, eh? That's a thigh bone, isn't it, and only a bit?"

"As you say. Fragment of leg." Reggie was working at the other lumps with minute care and study, but as the examination proceeded, his intent face became plaintive and dreamy. He arranged the lumps in separate divisions and contemplated the result sorrowfully. "Well, well!" he sighed and turned to the general with a look of bewildered reproach. "You have found something." He took up two of the smaller lumps. "What did you make of these?"

"Aha, they're very interesting," the general chuckled. "That's a bit of his spine, what? And the other must be a tooth, a huge tooth. How big do you think the fellow was, Fortune?"

"Very extensive creature. That is a vertebra, yes. But it came from a tail. Sorry. And the other is a tooth, but not human. Owner was an elephant. Not one of the elephants now living—"

"I should think not," the general squeaked.

"Oh no. No. Elephas meridionalis. Long extinct. Very sorry to disappoint you. But you have done extraordinarily well. It's a wonderful find. Museum pieces."

This anxiety to break the general's fall was superfluous. The bones of an extinct elephant, it became swiftly clear, were just as good evidence for an age of giants to General Duddon as a giant's authentic skeleton. He sped on into more fairy tales of dragons and elephants and giants all fighting together.

"As you say. Very picturesque," Reggie interrupted. "But you found something more than a bit of hind leg and tail and molar." He pointed to the second of his divisions of lumps. "What did you make of these?"

"They're bones too, aren't they?—small bones, more bits of him or another creature of his time."

"Yes, they are bones," Reggie said slowly. "Very distressin'. Not his bones, General. Not of his time. From another family still going strong. Bit of a pelvis, bit of a jaw—human, all too human. And much too new. Bones of a boy who was alive ten years ago."

"Good heavens, Fortune!" the general squeaked. "But that's preposterous. Oh come, too bad of you, you don't pull my leg like that. Fantastic nonsense."

"My dear chap!" Reggie's smile was rueful. "Not me. I wouldn't. The painful truth."

The general spluttered an angry exclamation. "That's enough. You don't expect me to believe a boy who was alive only the other day would be buried two hundred feet deep in the cliff, in among gravel laid down ages ago."

"Oh yes, I do. Always expect people to believe evidence. I am sanguine. But this is quite clear and simple. You saw the deep cracks in the cliff today. You said the cliff was always cracking. Some day about ten years back a boy, fifteen or so, went down into a crack there. Dead or alive, he couldn't get out. The cliff went on cracking, moving, slipping. His body was crushed in the earth movements, mixed with the deep gravel, same like the elephant's— and they came out together the other day."

"It's amazing!" The general stared at him. "A boy—only ten years ago— are you sure?"

"Oh yes. Not to a year or two. But quite a recent boy. I wonder." Reggie took up the scrap of jaw and handled it tenderly. "Why did you go into the crack?" he asked it. "Did you go down there alive?"

The general shuddered. "Ugh, don't talk like that, Fortune. It's gruesome."

"You think so?" Reggie's round face showed no feeling but curiosity. "Has nobody happened to think about him till now? Nobody noticed the elimination of a boy in these parts?"

"Ten years ago, you said," the general frowned. "That's long before I came down here, I shouldn't be likely—My God, Fortune! It was somewhere along the coast there that Tracy's boy was lost, his only son, don't you know! That would be some twelve years back, and he was near the age you say—a schoolboy home for the holidays. I never heard of any suspicions. People still gossip about it because Tracy's such a wretched brute, and they say he was all right till his son's death—that's what soured him. Everybody always believed the boy was drowned. Tracy himself hasn't raised a doubt. But the body wasn't found—never been found. You see? Never found—nobody really knew."

"I wonder." Reggie's long fingers caressed the boy's jawbone, and he sighed. "Queer world. The primeval elephant comes out of the grave to give me a job of work. Not a nice job, no."

The general chattered at him a medley of incoherent fancies and was sent away to ring up the police.

"Tell your haughty chief constable Mr. Fortune has some grave information for him. Only that and nothing more." Reggie sat down to collective study of the bones.

CHAPTER III *Evidence of a Girl*

THE GENERAL CAME BACK to the workshop fuming. "Supercilious ass, said he'd give you five minutes, if I'd bring you in at once. What the devil's this now?"

A car made itself heard and seen, sweeping by the window—a blaze of headlights, a long shining coupé. It was stopped with a jerk. Two people jumped out. The door of the workshop was flung open. "Hallo, hallo!" a fruity voice exclaimed. "Is the lion in his den? Yes, we've caught him, girlie. Come on. Here he is, growling over his bones."

This boisterous visitor was a little man in a great deal of fur coat. The face which emerged from it was long and fat, made to tell the world of simple jollity within, but its small eyes seemed to be looking into the distance. Behind him came a girl not dressed for a car of luxury; her tweeds were made to walk in and had done some walking. She went well with them—a buxom shape, heartily alive.

"How goes it, soldier?" the little man went on. "How's old man giant? I was telling 'em about him at tea and said I meant to come and have a look-see at his nibs, and the Allie girl got all het up—like her, ain't it?—so I brought the puss right along." His unmirthful eyes acknowledged the existence of Reggie. "I say, hope we don't intrude?"

"Oh not at all," said the general drearily and introduced Mr. Fortune to Mr. William Brown and Miss Alison Tracy.

"Pleased to meet you." Brown was exuberant. "Scientist, sir?"

"I wouldn't say that," Reggie murmured. He was contemplating the daughter of Tracy, and the singular gleam in her green eyes he has never forgotten. But she had a lot of color. The hair which came in waves out of her hat and made a big knot on her neck was copper red like her father's. It was set off by that cream complexion which red hair brings to the lucky, and something had made her cheeks rosy—an eager, fierce face, gaily excited.

"Do show us Goliath," she cried. "And have you found David too?"

The general caught his breath and choked.

"I'm afraid you're not being respectful, Miss Tracy," said Reggie.

"Oh, absolutely, sir," Brown laughed. "We're all thrilled. Come on, soldier. What have you got? Trot him out."

"Very sorry, Brown, very sorry," the general spluttered. "I'm afraid I can't go into things now. Mr. Fortune and I have an appointment. We mustn't stop a minute. Really now—"

"How horrid of you." The girl made a pout at him. "Do let me see."

"Not horrid of him," said Reggie. "The things are rather horrid, Miss Tracy."

"Why? What's the matter with them?" She frowned. "They're only like great big fossils, aren't they?"

"Never mind, my dear, not now." The general came to her. "Come along. We really have to go." He tried to shepherd her to the door, winking at Brown.

"All right, all right, soldier," Brown said.

"I don't believe there is a giant," she cried.

"Naughty temper," Brown laughed. "Come on with you."

She broke from them and ran to the worktable. "Are these the things? Oh, what a little giant!" She picked up the fragment of the boy's jaw and dandled it.

The general screamed, "My God, Alison, don't touch that!"

"The smallest giant ever!" She laughed and turned to Brown. "Giles said it was all rot, didn't he?"

"Giles says a heap," Brown answered. "Come on, you minx."

"Giles?" Reggie asked.

"Giles Aston," she said fiercely, and her flush was darker.

"Oh yes. May I have that now?" He took the piece of jaw from her. "Thank you, Miss Tracy. Good-bye."

"Good-bye. It has been fun." She swept away, called to the general, "You poor dear," and was gone.

Brown stood a moment, his small solemn eyes taking in the general's distress and Reggie's calm. "H'm. Pardon me," he said and followed her, and their car purred away.

The general wiped his face. "God bless me, that was ghastly, Fortune. The girl playing with her brother's bones! If she knew! If she has to know!"

"I wonder," Reggie murmured.

CHAPTER IV *Evidence of Glass*

For the headquarters of the police Durshire built in the nineteenth century an imitation of a medieval castle. This error of judgment enthroned the chief constable in a room all curves and points, gloomily vast.

His prim person against such a background was attenuated and incongruous, but he did not know it. He ignored the arrival of Reggie and General Duddon with official majesty and went on reading his papers.

"Sorry to interrupt you," Reggie drawled. "Callin' on you to investigate a death."

The chief constable raised his bald head slowly and stared. "I beg your pardon."

"Thank you," Reggie said, drew up a chair, sat down and put on the chief constable's table an attaché case. "Some of the evidence."

The chief constable turned away from it to the general. "What is all this, Duddon?" he asked contemptuously. "Be concise. I have matters of importance in hand. I am not to be occupied with your fancies."

"Ha! Occupied with this epidemic of burglars?" the general squeaked. "Not *in* hand but *out* of hand I should say. There's nothing fanciful about my business. It's developed in a most remarkable manner. This is Mr. Fortune, you know. I asked him down here for his opinion on the remains I found in the landslip—"

"And his opinion is that they are really dead," the chief constable sneered. "Most gratifying. Pray go on. Does Mr. Fortune also pronounce that they are the remains of a giant? Is that the death which I am called upon to investigate?"

"No, we are not amused," Reggie sighed.

"Not at all. You're treating duty matters with levity, Seymour." The general rebuked him in a military manner. "Just listen to me. We've come to the conclusion that the gigantic remains were of a bigger creature than a giant, an elephant, sir—"

The chief constable interrupted with a supercilious laugh. "I do congratulate you. What fertile brains! An elephant! But why stop there, Duddon? Why not a whale?"

"Because we work on evidence," said Reggie. "You're wasting time." He opened his case. "Bones of elephant not the only bones found in landslip. Also bones of a boy. How long have you been chief constable?"

The chief constable gave him a glassy stare. "More than a dozen years, isn't it, Seymour?" the general squeaked.

"Oh yes. Look at that." Reggie held out the piece of jaw. "Boy who died in your time. What do you know about him?"

The chief constable peered at the gravel-stained bone. "Why, but this is very old," he objected, "a mere fossil."

"No. Your mistake. Not much more than ten years dead. So it's up to you. Why was he buried in the cliff? How did he die?"

The chief constable looked up with a start, and his face twitched, and he bent again to frown over the bone. "Pshaw! It's quite clearly an ancient relic," he said with obvious relaxation of tension. "Not a subject for police enquiry."

"Oh." Reggie drew out the word. "That won't do."

"What do you mean, sir? It's for me to decide."

"Yes, primarily. That's why I came to you. Expectin' you to consider the evidence. Why won't you?"

"There is no evidence before me," the chief constable said angrily.

"My poor chap!" Reggie gave him a small sad smile. "Why not look? Why not think? Portion of jaw, portion of pelvis, other fragments—all belonging to a boy of fifteen or so and some ten years dead."

"You choose to say so."

"No choice about it. You won't get any different opinion—from a competent man. Boy's remains thrust out of the deep levels in your cliffs by the landslip. Therefore he went into the cliff down one of the clefts into which it cracks. Nothing to indicate cause of death. He may have been killed before his body went underground. Ten or twelve years ago. Do you remember the disappearance of any boy in your county about that time? Yes, I see you do." The chief constable's mouth had come open, and his stare was vacuous. "When did you remember? Before you announced that this evidence wasn't to be evidence?"

"Really, sir! That's a most improper observation," the chief constable stammered. "You must know that all this is quite irregular."

"Absolutely, yes. Never had such difficulty in persuading a police officer to do his job. What's the objection? You have in your mind that the son of a man Tracy vanished without trace along the coast near the landslip. I show you the bones of a boy of his age found in it. And you decide that you won't have any further investigation. Your mistake."

"Are you threatening me, Mr. Fortune?"

"Oh no. Telling you what will happen. This can't be hushed up."

The chief constable laughed at high pressure. "If I took you seriously—"

"You'd be wiser," Reggie told him.

"Your suggestions are preposterous." The chief constable was reduced to the plaintive tone of the righteous official justifying himself. "What have I to hush up? Nothing. That sad affair of Tracy's son—there was no sort of mystery about it. You are not acquainted with the facts." He rang a bell and commanded the presence of Superintendent Bubb. "When you hear them," he went on, recovering his self-assurance with oratory, "you will see, Mr. Fortune, that it would be mere futile cruelty to revive all the suffering of a tragic loss by making a sensation over these fragmentary remains which can tell us nothing."

"You think so?" Reggie smiled. "They have told a lot. If you'd only attend to 'em. The bones—well, they do want knowledge to understand. But you might have understood that." He took up an envelope containing the scrap of gravel which he had called to the general Exhibit A. "You see. Gravel from the deep levels, forest-bed gravel, very old, same like the stuff on the bones, and in it scraps of glass, quite modern glass, uncommon thin. Splinters of it also sticking to the bone. Went in at the same time as the boy."

"Tcht," the chief constable made a petulant exclamation, "it's as thin as paper." He frowned at Reggie. "What could it signify?"

"I wonder," Reggie murmured. "I want Mr. Superintendent Bubb."

CHAPTER V *Evidence of a Superintendent*

SUPERINTENDENT BUBB ARRIVED, and Reggie, blinking, felt that he had seen him before, which was enormously improbable. Nothing striking about him—a plump, neat man rather dark, rather solemn, well disciplined.

"Ah, Superintendent. You were in charge of the investigation of Charles Tracy's death," the chief constable instructed him, and Superintendent Bubb showed no sign of surprise at this sudden resurrection of an old case. "I want you to go over the facts concisely."

"Sir," said Superintendent Bubb and went on at level speed, "young Mr. Tracy was home from school for the Easter holidays. It was his habit to go birds'-nesting, especially on the cliffs, because some rare gulls come to breed there."

"That sort of boy," Reggie murmured. "Oh yes, I saw a black guillemot today."

Superintendent Bubb, with a respectful glance, said that name was mentioned. Young Mr. Tracy went out on the morning of April 15, a bright but showery day, taking his lunch, having told the head gamekeeper he was after guillemots' eggs, and he was warned, not for the first time, the cliffs were risky climbing. He never came back. After nightfall a search began, and in the morning the police were informed that he had disappeared. Nobody could be found who saw him after he left his home, but his egg-collecting box was discovered on the beach half full of sea water and battered. It was concluded that he had fallen from the cliff while climbing, and his body had been washed out to sea. After some years this was confirmed by the law courts giving leave to presume his death as regards the settlement of the estate.

"What was he wearing?" Reggie asked.

Superintendent Bubb smoothed his smooth hair. "My recollection is, sweater and flannel trousers."

"Very good recollection," Reggie smiled. "No coat?"

"I believe not, sir."

"Any sort of glass in the egg box—test tubes or what not?"

"Nothing like that. No glass at all." Bubb looked at him with interest. "Might I ask, what is the idea, sir?"

"Oh yes. The idea is that somebody did see him after he left home. Somebody does know how he died. And it wasn't by drowning."

"I don't know why you say that," Bubb remarked in a voice without expression.

"Hasn't it ever been said before?" Reggie's eyebrows went up.

"Meaning a suggestion of foul play?" Bubb's tone was still flat. "Not within my knowledge." He turned to the chief constable for corroboration or instruction.

"You never thought of it?" Reggie demanded.

"Certainly not," the chief constable said in a hurry. "There was no ground for any kind of suspicion. What?" he snapped at Bubb who stood silent.

"That was the conclusion, sir," Bubb answered.

"Would you be surprised to hear that his bones have turned up?" Reggie asked him.

Superintendent Bubb showed no surprise, looked quite incapable of it and said that he would require to see 'em and didn't know how anybody could be sure of 'em—it was getting on for twelve years ago, ah, twelve years next spring.

"Precisely," the chief constable exclaimed.

"Yes, I was accurate, wasn't I?" Reggie interrupted.

"Accurate! You gave a vague date. The rest is nothing but guesswork—a preposterous fancy."

"Everything's fanciful you don't want to look into, Seymour," General Duddon told him with gusto.

Bubb coughed. "As you say," Reggie smiled. "Little hands were never made to scratch each other's eyes. No. Consider the evidence. The young Tracy was a cliff climber. Superintendent, would you have thought him likely to fall into one of those cracks in the turf of the cliffs? No. Most improbable. I don't think he did fall. But that's where his body went, deep down into the cliff. And bits of it have just come out in the landslip. Here you are."

Bubb examined the remains. "I should take these for human all right," he said slowly. "They don't look full grown. That's as far as I get."

"As far as any man can get," the chief constable approved.

"Oh no. We have got much further. Why refuse the certain facts? Bones of a boy Charles Tracy's age. Went into the ground at the time he was lost."

"You're a medical man, sir?" Bubb enquired.

"Yes. Rather good on these things," said Reggie modestly. "Nobody better. My name's Fortune."

"I beg your pardon, sir." Bubb was reverential.

"My dear chap!" Reggie smiled. "Always happy to assist the active and intelligent police force. You were askin' how could anybody be sure what boy grew these bones. Quite simple. What boy vanished on those cliffs twelve years ago? Only one—young Tracy. My further medical evidence indicates that somebody caused him to vanish. He wasn't carrying any glass, unless he had a watch. But with his bones were found bits of very fine glass—you see—much too thin for a watch glass—splinters actually in the jawbone."

"It is thin," Bubb agreed. "Very thin. I don't know what it could be."

"Suggests nothing to your mind?" Reggie's eyelids drooped.

"Must have come from somewhere," Bubb said slowly. "Looks like scientific glass to me, those tubes they use. The boy wouldn't have that on him. I grant you it points to somebody else being present."

"Pshaw," the chief constable exclaimed. "Any collector fellow might have dropped his rubbish into a hole at any time. It might have been yourself, Duddon."

"I don't carry test tubes," the general told him. "Who does?"

"Can't you invent a prehistoric chemist?" the chief constable sneered.

"About dropping," said Bubb. "How would a splinter of glass get stuck in the poor lad's jawbone? That's more like a rough-and-tumble."

"Yes. Foul play is indicated," Reggie murmured. "There's your case, Chief Constable."

"I admire your imagination, Mr. Fortune." The chief constable spoke, biting his words. "You have certainly produced a wonderful case. It has no substance whatever—a structure of fantastic theory which defies all probability and has no meaning. I am obliged to you for an amusing half-hour." He made a show of taking up his papers.

"Oh no," said Reggie. "Not amusing. But suggestive. Not me defying probability. You. You've defied it comfortably for twelve years, insistin' the incredible was true. Boy, heir to a big estate, mysteriously vanishes. And you say nobody had any suspicions. No gossip. Not one unkind word. My poor friend! It didn't happen like that, you know it didn't."

The chief constable shifted in his chair. "I said there was no ground for any suspicion."

"Yes. *You* decided that. On what evidence? Proof that nobody ever had a row with the boy, the family of Tracy were all sweet and kind, and everybody loved 'em, and there wasn't any old grudge about anywhere?"

"These are scandalous insinuations," the chief constable exclaimed, but his alarm was visible.

"My God, Fortune," the general broke in. "You know—"

"So does he," said Reggie. "Not a nice case, no. Not a pleasant position for the chief constable. There were suspicions. It was decided not to look at 'em. Not to go over people who had a motive."

"There was no evidence against any person, sir," the chief constable said in a hurry.

"As you were sayin'. It was decided not to find it. It was decided not to have any evidence of foul play. And now the evidence has emerged. Very awkward for you. You'll have to act on it now."

"Act, sir? What action can be taken? Nothing can be made of these miserable fragments."

"Your mistake," Reggie smiled.

"I should like to know what you suggest is possible now?"

"Very interestin' question." Reggie gazed at him with closing eyes. "I shouldn't put any limits to the possible. Almost anything might arrive—as it's gone." He gave a little shiver. "Lots of forces at work. Not nice forces. However. No doubt what's going to be done. Look over the landslip for more evidence."

"Oh that, indeed." The chief constable was relieved. "Yes, that should certainly be done. Superintendent, you'll go over there in the morning and examine the ground."

"With me," said Reggie. "And then we'll rub out the case and do it again."

"It will be reviewed in the light of results," said the chief constable with some recovery of his dignity, but he looked away from Reggie.

"Yes, that is so," said Reggie. "Good-bye." And as he went out spoke to Superintendent Bubb: "Ten o'clock on the cliff? Right." He gazed at Bubb's plump face. "Have I seen you before?"

"Not to my knowledge, sir," Bubb answered. "Lots like me in these parts."

CHAPTER VI *Evidence of a Goddess*

WHEN REGGIE REACHED the cliffs next morning a cold mist was driving in from the sea. Shrunken into his coat he stamped to and fro and mourned the perversity of the world and his awful sense of duty and the lack of it in the police force. Everything was melted into a gray, dim, shapeless uniformity. Impossible to distinguish where the cliff broke in a gulf of air, where the land ended and the sea began.

Sounds approached, something darkly solid, and he made out a car from which issued Superintendent Bubb and two policemen, of a larger size, with spades. Bubb said that Mr. Fortune was very punctual, and Reggie moaned resentment and took his arm and walked him away. "Wonderin' if you'd been countermanded after all."

Bubb chose not to understand. "It's this run of country-house burglaries kept me," he said earnestly. "I believe we're up against a skilled gang."

"Well, well. So the burglary epidemic is real?" Reggie murmured. "Sorry. I have a nasty mind. I was afraid it was an excuse for doing nothing once again."

Bubb couldn't agree nothing was done before. Of course it was difficult when you had big people involved to handle a case; you must be careful.

"Not to find out too much. Yes. You were. Not blaming you. Sad world. Silly world. However. How far did you get? Ever been here before?"

Bubb's full face, rather red from the wet cold, turned to him with a shrewd, humorous look. "I have, sir."

"Oh my hat!" Reggie murmured. "Now I know."

"I don't get it, sir."

"My dear chap! Remember my asking last night if I'd seen you before? Thought you were like somebody. It was a fellow in the club down here, one Cope."

"Mr. Cope the banker?" Bubb was amused. "I suppose there is a sort of likeness. I'd never thought about it before. You see, it's not special to me and him. In these parts it's the ordinary make. The village where I come from, we're mostly this style. And Mr. Cope, his people were village folks away back—before his granddad set up the bank—regular out of the ground, same as mine. By long and by large it's only the gentry and the newcomers that's different."

"All men and brothers. Well, well. We were sayin'—you did go over this ground. Would you say young Tracy came along here to climb for his guillemots?"

Bubb looked this way and that through the swirling mist. "Here or hereabouts," he said. "Lord, I know this place like the back of my hand still, I worked it over that thorough."

"And found nothing. Yet you thought this was the place to work. Why?"

Again Reggie was given a knowing look. "You're keen, Mr. Fortune. It's like this. The land here used to be Mr. Aston's, and there was talk of his having had a row with young Mr. Tracy for trespassing and Tracy daring him. The families were like that, both of 'em."

"Oh yes. Possibility of another row indicated. But no evidence. Was evidence looked for?"

"I should say the matter was pursued," said Bubb with official solemnity and went on briskly to give Reggie the information which he had already received from General Duddon. Mr. Aston used to own all along, but just lately Mr. Brown bought up a lot in a mortgagees' sale. They did say Mr. Aston tried hard to keep it, and Mr. Tracy made a bid to get it too.

"Fancy that," Reggie murmured. "Who told you?"

"Everybody talks about land sales down here," Bubb answered. "Now come along a bit, Mr. Fortune." They walked past the gash of the landslip. "You see the fence just beyond? That's the boundary of Mr. Aston's estate now. But they're saying it won't be long. The land beyond is heavily mortgaged too, and Mr. Aston can't meet the payments though he's fighting hard for it."

"You do hear a lot," said Reggie. "Curious and interesting. And what is Superintendent Bubb's impressive conclusion?"

"I'm just giving you the facts, sir. I don't want to be hasty."

"No. I gathered that. You haven't been. However. One conclusion inevitable. Aston's not a lucky man."

"You may say so," Bubb agreed heartily. "His family's been going down for donkey's years."

"While the Tracys went up. Yes. Does make for hate. But I wasn't thinking of that. Everybody's telling everybody he's desperate anxious to keep these cliffs to himself, and they fall down just when he's lost 'em and display the dead boy's bones. Very unlucky."

"You can put it nasty," said Bubb. "But that don't make proof. And if you ask me, we have to remember young Mr. Tracy and old Mr. Tracy had their rows too, and the father did stand to gain by the son's death. There was big money passed to him."

"Oh yes. Kind people talked about that too. Neither the Tracys nor the Astons much loved by the ordinary man. You're beautifully fair."

"The truth is," said Bubb slowly, "I never have satisfied myself."

"My dear chap!" Reggie spoke with affection. "I'm goin' to like working with you. We will now begin. From the beginning. Twelve years ago, when you worked over this cliff top, it looked much the same, what? Cracking all along the edge, lots of cracks gaping wide enough to take a body both sides of the fence."

"That's right, sir. And there didn't use to be any fence. Mr. Brown had it put up when he bought."

"Oh yes. I saw it was new. After a lapse of time the fellow who put the boy down a crack wouldn't be quite sure where the body had got to. If it was Aston, he'd still want to keep the land beyond the fence. Whoever it was, he couldn't tell what the landslip would do with the remains. He'd want to have a look at the debris. Aston has had a look, with Mrs. Aston. I saw 'em. I don't think they found much that trip. The general had collected the obvious relics, bless him. And Aston hadn't a thing in his hands, and there had been no digging except General Duddon's. But Aston may have got busy since. Now we'll go and see."

"If you please, sir." Bubb called to his policemen. "You're rather pressing it against Mr. Aston."

"Not me. No. The mind is quite open. Same like the mind of Superintendent Bubb. But anxious. I don't like this case. Not a nice case."

The mist was breaking as the sun gained power. Gleams of light came on the sea, the cliffs thrust out of their cloak. Bubb looked over the tumbled masses of chalk and sand on the beach. "By gum, it's a big fall. I don't know how General Duddon happened on anything in that mess. A bit of a miracle, I'd say."

"Oh no. Only rational investigation. He went for the stuff from the deep levels, at the cliff base. You see? That's his little digging." Reggie led the way to the place. "And nobody else has dug."

"I didn't expect it myself," said Bubb complacently.

Reggie was frowning at the gravel. "My only aunt!" he moaned, took off his gloves and bent down.

"What have you got, sir?" Bubb came to look. "Some more glass?"

Reggie stood up again and showed in the palm of his hand a small, flat, pink thing. "Not glass, no," he said. One long finger turned the thing round. "I've got a goddess. Goddess Athena. Complete with shield and helmet. Well, well." He gazed at Bubb, and his round face was plaintive and reproachful.

"But what is the thing?" Bubb asked.

"Oh my Bubb! Don't you see? Goddess carved in low relief. Cameo. From a ring. Not a good cameo. Cut from shell. However—"

"Well now, where are we coming to?" Bubb gave a chuckle. "First you find some funny glass with the bones, and now you've got a bit of an old ring buried with them."

"No, I haven't." Reggie was aggrieved. "Nothing like that. Not old. Wasn't buried with 'em. Quite fresh. No gravel stains. Also—and moreover—and especially—it wasn't here yesterday. It's been deposited since I inspected the site. That's very distressin'."

Bubb was not impressed. "You mean to say somebody's been poking round and lost a stone out of his ring. But who would come between yesterday and now? There's been hardly any daylight."

"I haven't the slightest idea." Reggie gazed at him with large, pathetic eyes. "Does anybody happen to have been told that the bones of a boy had turned up here?"

"Not by me, sir," said Bubb sharply.

"Rulin' that out," Reggie drawled, "who would come?—as you were saying. Who wears a cameo ring?"

"I couldn't tell you," said Bubb.

"Oh." Reggie's eyelids drooped. "Not one of the things everybody talks about. Pity. Well, well. Be good, sweet maid, and let who will be clever. Tell the constabulary to dig."

They dug, and Reggie wandered about them like a curious but bored dog. They found some more portions of the bones of a boy. At the demand of Bubb, Reggie gave an anatomical lecture on them which concluded, "So we have a good deal of him—enough to show he must have gone into the cliff complete. I dare say you won't get any more."

"That'll do," said Bubb. "It makes a case to start on. Good work, Mr. Fortune."

"Good?" Reggie's voice went up. "My only aunt! Don't tell anybody you think so."

"What's worrying you?"

"The goddess. Very distressin'. Tell 'em that if you like."

"I don't talk, sir," said Bubb severely.

CHAPTER VII *Evidence of a Ball*

THAT EVENING Reggie lay long in his bath and when General Duddon came knocking with nervous anxiety explained that he was composing an ode to melancholy. "Same like the late Keats'. But different. Main theme, the miserable folly of wantin' to do anything, with cursive embroidery on the horrid opportunities fellows give you."

"Don't forget—" The general's shrill admonition was cut short by the strains of a vulgar song from the bath:

> *"All the jungle folks have habits of their own*
> *I'm not afraid of the big bad wolf*
> *But the elephant never forgets!"*

"The elephant and me. Poor beggars!" Reggie crooned. "The downy owl won't drown the wakeful anguish of our souls. No, Mr. Keats."

"I don't see the joke," the general rebuked him. "There's nothing comical about the discovery of the elephant."

"Oh, my dear chap," Reggie gurgled apology. "Not suggested. No."

The general was unappeased. "Just remember we're going on to this ball after dinner—if you ever come down."

"I do, we will, I will." Reggie cried, and the general retired hurt.

The useful opportunity of seeing the county people at the county ball was in fact one of the causes of Reggie's languid melancholy. The other was the goddess.

When he talks of his conduct of the case, an event not uncommon, for it makes him very pleased with himself, he never fails to explain that the storm of ghastly difficulties which he had to fight arose from things being made too easy.

This has been derided as one of Mr. Fortune's paradoxes, but he maintains it solemnly, thus:

Everybody concerned was either so silly or so clever that they all began to give themselves away as soon as the extinct elephant drew his attention to them. The forces of nature which, having exhumed the elephantine leg and tail, then held the county ball, cooperated with them to provide excessive assistance.

Before he went down with Superintendent Bubb to the landslip, he insists, his mind had obtained all the evidence which was necessary to solve the mystery of the boy's bones, and he knew enough of it to work out the case to a swift and lawful end if the wretched people and the nature of things had not interfered.

Superintendent Bubb, discomfited at the end which was reached, declined to believe this and swore in the bitterness of his heart that Mr. Fortune hadn't the right to think so much of himself, he wasn't so wonderful as he set up for. Nobody could be. But Superintendent Bubb was then unable to do anything about it.

Reggie does not claim that anything which he did was wonderful. He admires his operations as a model of the uses of pure reason in crime, pointing out with pride that he gave every fact its value, however inconvenient, and drew the logical, awkward inferences and took the unpleasant action thereby compelled. The delays and casualties of the investigation, he contends, were not his fault, they broke in because the facts thrust upon him were far too many and confused. So he makes the case demonstrate both the strength and the weakness of being reasonable in a far from reasonable world.

As he emerged from the bath he was equally bothered by the presence of the goddess of the cameo and the prospect of the ball. The goddess he felt inexplicably superfluous. From the county ball he anticipated more than his usual woe at balls. Yet both gifts of fate had to be accepted. The goddess must have a meaning. His ruthless sense of duty bade him go and inspect the county people.

"Do the painful right," he admonished himself and slid swiftly into his clothes and went down and soothed the injured general with archaeological small talk. Taking extinct elephants seriously was quite enough to divert General Duddon's mind from curiosity about more recent death.

The county ball of Durshire is still held in the town hall which Colsbury built when last century was young, a structure cunningly constructed to be both dowdy and cavernous. The main cave, the big hall wherein they danced, was already populous when Reggie came wistfully to the threshold. A resplendent scene: the maroon walls were hung with red, white and blue, strident in a blaze of light from pitiless lamps in the curved roof which brought out the top half of man and woman—sharper in shape and color and sheen than nature or artifice had intended—faces emphatic, and shoulders and chests magnified whether bare or black and white; the rest was lost in shadow; they had no legs.

Reggie remarked to himself that it didn't matter, they didn't want 'em. He had never seen so many people come to a dance who weren't dancing. The gliding couples obtained only a small part of the floor. Parade and conversation required the rest.

Yielding to the sway of people showing themselves and seeking the right people, he detached himself from General Duddon and wandered, watching and listening.

Not a word came to his ears of any scandal about the landslip. Whoever had left the cameo goddess there, whatever the motive for the visit, the revelation of the boy's bones was not yet common knowledge. If it was a leakage from police headquarters which sent somebody to the site, the leak had been guarded with discretion. People were talking abundantly of the police and unkindly, but the theme of their stories and their indignation was the uncaught, unchecked burglars.

Reggie coasted round a group which listened with joyous horror to the plaint of a victim and saw among them the dreary, handsome head of Aston. He was almost erect; he looked almost alive. He was being friendly; he spoke of his own accord; he showed interest. His wife had a lot to say.

However poor they might be, they had not lost standing. They were treated as people of importance, and they made a good show. Aston had the presence of a man who knew he was a fine fellow when he remembered. Though his wife was wasted and sallow, the years had not robbed her of grace, and she could still wear the diamonds in that heavy, old-fashioned setting on her shrunken neck and gray hair as if she had a right to jewels.

But Reggie suffered from a sense of wrong. If the Astons still had family jewels like those, why did people talk of their being desperately hard up? They could buy a lot of cliff land for the price of that dog collar. Still more confusing facts! He turned sorrowfully away as Aston moved out of the group and saw on Aston's left hand a cameo ring—something in reddish-yellow—a Greek head.

Reggie wandered out of the glare of the ball into the corridor from which other dimmer caverns opened. His round face was woebegone as a child's who cannot understand why things should be so unkind.

"Hallo! Hallo!" He was slapped on the back. "Happy days!" He turned to see the long, fat face of Mr. Brown, grinning. Behind it rose the bulk of a large woman in purple. "Meet the wife, Mr. Fortune," said Brown with pride.

As Reggie bowed to the overwhelming purple, a small and gentle voice issued from it: "I do hope you're having a good time." He looked up past a pink bosom draped with pearls into a shining red countenance which greeted him like an anxious mother.

"Delightful," said Reggie.

"All really very friendly," Mrs. Brown went on. "Aren't they?"

"That's right," Brown nodded. "But I know what you want, Mr. Fortune, eh? We'll just have a gargle, dearie!" He linked arms with Reggie and drew him off. "Well, how's things?"

"Thanks very much. Doing as well as can be expected. No further bulletins being issued."

"Good for you." Brown gave him a confidential pinch. "Let sleeping giants lie. That one did, didn't he?"

"You're very witty. The general wouldn't like it at all."

"Poor old soldier man. One of the best, though. You know, I've seen something in my time, Mr. Fortune, and I've come to think the fellows that have stuff in 'em mostly run to some kind of craze. What do you say?"

"Notice that in yourself?" said Reggie.

"Me? Not much," Brown guffawed. "I've always had too many things in hand. I'm just a business man. One damn thing after another, you know, and making the show work. No time for getting ideas."

"Interestin' life," Reggie drawled.

"Not for you, eh? You're scientific. You want to bring out the truth all the time. It don't matter to you about having the show work smooth."

"You think not?" Reggie's tone was without expression.

"I wasn't meaning anything personal." Brown compressed his arm again. "What I was getting at is the sort of fuss that brings out the truth of what really happened though it's going to do more harm than good. I mean to say, it ain't so much what the truth was that matters as what it 'll make of things now."

"You're a philosopher, Mr. Brown."

"My Lor'! Nobody ever called me that before. I must tell the wife that. That's a good one. Come on, let's drink to it." He conducted Reggie into one of the minor caverns which was a bar. "What's yours?" Reggie asked if he could have seltzer water. "You don't mean it?" Brown was horrified. "The stuff's all right here, believe me. I don't say as good as I'd give you at home, but no dirty work." Nevertheless Reggie insisted on water, and, since seltzer was unknown to Colsbury, drank soda water pure with a satisfaction which made Mr. Brown, so he said, feel wicked, and he retreated to look, as he also said, for his wife.

Reggie remained in plaintive meditation over further unsought, confusing facts. Brown was both too obvious and too elusive. His philosophic advice could mean nothing but instruction to damp down investigation of young Tracy's death. Impudent fellow. And why should he meddle? If he had something to be afraid of, he was a fool to thrust himself on the police expert with advice that nothing must be found out. And, if he wasn't involved, the more fool he to mix himself up in it. No just cause or impediment why a get-rich-quick man shouldn't be a fool. But the brooding, far-gazing little eyes in Mr. Brown's head did not fit into that explanation of him. He wanted something and meant to get it. Deuced impudence. No, not a fool. Quite a lot in his fat head. "Let sleeping giants lie. That one did, didn't he?" Very clever of Mr. Brown. Too clever by half. Why did he butt in with the Tracy girl at Mr. Fortune's examination of the remains? Why infer from the sight of a bit of human jaw that inconvenient things might be done about it?

Perhaps there was a leak in the chief constable's office which came to him. Some way he knew more than he ought. He was quite sure that if the truth about young Tracy's death came out it would cramp his style. But how? He couldn't have had a hand in murdering the boy—if it was murder. Deuced elusive fellow. And he meant to interfere. He was going to be a nuisance. Another one!

In the course of this analysis of Brown—which he still admires—Reggie became aware that young Tracy's father stood at the counter of the bar and was working steadily. It had no visible effect on the stolidity of his countenance, but either liquor or temper was making him snarl at anyone who dared speak to him. He was in a state very different from Aston's. That could be seen without taking his temperature, which was much too high for enquiry into what had sent it up.

Impossible to guess whether the man was by habit a hard and surly drinker or under stress of anxiety. The company at the bar were leaving him to himself and did not appear to think him more repulsive than usual. But a newcomer's effort to be friendly and confidential Tracy rejected with violence which produced some nods and winks and grins.

The scorned friend drew away with a glass of sherry, and for a fleeting moment Reggie thought it was Superintendent Bubb. Then memory recalled the man so like Bubb, the man in the club with Tracy and the chief constable—Cope, the banker. Of course it was the banker. A fellow who wore those old-world horsy clothes in the daytime would have evening dress with high shoulders and a lot of collar and tie and tight trousers like a buck of last century.

Cope observed Reggie's attentive eyes and came to him sociably. "Good evening, sir. Do you care to try the sherry or … Why, what's that you have, soda water? God bless me! Well, every man ought to know what he's fit for. I hope you're being looked after."

"Thanks very much. Everybody very good to me," Reggie said. "Uncommon kind."

"Glad you think so. We are a genial crowd down here, as people go, I think. No damned nonsense about." Cope's grave eyes twinkled. "I wouldn't answer for Duddon's antiquities, though. I dare say his giant was a devilish exclusive fellow, eh? Where's Duddon got to? He ought to be showing you round us moderns."

"I'm afraid we drifted apart," said Reggie.

"Too bad." Cope was more amused. "Dear old fellow, the general, but he does ride his hobbies hard. Do you remember the fellow at the bar there?" He nodded toward Tracy's red head, "Jim Tracy, you know, he was with

Seymour and me at the club when Duddon introduced you. Very good chap, one of the oldest families you'd find and still on top, though he does know it rather too well. Duddon fairly raised his gall over this giant in the landslip. Dam' silly of course. But they don't like digging up the sacred past, these fellows whose people have owned the land since the Flood. Have you met Francis Aston?"

"No, I haven't. No. Why?"

"He's another of 'em," Cope chuckled. "As different from Tracy as you please. Casual, inconsequent sort of fellow, scholar and all that, and always on some wonderful scheme to make his fortune. But he traces back to Adam and Eve and mad about the family land—what's left of it. He flew right up in the air over Duddon's giant. Took him as a nasty scandal on the Aston reputation, don't you know."

"Very odd. As you say," Reggie murmured. "Tracy and Aston—heirs of all the ages—in a holy alliance against the disturbing excavator. Very surprisin'."

Cope shook his head. "No, no. I didn't say anything about alliance. That would be a surprise. Astons and Tracys have always been cat and dog to each other. Noblesse oblige—hate for the honor of the family—and these two keep it up in the grand style. The only thing they could agree about is damning a poke into the old times."

"Then they bury the hatchet in the investigator. Alarmin' prospect. Nasty temper." Reggie contemplated Tracy's red head. "And that is your Mr. Tracy. He seems to be getting on with it. Drownin' care—or not."

"A hard case," Cope agreed. "He ought to pull up. His daughter's here, you know. I'll have another shot at him."

Reggie watched the effort. It was not well taken. Cope turned from this second repulse with a shrug and a smile and went out. If he was going to warn Miss Tracy of the progress of her father's potations, Reggie decided that the result might be instructive. Whether or not, he desired to know what the girl was doing. She and her association with the elusive Brown did not please him. He strolled after Cope along labyrinthine corridors and stairs and at last saw the man check and stop before Brown and Mrs. Brown, who seemed to come out of the wall.

The situation elucidated itself incredibly. They had risen from a dark recess. Cope was jovial with them. "Very cozy, Brown. You old rascal, how many have you sat out with her? I don't blame you, but it's too bad of you, ma'am, to let nobody else have a turn. Some of us young fellows have got desperate." Brown guffawed and threw back chaff, and Mrs. Brown was shy. Into the midst of this noise came a girl, with a green frock and cream shoulders and dark red hair—Alison Tracy. She had a man behind her, a tall, fair, young fellow looking haughty. It was obvious that they had been in some cozier corner beyond, using the Browns as an outpost. But Brown exclaimed,

"Why, Allie, where have you sprung from? My word, don't say you've had to look for me."

Alison took the cue. "Oh yes, I have. You're abominable. Faithless, shameless person." And Mrs. Brown's small voice carried on: "Don't you forgive him, my dear, I never did."

Cope laughed. "Well played!"

Alison made a melodramatic gesture at Brown. "All is over between us. Take me away, Mr. Aston."

"Sorry, Giles." Cope intervened with a hand on her arm. "I've just had a word with your father, Alison." He lowered his voice, and Reggie, who could not hear, could see her annoyance.

"Thank you very much," she cried. "It doesn't matter." She whirled round on Mrs. Brown. "You'll give me a lift home, won't you?"

"Why of course we will, dear." Mrs. Brown patted her. "You dance as much as you like."

"Thanks awfully," said Giles Aston and went off with Alison.

Cope watched their departure with a look of cool, humorous calculation like a shrewd judge pricing horses. "Go well together, don't they?" he said. "Make a good pair."

"D'ye think so?" Brown answered.

"Now I don't like that sort of talk," said Mrs. Brown.

Cope begged her pardon and asked for a dance, and Reggie removed himself.

He felt dazed by an embarrassment of evidence. Everybody insisted on bearing witness, and it was all infernally relevant and desperately incompatible. Everything meant too much, and nothing meant anything. A crushing chaos of a case.

Through the labyrinth of the town hall he wandered in a sleepwalking manner, lost himself and found at last the brilliance of the main cavern. No Aston old or young was visible, no Tracy. Fewer people were dancing, and more people talking than ever, and they still talked burglaries.

He descried General Duddon and sought him and sighed into his ear: "Take me home."

"What? Fortune! My dear fellow, by all means. Aren't you well?"

"No. No. The world is too much with us. Such a lot of world and such a mess. I want to go home. I want my bed."

"Dear, dear. You do look tired. We'll push off at once. Come along." The general bustled him away. "Have you heard the news? There's been another burglary tonight—out at Ningbourne."

"What?" Reggie stared at him vacantly. "I don't mind."

"No, of course not. Not your affair. But it is a scandal the way these cases go on. Our police are a flock of sheep. There must be gangs of rascals at work. This business—only a couple of hours ago, and they're clean away with every bit of Lady Werne's jewelry that she wasn't wearing here."

"Well, well. Then nobody who was here was the burglar. Thank heaven."

"Good Lord, Fortune, you didn't suppose—"

"Suppose nothing. Thankin' heaven for something that isn't relevant. I thought the whole wide world was going to be." Reggie yawned. "There may be an end in the end. Hope on. Hope ever!" He gazed vacantly at the general's alarm. "So runs my dream. But what am I? The mind is wholly futile."

CHAPTER VIII *Evidence of a Burglary*

THE CHIEF of the Criminal Investigation Department, in remarks upon this case designed to annoy Mr. Fortune, has contended that in assuming this Ningbourne burglary to be irrelevant he made his first mistake.

Reggie's comment was, "No rise, Lomas," and when the criticism was pressed he added, "Don't be silly. Not the first mistake; there weren't any others; also it wasn't a mistake at all. Think again. I should say, think. Then you have to find I was never wrong. Work of pure and faultless reason. Very instructive. Exhibitin' the power and the limitations of rational action. I wasn't right quick enough. Though ultimately adequate."

"Adequate!" Lomas scoffed. "An irresponsible providence at large."

"My dear old thing!" Reggie remonstrated. "Only the absolute opposite. Providence, yes. But with the strongest sense of duty. Wholly logical and moral. That's me. Poor Reginald. A hard life."

But he is ready, even eager, to acknowledge that he had a shattering surprise on the morning after the county ball. While he sat at a late breakfast, the general's manservant brought in a telephone enquiry from Superintendent Bubb: was Mr. Fortune there, and if he was could he wait till the superintendent came round? "I could," Reggie sighed. "I will. And I hate him. Tell him so."

The general said that Bubb was devilish active all of a sudden. What did Fortune suppose had happened?

"I haven't the slightest idea," Reggie said and went to the sideboard for another sausage. "Anything could arrive. Might be angels. However. Meet 'em serene and full."

He had attained that state; he was smoking his pipe to a desultory chatter from the general when Bubb was brought in. The general jumped up to make a discreet disappearance. "Don't you disturb yourself, sir," said Bubb. "I'm hoping Mr. Fortune will come along with me, if he could give me an hour. I have a car here."

Reggie groaned and followed him out and saw a little two-seater in the swirls of a snow shower. "Oh my Bubb!" He shivered and huddled into a fur coat. "Do your worst. What is this horrid zeal?"

Bubb spoke into his ear. "Mr. Aston's place was burgled last night, sir."

"Oh no." Reggie drew away, staring reproachful horror. "Not Aston's place. Some other place."

"Both, sir," said Bubb. "If you don't mind—" He urged Reggie to the car.

"I do. I mind bitterly. It's not in my line, and it's nasty cold." But he allowed Bubb to put him in the car and drive off with him. "Why?" he was piteous. "Why?"

"Now you're asking something," Bubb said. "But there's another question first, Mr. Fortune. Who? That's what I want to begin from. Who? Look here, we've had a nasty run of burglaries round the gentlemen's houses, and we're pretty sure it's one little gang of old crooks working from Hartlemouth. Now last night somewhere between nine and eleven they got into Lord Werne's place and made a big haul. I ask you, would you expect another job the same night? Of course you wouldn't. If there was one, would you think it likely to be right the other side of the county? You would not. Matter of fifty mile from Lord Werne's place to Mr. Aston's. Very well. We had a report of Lord Werne's burglary before midnight and from that time on the roads were watched. This morning about nine o'clock, Mr. Aston rang up to say he'd had burglars, and all his wife's diamonds and his collection of cameos had been taken. Well, that was a staggerer to me. He told us he and his wife didn't get back home till well after midnight and went to bed about one. I've checked up on that, and it's all right. They were at the ball till close on twelve anyway. See what it comes to. Mrs. Aston's diamonds didn't get put away before one o'clock or so. And so, following on Lord Werne's burglary, with motor patrols out and all our men on the jump, burglars went round to Mr. Aston and cleaned out his place and got away with it. What do you say to that, Mr. Fortune?"

"It wasn't me," Reggie said. "I have an alibi. Four corners to my bed, four angels round my head. You ask 'em."

"Very funny," Bubb rebuked him. "But I don't care for joking over a case."

"My poor Bubb! What a life! When things laugh at me, I like to laugh back. And they are laughing—like hell. However, I wasn't being merely funny. Your question was: who burgled Aston? And I gave you the only information I have—I didn't."

"I was asking for your opinion, sir," said Bubb severely. "Look here now. It isn't likely a gang that had made one good haul would go right across the county to try for another. Such a thing was never heard of, I reckon. And if they did they were running through patrols which had been warned to look out for them. A thousand to one they'd be held up. You can say there's another gang at work. That isn't likely either. And again there's just the same odds they'd be stopped. What's it look like to you?"

"Nasty mess. Confusion worse confounded. Why do you do it?"

"Sir?" Bubb made it clear that he was affronted.

"Oh yes, you do. Same like everybody. Pushin' on me more superfluous, unwanted evidence. Tiresome case."

"I haven't pushed anything on to you," Bubb exclaimed. "I've just given you the facts as they are."

"With a question," Reggie drawled. "Leading question. You asked me who did the burglary. Indicatin' it wasn't burglars. Indicatin' the man Aston burgled himself."

"I didn't say anything like that," Bubb protested. "I can't help it if you think so."

"I wonder," Reggie murmured.

"I don't mind owning the whole thing beats me," said Bubb earnestly. "That's why I wanted to see what you'd make of it, Mr. Fortune. I do think this second burglary looks a very tricky business. But I'm not saying Mr. Aston faked it. There's no evidence of that. And he's a gentleman."

"Yes. So I've heard. Very awkward. Does it beat the chief constable?"

"Mr. Seymour takes a very serious view, sir." Bubb spoke in his most official manner. "He said to inform you of the facts."

"How kind of him." Reggie sighed. "Everybody is so kind."

"That's what you said before. I don't know how you mean everybody," Bubb complained. "Do you think this burglary is somehow connected with young Tracy's remains?"

"Me? I don't think. I wouldn't presume. The chief constable does the thinking—with him, Mr. Superintendent Bubb. I only wonder. Why was I to be informed of these tiresome facts? I don't hunt burglars. The official mind thinks Aston's burglary has to do with young Tracy's bones and would like me to make it so. I resist these suggested thoughts. The mind will not act."

"There's no liking about it," Bubb retorted sharply. "I don't want to influence you at all. It's no jam to me to find a crime looks faked—and with county people. I can't see any sense myself in linking up this burglary with the boy's bones coming up. 'Confusion worse confounded' you said, and I agree. But there it is. You can't help putting the things together."

"And two and two make forty-four and nothing," Reggie murmured.

"That's just about how I feel," said Bubb. "I'm coming to it with an open mind. I give you my word."

"Bless you." Reggie smiled, and Bubb snorted and fell silent.

CHAPTER IX *Evidence of a Parlor*

SUPERINTENDENT BUBB'S DIGNITY still maintained silence as he drove Mr. Fortune on up the ridge of chalk and turned through Aston's unhinged gates across the treeless park to his house.

Out of the gray gloom of swirling snow it rose—a shapeless, vague bulk. The garden below had been elaborately planned but was decayed and ragged. In a range of glass at the side no color could be seen, not a man at work. The house itself, with innumerable casements shut and blank against drawn drab blinds, looked empty. But as the car turned over moss-grown gravel to the porch, Aston came out. He looked more of a man in shabby tweeds than Reggie had ever seen him. He let loose a haughty rage.

"I expected you hours ago, Superintendent. You've given the scoundrels time to get to the other end of England by now. This delay is a scandalous neglect of duty."

Bubb was sorry to hear Mr. Aston talk like that. But perhaps he didn't know that the burglary at his house wasn't the only burglary last night.

From Aston's scowl it seemed that he was surprised and disconcerted. But after a moment he went on blustering. That showed the inefficiency of the police. Two burglaries in one night! A fine reason for not taking prompt action! Where was the other, pray? Had the fellows been caught? Ha, no need to ask!

Bubb said that what he was asking himself was how the same burglars could have cleaned out Lord Werne's house and then Mr. Aston's all in one night.

"Ask yourself what the police are worth," Aston told him. "The wonder is there's any house in the county not been robbed."

"Thank you, sir. Now if you don't mind we'll have a look at what was done to yours. This is Mr. Fortune. You may have heard of him, Mr. Aston."

Aston inspected Reggie with frowning curiosity which did not hide recognition and discomfort, but all he said was, "I seem to remember your name. You come from Scotland Yard, don't you?"

"Not officially," said Reggie. "I'm quite accidental. I was invited down to look at your landslip. So my friend Bubb dug me out for my accidental opinion of the irrelevant burglary. If you don't mind."

Aston was in a hurry to say that he would be very glad for the police to have expert assistance. His scolding wrath passed off into anxiety to talk about the burglary and to be hospitable. There must have been a very clever gang at work. It seemed to be just like all the other cases, and they'd been infernally successful; they'd taken things which couldn't be replaced—family heirlooms and a collection that was the work of generations. But it was very cold, a glass of sherry now and a sandwich—

He left Reggie and Bubb in the noble Elizabethan hall which had no fire on its big hearth and bustled away to return with his wife and sherry and biscuits. Reggie's smarting tongue reported that the sherry was as much like sherry as the biscuits like sandwiches.

Corroborated at each sentence by his wife, who was faintly purple from cold, Aston went on with his tale. They had got home from the ball about half-past twelve, drunk some soup and gone to bed. Everything was in order, everything quiet then. Mrs. Aston took off her diamonds—

"One moment," Reggie interrupted. "Had you heard of the burglary at Lord Werne's place when you left the ball?"

"No sir, I had not." Aston's answer was quick. "Not a word about it." Then he stopped while his wife twittered agreement. "Was it known at the ball?"

"Oh yes. I heard of it there," said Reggie. "But I think you left before I did."

"What time was Werne's burglary then?" Aston demanded, and Bubb told him it was before eleven. "I wish I had known the rascals were busy last night," Aston said with some vehemence.

"Naturally. Yes," Reggie murmured. "By the way, did your son come home with you?"

Aston frowned. "My son is assisting Mr. Brown in some farm development and staying over there for the time." Mrs. Aston made haste to add that Giles was so interested in farming, and there were only the servants in the house, and they hadn't heard a sound.

"Pity," Reggie murmured. "However. To resume—Mrs. Aston took off her diamonds—"

And Aston resumed eagerly. That was about one o'clock. His wife put the diamonds away just as usual in the cabinet in the wainscot parlor and locked them up. "Yes, I'm quite sure I did," Mrs. Aston chimed in. "But they had better come and see, hadn't they, Francis?" She drew her cashmere shawl more closely round her and led the way up a stately and drafty staircase to a long, bare corridor in which were many windows and doors rattling to the wind.

Aston opened one door and gave them a glimpse of a bedroom hung with faded tapestry. "That's our room, the great chamber it's called." He crossed the corridor and flung another door wide. "This is the wainscot parlor, you see, meant for the privacy of the master and mistress of the house."

It was a small room with dark paneling in a rectangular pattern and a molded ceiling on which coats of arms had faded. The casement swung creaking. "That's how it was found this morning," Aston explained. "It was shut last night. But you'll see …" One pane of the glass was gone. "Now this is where the jewels have always been kept." He brought them to an old cabinet of walnut inlaid with lighter woods and was expounding that it was a seventeenth-century piece and was made for his family and had never been moved, till Bubb began to pry into it.

The doors had been forced, and the lock torn away. A range of small drawers was displayed, most of them open, and those which were open were empty.

"Who did this?" Bubb interrupted Aston's lecture.

"What? Oh I see what you mean. The housemaid found the window open and the door of the cabinet broken just as it is and told me. Then of course I came at once to see if anything had been taken. I opened the drawers."

"Then your fingerprints will be on 'em. You won't mind our taking prints of your hands—just to eliminate you?"

"Certainly, naturally, I've no objection, of course," said Aston. And his wife added that they had better have hers too—she was touching several of the drawers last night—and husband and wife made a duet of further information. Her tiara had been put in one drawer, her necklace in a second which also contained other jewelry. In a third was a collection of cameos, some thirty pieces, most of them very beautiful, apart from intrinsic value. The duet was becoming affectionate over the beauty of the cameos when Bubb interrupted again. "Yes, I'm sure. But I must ask you to give me a list of what's been taken. I suppose you were insured, Mr. Aston?"

"Of course I am," said Aston. "With burglaries all round us, I wasn't going to omit that. But it's no sort of compensation. The things were insured for £5,500, a mere commercial value. They're priceless to me." And Mrs. Aston echoed him in a wail.

"I understand your feelings, I hope, sir," Bubb answered. "If you show me the policy and the specification I can make a note."

Aston fussed at a writing table and produced papers. Bubb sat down to them with Reggie looking over his shoulder. Laboriously Bubb copied particulars of the jewels; Reggie was more interested in the list of cameos. They were all specified as Greek or Roman with the names of the stones in which they had been cut, sard, cornelian, onyx. "Fine collection, sir." He looked up at Aston. "A work of scholarship."

Aston stroked his mustache complacently and said he had not quite forgotten his classics, and Mrs. Aston added with affectionate adoration that he cared for them more than anything in the world and exhorted Mr. Fortune to look at his books.

Reggie looked and saw a Chippendale bookcase and sighed. A good piece in itself but wrong in that Tudor room. So were the books: college prizes bound in vellum.

Yes, Francis Aston had read some classics in his time and his father before him; "Presented to Francis Aston, scholar of Coena Domini College, Oxford, by the President and Fellows" for a first class in the Final Classical School; Homer; Aeschylus; a whole string. They had been read too. Reggie glanced at Aston's sentimentally handsome face and remarked to himself that the world was a strange world, and his eyes were caught by something else which did not go with the room—a portrait of Aston. Oil painting, very shiny, made the man look like a fashion plate. Probably he did, before he got woebegone and ravaged. The gentleman of blood in riding clothes, adorned with buttonhole: pink sweet peas. Reggie gazed at the picture in plaintive horror—continued to gaze though Bubb had finished his notes and gone to the open window with Aston, and Aston was demonstrating how the burglars broke in.

One of the panes of the casement had been cut out with a glazier's diamond—there were the marks—obviously for a hand to come through and open the latch. Quite easy to climb up to the window; it was only the first floor and plenty of handholds on the bays below and the moulding. No need of a ladder, confound them. Just the same way as they got into George Holne's place. The usual way—cat-burglars, they were called, weren't they?—all the cases were the same. Aston supposed the burglary at Lord Werne's was done from an upper window too.

"It did look like it," said Bubb. "You have got the way of these cases clear in your head, sir."

"Why, of course, we've been so worried about them," Mrs. Aston cried. "Everybody has. It's dreadful."

"How much longer is it going on, Superintendent?" Aston demanded. "That's the question. Have you any clue to the fellows?"

"I don't mind saying I have hopes now," said Bubb. "I'll have a look outside, if you please." He went out, and Mr. and Mrs. Aston followed.

Reggie was still contemplating the picture. He drew nearer …

When Bubb and the Astons came back he had not moved. "Oh, do you like that portrait?" Mrs. Aston asked. "I think it's so good. Of course it was done a long time ago."

"Very good, yes," Reggie murmured. "You haven't looked at it, Bubb."

Bubb approached and looked stolidly and said without any conviction, "It is a good likeness."

Aston gave a self-conscious laugh. "Not now, my friend," and he quoted Greek: "The spring has gone out of the year."

"Oh no! No," Reggie said. "Others to come, sir." He turned to Bubb. "Well, well. If you've finished—"

A hint as broad as that Bubb was capable of taking. "I have, sir, for the present. I'll be coming back soon with the fingerprint men, Mr. Aston."

"But what do you think of it, Mr. Fortune?" Aston demanded.

"As you were sayin'. Your local type of burglary. Good-bye." Reggie's mumbling tone changed a note as he added, "Good-bye, Mrs. Aston."

CHAPTER X *Evidence of a Buttonhole*

THE SHOWERS HAD BECOME a drizzle of sleet. As the car started Reggie rubbed the side window and peered out at the range of greenhouses. "Lot of glass," he murmured. "Used to be very horticultural." He turned up his fur collar and slid down till his knees were under the dashboard.

"Well, what are you going to tell me, Mr. Fortune?" Bubb demanded.

"Oh my Bubb! A sad world."

"Do you advise me now to take that as a genuine burglary?"

"My dear chap! I never advise grandmothers how to suck eggs."

"Pretty bad egg, eh?"

"Yes, I think so. You have my sympathy. I should say there were no burglars. But I found no flaw in the evidence of burglary. Did you?"

"I have to own I didn't. There's scrabbling on the gravel below the window like there ought to be and not one clear footmark. If we do get Mr. Aston's fingerprints that won't signify. If we find no others, he can say the burglars wore gloves. And that's how this gang down here has worked all through. A burglary could have been done easy by the window, and it would be exactly like the others. Of course we can argue keeping valuables in a cabinet in an empty room looks fishy, but that won't get us anywhere. People do it; we've had the same kind of thing over and over. We can say it's queer him and his wife didn't hear anything, sleeping just across the passage. But the like of that's happened before, and last night there was a lot of wind blowing, and you heard how the old place rattled. Then you saw the date on his insurance policy; he's only just taken it out. But he has his answer again, he got nervous over the run of burglaries and insured. That's reasonable enough. I wouldn't mind betting there's been a lot of fresh insurance down here."

"Quite likely. Yes. The police have their uses, Bubb. Stimulate insurance business."

"I don't see the joke," Bubb complained. "His insurance company will have to pay up if we can't break down his story, and there's no way to begin. The one thing we have hold of—it's pretty well impossible the usual gang, the gang which cracked Lord Werne's place, would have got to Mr. Aston's— we can't do any good with that. Even if we caught 'em and proved they didn't, who's to say there wasn't imitators? We couldn't so much as challenge a man like Mr. Aston without a strong case. Nor could the insurance people. You know it. And yet you don't believe he ever had any burglars,

45

though you were sniffy when I hinted he hadn't. You're sure now. And all the same we've got to sit pretty and let a fraud go through."

"My Bubb! You're quite hot. Lucky fellow. I am not. Oh my hat, I am not." Reggie shuddered and cuddled himself together. "One other little bit of evidence. Also no use. When I came down here, our Mr. Aston was on the train, conspicuously anxious not to be observed. That's why I observed him. Well. He'd been in London and didn't want anybody to know it. What had he been doing? Taking out the insurance policy, yes. No need to go up for that. He could have had the diamonds and cameos valued down here. I should say he went up because he hadn't got 'em, because they were in pawn, and he didn't want to be noticed because he felt mighty clever and horrid frightened. Why frightened? I regret to say the official mind may be right. Burglary may be product of boy's bones. Aston was going to lose the rest of the cliff unless he could meet the mortgage on it. Well, he clings to his land desperate anyway. Perhaps he was only frightened of losing it. But we saw him very interested in the landslip. He may be panicking about the boy who went into those cliffs. No certainty where bits would come out. Better to keep all the ground he could. Your epidemic of burglaries he saw his way to use beautifully. Insure the jewels, fake a burglary to pattern, collect the full value in hard cash to pay off his mortgage and still have 'em all in the family. So he showed Mrs. Aston wearing 'em at the ball to prove possession and had his burglary good and quick. Very neat. Only one flaw. Flaw which attracted the acute eye of Superintendent Bubb. Aston shouldn't have had his burglary on the same night as my Lord Werne's. But he didn't know about it. He left the ball before the news got round."

"That's all right," said Bubb gloomily. "I always suspected it went like that. But what's the good of talking? Suppose we could prove he did go up to take the diamonds out of pawn. What then? He's got his answer ready. He did it so Mrs. Aston should have 'em to wear at the ball. That sort of thing's common—family jewels in pawn from one big do to another."

"Oh yes. Yes. He's managed quite well. I should say his insurance people will have to pay without one little kick. Are we downhearted? Yes. But not over their troubles. Once upon a time a boy died underground. Rather forgetting him, aren't you?"

"You've no need to say that, Mr. Fortune." Bubb was resentful. "You don't help us with young Tracy's case just telling me that the burglary is a fraud that won't ever be proved."

"I am futile, yes," Reggie agreed. "Not as futile as that. Evidence confused and confusin'. However. Heard are the voices—we bid you to hope. Direct the intelligence of Superintendent Bubb to our Mr. Aston's wainscot parlor. Which throws some new light on Mr. Aston, his nature and habit."

"How do you mean?"

"My Bubb! I made you look at that picture. Very instructive. Aston is the sort of man who keeps his own portrait in his den. Tryin' sort of man. And a very tryin' portrait."

"I don't know," Bubb objected. "I'd call it a handsome likeness. He is a good-looker, there's no denying."

"Yes, noble injured hero, yes," Reggie sighed. "I thought you thought so. Why did you go looking at the picture like a horse offered a jam tart?"

"I don't get that." Bubb was offended. "You can take it I saw no sense in fussing about his portrait."

"My dear chap! Oh my dear chap! I thought you were putting that on to beguile the Astons."

"You're being very clever," Bubb complained. "Mr. and Mrs. Aston weren't bothering about the picture at all."

"Not till they saw I was, no. And then they couldn't think why I did. But they don't know what we know. You saw our Mr. Aston was painted with a buttonhole."

"What about it? He would be. He always used to go about with a button-hole; I can remember him myself."

"Oh Bubb!" Reggie reproached him. "And you never told me. Your error. Your grave error. However. Now repaired. I thought it was a fellow with a buttonhole who assisted the boy Tracy underground. And our Mr. Aston kindly informs me that he used to wear one."

"Here—I can't make this out," Bubb said slowly. "How do you mean you thought of buttonholes over young Tracy's bones?"

"The glass," Reggie murmured. "The glass with the bones, the uncommon thin glass. Suggestin' a tube, as you remarked. Suggestin' also the tubes holding flowers in a buttonhole with water to keep 'em fresh, as worn by lovers of flowers in the days when our Mr. Aston was young. And it goes on record that he did wear one. You saw his pink sweet peas in the portrait. Careful photographic painter got in the metal leaf of the holder and the gleam of the glass tube. Didn't you notice?"

"By gum! That's a good one," Bubb said heartily. "You do get on to everything, Mr. Fortune. And now you put it together it looks so easy. Of course Aston did always have his flower in a buttonhole thing like you say—till he stopped growing flowers. Then those bits of glass with the boy's bones, they point to him having had a scrap with young Tracy—and his cameos too. You said those bits we found on the dig in the landslip were a broken cameo. You're getting a real case together."

"I wonder," Reggie murmured.

"I'll put it up to the chief constable right away, sir," Bubb said with gusto.

"Yes. You have to do that. Yes." Reggie was mournful. "Did you say it looked easy? Oh my Bubb!"

CHAPTER XI *Evidence of Ye Catte's Cradle*

IT IS CONTENDED by Mr. Fortune that the most brilliant thing in all his work on this case was the decision to look through Ye Catte's Cradle.

In dreaming complacent exposition of the processes of his mind, he will remark that this resolve seems like inspired imagination, its importance was so far beyond comprehension, so trenchant. But it wasn't really suggested by imagination, because he hasn't any; it was the product of pure reason—a very good effort—reasoning raised to the power of genius.

This is not taken seriously by his wife who prefers, in public, the explanation that he never could pass an old curiosity shop. But she finds the case too tragic for talk and in his conduct of it the Reggie Fortune whom she must laugh at—or fear.

The plain fact is that he did not come upon Ye Catte's Cradle by chance but sought it.

When Bubb returned him to General Duddon the general found him indisposed to talk and respecting his discretion entertained him at lunch with antiquarian chatter all about the museum of Colsbury: ice-age bones and flint arrows and stone axes and Celtic pots and Roman pans. Not by chance would Reggie have submitted without a struggle to a drive on a cold day to look at a museum like that. But he went amiably, and amiably he endured the general's demonstration of the crowded medley of odds and ends. Only when they had worked through to the stuffed birds and beasts did he grow restive. "Remarkable show. Yes. Ought to be some good old things about in the town. Is there an antique shop of class?"

"Yes, there is." The general was pleased with him. "You'd like to go round there next. Come along. Ye Catte's Cradle, they call it."

"Oh no!" Reggie was horrified.

"It's not so bad, I promise you. Quite shrewd, enterprising people. Ladies, you know."

"They would be," said Reggie, and, nevertheless, he went.

The name of Ye Catte's Cradle was the only offensively modern thing about it. It stood in Marygate, a lane off the market place, where ancient houses thrust out their upper stories beyond the lower, and their dark little shops were kept either by craftsmen working for country folk or people cherishing the old-world style for the attraction of tourists to picture postcards, Durshire pottery, a Durshire tea.

Ye Catte's Cradle hung out a painted sign of two pairs of hands, male and very female, making a net of string for a kitten who played with it. Underneath, between a saddler's and a gunsmith's, the window of bull's-eye panes exhibited old silver and samplers, some glass which might have been cut long ago and a suit of armor which was not obviously made last year.

The general opened the door, and a bell rang. A woman with pompadour hair, who was also painted in the eighteenth-century manner, came undulating to meet him and was arch. He shied at the exquisite medieval piece to which she lured him, a coffer so rough-hewn that Reggie murmured in his ear, "I did it with my little hatchet."

The general was more delicate. "You must have a heart, Miss Brabazon. Don't tempt me. I'm only a poor old half-pay officer. I just brought my friend in to look round, if you don't mind."

"Oh quite," Miss Brabazon drawled, "by all means; that's just what we like, General," and developed all her power of refined seduction, switching lights on and off again through the crowded purlieus of the shop. She did not find Reggie a good subject. She had already begun to let it appear that she thought poorly of him when, as she fussed over a table of china, she saw him looking at a picture. "Do you care for that?" she asked. "Quite Dutch, isn't it? I mean there's a style, a simple truth. I'm quite sure there's a great future for our best early nineteenth-century work. So earnest, you know, so sure. The eternal dignity of life."

"Yes, very earnest. As you say," Reggie murmured. The artist had the naive photographic method of Aston's artist. His picture showed a group of people on a lawn, and each of them stood out in separate focus. It was labeled "Coronation Fête Committee." There was a mayor in robes, the others wore plain clothes. What held Reggie's eyes was the discovery of Tracy among them, for Tracy was depicted with a rose in his buttonhole and the shimmer of a holder below.

"That came from the mayor's house when he died," said Miss Brabazon, still hoping. "A Simpkins. He did a good deal of work down here. Such an elegance of veracity. I've had a great many offers."

"You should have," Reggie nodded. "I wonder the people in it haven't snapped it up. I suppose you get a lot of 'em in here."

"Oh quite," Miss Brabazon drawled. "There's a very high level of taste in the county."

"There must be," Reggie smiled. "Do you do anything with jewels at all?"

"Indeed yes." She thought she had him at last. She minced across the shop to a glass-topped case.

He readily admits that he did not expect to find the inconvenient evidence of this second buttonhole. Another proof that his mind is without imagination. But he denies that the discovery of the picture was mere luck, explaining it as the deserved by-product of rational enquiry into the presence of cameos in the Aston affairs.

Miss Brabazon exhibited jewelry which she told him was very artistic; modern stuff, with semiprecious stones in settings which inadequate craftsmanship had copied from ancient design. Reggie was vaguely complimentary, and she tried him with hideous Indian gauds and garnets and jade. But he had seen a little tray of pendants, seals, odds and ends and asked for that. "Oh quite!" Miss Brabazon said again. "You are a connoisseur. These are very choice." She brought them out and with ruby nails pointed to a lump of rock crystal with a handle which might have been gold. "That was Sir William Temple's—it has his cipher, he sealed all his famous love letters to Dorothy Osborne with it."

"Systematic fellow," Reggie murmured. He was bent over the tray; he had found some cameos in brooches, in rings and unset. "Where did these come from?"

"Ah, those are quite ancient, classical, you see, all classical. Roman and Greek." Miss Brabazon expanded. "That is the goddess Venus, and here is Bacchus, and that is the Roman wolf with her twins," she giggled. "And that, that gentleman, that is the poet Homer. Isn't he venerable?"

Reggie scrutinized one after the other. "I was askin'—where did you get them?"

Miss Brabazon told him that she always took her holidays abroad—Italy, all over Italy, so refreshing, quite exquisite—and one picked up treasures here and there.

"Oh yes. Yes. Much of a market for cameos here?"

Miss Brabazon tossed her head. People came to her from all over the country.

"They would," Reggie soothed her. "I was wondering, have you had anyone after these?"

Miss Brabazon assured him she didn't expect to keep them long. People were pricing them every day.

"I rather like the Venus," said Reggie.

Miss Brabazon was very arch. "She is attractive, isn't she?"

Reggie haggled for her weakly and bought her for five pounds, and having thus engaged Miss Brabazon's interest asked if there had been any others of the same sort. Miss Brabazon was sorry—one or two, yes, she didn't know who bought them—but she could get other examples from her correspondents in Italy.

Reggie didn't think that was worth while. Reggie took Venus and the general away.

"Oh my hat! What a female! What a scent!" he moaned. "Tea is strongly indicated." The general talked of tea at the club. "Not that, no. Too virile.

I'm not strong enough. Sweetness and light, my need. Look." He led the general to a beetle-browed shop which had comely pots of honey and cream in front of pale blue curtains and willow-pattern walls behind. "Same like the king's daughter, all glorious within."

This Willow Tearoom was a place of many corners arranged for intimacy. They had taken one. Reggie had shocked General Duddon by his demands for cream, cakes and still more cream and honey, when he became sadly aware that the two young people whose heads were very close together in the farthest corner were Alison Tracy and Giles Aston.

Their conversation seemed vehement rather than sentimental. Both of them were often talking at the same time. But they had no quarrel, they held a conference of excitement; their flushed, eager faces told of an alliance in which the only point of difference was likely to be which should do more for the other, or how they should do it.

They were still talking hard after Reggie had satisfied his desire for sweets. He catalogued that as an extraordinary, an instructive proof of devotion and caught the eye of the waitress and beyond her saw Tracy coming into the tearoom.

Tracy stood still and swept a choleric stare round the cozy corners, detected his daughter and made for her. What he said was in a hoarse growl.

Paying the bill Reggie heard something about catching her, and a young blackguard, and a lying little minx and an order to get back home. Her answer came clear enough. "Don't be idiotic. You know I'm not afraid of you. If you want to make a scene, you can have it." She stood up. "You won't! You daren't! Come along, Giles. Come with me."

For Giles had felt that dignity required him to stop and challenge her father. "If you've anything to say to me, sir, you know where to find me." Honor thus satisfied he obeyed the girl's hand, and Tracy let them pass and followed heavily.

"Well, well." Reggie came to the door and saw the two vanish into the market place with Tracy lagging far behind.

"Most unpleasant," the general squeaked.

"Yes. As you say. Fathers, love your children and be not bitter against them."

"That's not what the Bible says, sir," the general protested. "The text is husbands love your wives. Children are told to obey."

"By the letter of the regulations, yes."

"Certainly the man is a brute. But his daughter shouldn't treat him like that."

"I wonder," Reggie murmured.

CHAPTER XII *Evidence of Contradictions*

THE SNOW AND SLEET of the morning had blown away. Under a clear frosty sky twilight yielded slowly to dusk. As the general drove him back from Colsbury Reggie watched a hillside on which the white shape of a giant, the "Long Man" of Igdon, was cut out of the turf. It grew dim and faded into the form of the hill. Against the steel-blue light in the west the hilltop stood sharp, bulging with the mounds of ancient burial and fortress. Reggie let himself see ghosts, toiling and moiling there for the honor of their kin and their sacred right to the land. His dreamy watch on the hill delighted the general, who seized the occasion for another lecture on Durshire giants, the Igdon giant, the wonderful pits of Giants' Graves up there beyond, above the black land by the river, and so brought him happily home.

There the general's manservant reported a telephone message. "The chief constable's compliments to Mr. Fortune, and he would be glad if Mr. Fortune could call on him tomorrow."

"My compliments to the chief constable, and I was going to," said Reggie.

Through dinner he remained pensive and vague. To the dinners of General Duddon he has applied the French criticism of marriage, "good but not delightful." They are respectable—this one was cod and cutlets—they commit no offense, they omit to interest. The general's wine did not supply charm. There was only sherry and port; the sherry was merely blameless, and for port Reggie is incapable of affection.

He lit his cigar in a state of somnolent depression.

While the general, who had not found so good a listener through a long and talkative career, chattered wild antiquarian fancies and anecdotes of the army, he continued to see ghosts: gloomy Nordic blonds like the Astons and fierce redhaired enigmas like the Tracys chasing one another over black land and white land, with swarms of full-bodied brunettes like Bubb, like the country folk, playing in and out among them.

Although he insists that at this stage in the case, by his visit to Ye Catte's Cradle, he had already obtained the crucial evidence, the evidence which sufficed to explain everything, he confesses that he had not then the slightest idea what it meant. His state of mind was like that of the man of science who, having observed a new and surprising fact in astronomy, physics, biology, knows that he has made hay of the good old laws but cannot see how to make any others instead.

So he could only find comfort as he went to sleep by telling himself that he need not eat any more of the general's dinners; he had done all he could do for Durshire. He must go back to his laboratory where sections of warts were crying out for him and to his own cook, the admirable, the unique Elise.

When he came next morning into the vaulted room of the chief constable, he blinked. That prim official had started up to meet him, held out a hand, smiled with many teeth. "Good morning, Mr. Fortune. It's very kind of you to let me have a conference with you."

"We are getting on, aren't we?" said Reggie, accepting the limp hand with a glance at Superintendent Bubb, who stood by. "How do you do?"

"There have been remarkable developments," the chief constable went on. "I shall be glad to have your opinion. I must acknowledge that the insight which you showed on the first discovery has much impressed me. Now let me review the present position. You have advised the superintendent that the bones found in further excavation complete adequate evidence of a boy of the age of Charles Tracy having been put into the cliff about the time that Charles Tracy disappeared."

"More than adequate. Conclusive. But no indication of cause of death. There won't be."

"I appreciate that point. The fragments of the cameo which you found on the site were not there, in your belief, when you made your first visit."

"Not belief. Certainty. They weren't there before. They're freshly fresh and newly new."

"I am not contesting your statement, Mr. Fortune. We must therefore draw the inference that someone with a cameo had been busy on the site since the first bones were discovered."

"Oh yes. I did. I do."

"Now let me pass to the burglary. The superintendent informs me you agreed with him in concluding that there was no burglary, that Mr. Aston himself made away with his property in order to claim the insurance money and provide funds for saving the rest of his cliff property."

"One Aston or another," Reggie corrected. "However. No proof. I should say you'll never get any. Unless somebody splits. Neat job."

"A deplorable affair," said the chief constable. "But we have to do with something much more serious. Now let me return to the cameo. I was myself aware that Aston often wore a cameo ring. He used to be a good scholar. I believe he still keeps up his classics. These fragments appear to be the head of a Greek goddess."

"Oh yes. Athene. The conventional Athene."

"Quite so. I don't know of any other man in the county who wears a cameo. We have already inferred that Aston arranged for his cameos to disappear in a burglary."

"As you say. Curious and suggestive," Reggie drawled.

The chief constable gave him a look of solemn surprise. "You take the matter very coldly, Mr. Fortune. I cannot do so. There are the gravest issues. Let me go on. I come now to the fragments of glass which you found with the poor boy's bones. Am I to understand you feel certain that glass came from a flower holder such as you saw in the portrait of Aston?"

"Yes. Absolutely. Exact correspondence to small buttonhole tubes."

"In fact you had concluded that the broken glass came from a flower holder before you discovered that Aston used to wear one?"

Reggie smiled. "It was in my mind. Obvious possibility."

"I could not call it obvious. I should say a most impressive example of insight. So now we have established a strong chain of circumstantial evidence that Aston was concerned in young Tracy's disappearance."

"Looks like that, yes," Reggie murmured.

"It is a terrible case, Mr. Fortune," the chief constable reproved him. "But there is more yet. As you know, Superintendent Bubb returned to Aston's house for further investigation. …"

"Yes. I was waitin' for that." Reggie sat up. "What did you get, Bubb?"

Bubb gave a disciplined look at his chief and received permission to speak. "I got more than I bargained for, Mr. Fortune. More than Mr. Aston did either. There were no fingerprints at all but his and hers. I put the servants through it, and that was no good either. I don't believe they know anything. But while I was working at 'em, young Mr. Aston turned up, and him and his father fell to—hammer and tongs. I couldn't get to hear more than bits of it, but they're in a rare old fury with each other, and the root of it is that the young man has been going with Miss Tracy, and the old man won't stand for it. Mr. Giles came over because he'd heard of the burglary and wanted to know about it. He seemed to be thinking it was fishy. I couldn't swear to that, but somehow his father flew off the handle and damned him for staying with Brown. What right had he to talk? Where was he when the burglary was done? Then they got onto this Miss Tracy business, and Mr. Giles said right out he'd fallen for her and her for him, and the old man swore he wouldn't have it and got cursing wild, giving the Tracys dirt. Then the young one hit back. What was it he'd got against the Tracys? He couldn't put a name to anything, dared him to. And on that the old man pretty well kicked young Mr. Giles out of the house, and I saw him at the door looking like a corpse."

"The father?" Reggie asked.

"That's what I mean," said Bubb. "The son was just not giving a damn. Of course I couldn't take it up with 'em. I hadn't what you might call a locus standi in it."

"Oh my Bubb! I wouldn't," Reggie protested.

"Well, there you are; it's nasty stuff," Bubb concluded triumphantly.

"Yes. Very painful," Reggie murmured and again made the misquotation which distressed General Duddon. "Fathers, love your children and be not bitter against them."

The chief constable cleared his throat for oratory. "I am in agreement with you, Mr. Fortune. This quarrel between the Astons can only bear an ugly interpretation. We had already felt bound to recognize that you had produced weighty evidence compelling us to suspect Aston of guilty knowledge of Charles Tracy's death. I put it no higher. But now all the results of our investigation have been laid before you. What are we to infer from the course of this quarrel, the elder Aston's violent animosity against his son's connection with the Tracys, the son's challenge to give a reason for it which roused the father to desperation?"

Reggie contemplated him with closing eyes. "I haven't the slightest idea," said Reggie.

The chief constable's mouth came open. He put his handkerchief to it. "I beg your pardon, I don't follow," he complained. "You were remarking that the quarrel added a most painful element. Quite so. Surely you meant me to understand you were forced to the conclusion that the elder Aston's ferocity and alarm confirmed the circumstantial evidence?"

"You want me to say you ought to work up a case against him," Reggie smiled. "No. I shouldn't do that. You'll have to work. But you'd better avoid the fixed idea."

"I quite fail to understand you." The chief constable was offended.

"Yes, that is so. Sorry. Not wholly your fault. You said all the results of your efforts had been laid before me. Thanks very much. But I made some too. And I had other results. Inconvenient results. Quarrel between the Astons not the only family quarrel. Father Tracy also furious with daughter Tracy and cursing Aston the son. I heard him. In a tea shop."

"Did you indeed! It does not surprise me," the chief constable sneered. "And let me point out to you it is only further evidence of the bad blood between the families."

"Between the old ones—which we knew before—yes."

"And of a particular suspicion," the chief constable insisted.

"You think so? Son Aston challenged his father. Daughter Tracy challenged hers. Said he daren't make a scene about her affair. What young folks in love say to cross parents may not be evidence. But Father Tracy did gain by his son's death. However. Further confusin' results. Father Aston wasn't the only man who used to wear a flower holder. In that sinful shop here, Ye Catte's Cradle, there's a picture of a group with Father Tracy wearing one. Did you know he did?"

"Certainly not," the chief constable exclaimed. "I have no recollection. Have you, Superintendent?"

"I don't call it to mind, sir," said the faithful Bubb.

"We must recognize, Mr. Fortune," the chief constable told him, "that such things were not uncommon years ago."

"Yes. I do. But you didn't when you made it evidence against Aston."

"I cannot let that pass." The chief constable was indignant. "It was you, Mr. Fortune. You pointed it out to the superintendent as indicating Aston's guilt."

"That's right, sir." Bubb nodded.

"Not indicatin', no. Suggestin'. *You* said it looked easy, Bubb, not me. And then I didn't know our Tracy used a flower holder. Deeper and deeper yet."

"Surely, Mr. Fortune," the chief constable stammered, "surely you don't mean to imply suspicion of Tracy himself—his own son—"

"One of the possibilities," Reggie drawled. "Always was. Yet another result. Aston's cameos, according to the valuer for insurance, were genuine old stuff. Cameo found broken in the landslip was not. Modern copy. Aston's were stones. The cameo found was shell. Cassis rufa. As made in Italy now. As sold in your horrid shop, Ye Catte's Cradle. I bought one myself yesterday. There you are. And the female told me she had sold one or two others lately. So the cameo isn't evidence of Aston's interest in the landslip. Evidence somebody else wanted us to think Aston was interested. That's the real case—as far as it's gone." He smiled upon the chief constable. "You have a lot of work to do yet."

The chief constable leaned his head on his hand. "It is a most distressing affair." He spoke disconsolately. "All this new matter makes it more difficult than ever. I did think we had a clear line of enquiry," he looked up at Reggie, "painful as it was, very painful. But now I don't see my way. What is your opinion, Mr. Fortune?"

"There isn't a way. Not one way. You've got to work every way. With a free mind. Go over Aston and Tracy again—somebody ought to remember something about the morning the boy vanished, somebody should have seen him and them. Go over the sham cameo. Who bought it? Go over the whole place. Who went to the landslip between the night I left it and the morning when Bubb got there? Lots of work. Get on with it. I'm going back to London, but I shan't forget. Let me hear what you turn up. Good-bye."

So he returned to the warts in his laboratory, human and other, and heard nothing more from the chief constable. For the next thing which turned up was the chief constable's body—dead in a ditch.

CHAPTER XIII *Evidence of a Retriever*

REGGIE WAS CONCENTRATED upon a microscope when his assistant brought him the telegram from Colsbury.

REGRET REPORT CHIEF FOUND DROWNED LAST NIGHT, BUBB.

He read it and continued to gaze at it for some time. "Well, well." He rose slowly and turned large, reproachful eyes on his assistant. "A sad world, Jenks. Wasteful world. Superintendent Bubb isn't. Very economical, our Bubb." He wandered out of the laboratory and rang up the chief of the Criminal Investigation Department.

"Fortune speaking. Morning, Lomas. Have you heard from the Durshire police? No, I thought not. It sounded like that. Curious. They've been and drowned their chief constable. No reason given for rash act. But they might have asked for your eminent assistance. And they only ask for me—or not even that. Just a polite intimation that he has passed hence. Very exclusive people, the Durshire police. ... Yes, that is what I'm talking about—the bones and the burglary and happy families. ... As you say. Queer turn. Not a nice case. Never was. ... Yes, I did think the defunct chief constable was particularly shy of doing anything. I parted from him with powerful exhortations to get busy, and he goes and gets dead. Obstructive of him. And confusing. This case is continually confounding confusion. What? ... Bless your sweet innocence, no, nothing like that. I did not set him onto any particular person. On the contrary. I restrained him from such. He was yearning to make a dead set at the burglary faker and all bothered and worried by my nasty, reasonable objections. I told him to go for everybody in the perishin' vicinity. And the consequence is his superintendent finds him drowned. What? ... Result of taking advice from me? That has never drowned you yet. I'm sorry. Not my job to make the world safe for policemen. My job to be right. And I was. So far as I got. I can't help where he got to. ... You think I'm not sympathetic? No, we have no emotions. At present. I keep mine for deservin' cases. He may deserve a tear. The mind is open. Quite likely he meant well. Did it all for the best. That sort of man. ... Cryptic? My dear chap! It is. Partly his fault. Puzzle-headed, as only you officials can be. ... No, I never thought you meant well. You have some intelligence. … Oh yes. Yes. I shall go down. I must. Bother him. I don't know whether I'm a mourner or a nasty detective. What is life that one should seek it? Good-bye. You have no heart."

The next morning his own large car—he was determined never again to endure the pitch and toss of Superintendent Bubb's—twisted through Durshire lanes with a sucking gurgle of black mud as the directions of Bubb to his reluctant injured chauffeur ordained.

They stopped by the gate to a sodden field from which a crop of roots had lately been eaten by sheep. "You can turn here, my lad," Bubb told the chauffeur who, without moving his lips, said something improper.

Reggie stood surveying with dislike the field's untidiness and dirt. "What a place to come and die in," he murmured.

Bubb reproved him in the very manner of the chief constable. "That's a hard way to talk, Mr. Fortune. I reckon he didn't pick it, poor gentleman."

"You think not? Whose land is it?"

"It's all Mr. Tracy's estate here," said Bubb. "Now if you'll come along with me, I'll show you." And as Reggie picked his slow way across the filth of the field he filled out the details of the story.

The chief constable always took a day's hunting when he could. He was a good horseman but no thruster. He'd gone out as usual with Lord Werne's hounds, and they had a fair run all up the valley and lost their fox on the downs. Gentlemen said the chief was going all right, but he gave up before the end. Nobody seemed to have seen him after. His straight way back to Colsbury might be across those fields. About dusk one of Mr. Tracy's keepers was going along the lane and saw a saddle horse in the field without anyone on it or about. Of course he guessed somebody had taken a toss and went to have a look.

He had a dog with him, a retriever, and the dog worked over to the ditch and hunted along and went in and gave tongue. When the keeper got there the dog was tugging at something in the water, and he found it was a man's body. "Here, this is about the place, Mr. Fortune," Bubb continued. "You see there's hoof prints each side—and that trampling and scraping, that's where his body was dragged up."

The ditch was wide and deep, a drainage cut full of dark oily water eddying through reed banks. Pollarded willows grew along the banks, and some had slipped down and lay like dams. "He was caught against one of them—that one there," said Bubb. "Where the twigs are broken."

"So I thought," Reggie murmured. "Nailed boots on the trunk. The rescuin' keeper. Yes." He looked to and fro; he wandered each way along the bank. "That's where he was found. How did he get there? What is the theory of Superintendent Bubb?"

"It looks to me the keeper was right first off; he took a toss," Bubb said.

"It's a good big jump. Say the horse refused, the chief was thrown over his head and stunned and lay there and drowned. That's likely enough. That accounts for everything."

"Yes. It could be. Assumin' he was alone when he came here. Was he?"

"No reason to think otherwise, Mr. Fortune. No one's come forward."

"Oh my Bubb! Nobody would—if there was anybody. You're also assumin' he was drowned."

"I beg your pardon, sir. No assuming by me. That's why I sent word to you. I want to make sure everything's quite straight. I'm in charge, him being gone, and I have a duty to him and a kindness, if I may say so. I reckon I'm all right if I go by your opinion."

"Yes. You will be," Reggie said. "However. Materials for opinion not yet adequate. Take me to the body."

It was dark when he came out of the mortuary and woke his chauffeur from a doze of hopeless resignation to the new sorrow of returning to police headquarters.

Superintendent Bubb had established himself in the chief constable's medieval room which was not a harmonious setting for his plump matter-of-fact person.

"Well, well." Reggie gave him a crooked smile. "Here we are again. One being taken away, another is not lacking."

"You needn't rub it in, Mr. Fortune. I know there's a good man gone, and his place is a big one for me to fill."

"I wouldn't say that," Reggie murmured. "However. Cause of death of the predecessor. Medical evidence definite on that. He went into the water alive and he was drowned. But the medical evidence cannot say whether his death was accident, suicide or murder. Immediately previous to death he took a knock on the left temple sufficient to stun him: such a knock as might be caused by fall from horseback, voluntary dive into that stream or attack with a blunt weapon. No other injury. But he had a bad heart. He might go queer or faint when tired. It wouldn't have taken much to knock him out; he wasn't likely to come round quick. Somebody may have known all that and counted on it. Considerin' all considerations we reach a probability that death was accidental. I should have to say so if asked at the inquest."

The strained attention with which Bubb had listened was let off in a puff of relief. "Thank you, sir. That's very thorough. I didn't care to say so to you before, but our police surgeon had no doubt it was accident. I only troubled you because I wanted to have the highest authority."

"Wise man. Yes. I couldn't say there's no doubt. Neither suicide nor murder eliminated by the medical evidence. Passed to you. Matter for the police."

"How could it be suicide, sir? A man who meant to drown himself wouldn't do it by riding out to hounds first."

"Not likely, no. But the decision to kill himself might have been sudden. He may have heard something while out which made him feel desperate."

"I don't know how you can say a thing like that!" Bubb was indignant. "The chief hadn't anything to be afraid of, not from any man alive."

"Afraid," Reggie repeated. "Well, you ought to know. But he was bothered, wasn't he? Badly bothered by the Tracy-Aston business; then rather relieved by the converging of evidence on Aston; upset again when I pointed out it *didn't* converge, and he mustn't confine himself to making a case against Aston."

"As if he would!" Bubb was indignant. "It's such a blind muddle—that's the only way it got him. He was as straight as a die. I do wonder at you."

"My Bubb! Very proper of you. Very loyal. Passin' from suicide—any reason to suspect foul play?"

"None in the world, sir. Everybody liked the chief. He hadn't an enemy."

"What a life!" Reggie sighed. "And what a wonderful policeman! Didn't anyone ever feel annoyed by his activities? I suppose he had got active in the bone business?"

"Enquiries were going on," said Bubb with official dignity. "Nothing had been made out."

"Well, well. Who else went hunting on this last hunting of his? Have you made out that?"

"I took care to obtain a list of the gentlemen, naturally I did. No one could tell me anything except that he gave up and dropped out."

"As you said. Yes. Who was there?"

Bubb read out names from a paper. ...

"The young Aston. Oh," Reggie murmured. "Not old Aston. Nor old Tracy. Conspicuous by their absence, if your list is full. Nor young Aston's patron, the busy Brown."

"He's no hunting man," said Bubb with contemptuous surprise. "He's gone back to London too. I don't know why you drag him in."

"I didn't. He dragged himself to my notice. However. Also absent. Only the young Aston—of those known to the police. Well, well. Now what exactly had you been doing—previous to this distressin' death?"

Bubb talked at length. They had communicated with Aston's insurance company and the insurance company with them, and an assessor had visited Aston's place and gone over everything and met them afterward and said he couldn't advise his people to fight it—they had no firm ground—but he quite agreed it was a very fishy case, and they'd go slow in settling the claim.

"That is unusual," Reggie murmured. "However. I wasn't worrying about the sorrows of insurance people. I asked what you'd done."

Again Bubb had a lot to say, but it contained nothing—a catalogue of interviews with country people about the boy's disappearance which only reestablished what was already known.

"How useful," Reggie murmured.

"I'm sorry you're not satisfied," said Bubb tartly. "We were acting as you advised. I never thought it would get us anywhere myself."

"You do like advice, don't you?" Reggie drawled. "I suppose it hasn't occurred to you that there ought to be an inquest on the boy's bones someday?"

"Of course it has," Bubb exclaimed. "You said yourself to enquire further first. The chief thought best to go through with that and the coroner agreed. I may tell you we've taken our own surgeon's opinion on the bones, and he agrees with you they're quite recent."

"So he told me. Very gratifying. Then why didn't you open the inquest and adjourn for the enquiries?"

"That's what I should have preferred from the start," said Bubb with defiant emphasis.

"Oh my Bubb!" Reggie reproached him. "I am the obstructionist? Not so, but far otherwise. You're not doing yourself justice. Tell me all. I did suggest particular enquiries. Your modesty leaves out your brilliant results. What about the sham cameo? Who has been buying cameos at the nasty Catte's Cradle?"

"That line goes nowhere," Bubb told him. "The chief had Miss Brabazon in, and she couldn't recall any particular person buying one. She couldn't swear to the bits found as ever having been in her place."

"Well, well! Tryin' female. Evasive female." Reggie's eyelids drooped. "However. Enquiries being thus futile, pressure is indicated. Hadn't that occurred to the chief constable?"

"How do you mean, pressure?" Bubb looked blank.

"Bless your sweet innocence!" Reggie's smile was not amiable. "I mean publicity. You haven't found the right witnesses, or—if you have—they won't tell the truth. Openin' an inquest on the boy's bones will make everybody sit up and take notice. People who wouldn't help you might think again. People you've omitted to try should appear."

"Nobody's been omitted." Bubb was indignant.

Reggie's eyes opened wide. " 'Dear Clarence that cannot be true,' " he quoted. "You shouldn't say it. Shakes confidence in the intelligence of our conscientious police. Obvious that somebody was omitted—person who bought the cameo—person who visited the landslip privily and by stealth to deposit same so that you and me should find it. That person is the key to the whole confounded confusion. Didn't the chief constable perceive it?"

Bubb sat silent in frowning meditation and at last announced: "The chief was bothered about the cameo, of course. What he said to me was he couldn't see his way. If I understand you, Mr. Fortune, you're putting it the cameo was planted on us to fake evidence against Mr. Aston. Supposing it was, how can you expect the person who did so to come forward and tell us? That's not sense."

"Oh my Bubb! I expect nothing without work for it. Neither the late chief nor you had any suspicion of anybody. Happy condition. However. The cameo was planted very late one day or very early the next, almost certainly the latter. After the discovery of the boy's bones was known to police headquarters. That suggested nobody to you. Pity. Remains the possibility this cameo person did get noticed out so bright and early on a beastly morning. Wasn't anything done about that?"

"I myself asked round the houses near the landslip," Bubb said sulkily.

"And the chief constable?" Reggie murmured. "Whom did he ask?"

"It wasn't for him to make enquiries himself," Bubb protested.

"Not running round, no. Yet he did do something. He dealt with Miss Brabazon. Nobody else?"

"Not to my knowledge, sir. It wouldn't be like him, either."

"Well, well." Reggie's eyelids drooped again. "You have done something. You've left no possible justification for delayin' the inquest any longer. And now you'll have to hold two inquests. That is satisfactory. One on the unfortunate chief constable, one on the unfortunate bones. You'd better take the bones first. More instructive sequence."

Bubb scowled at him. "The way you talk isn't hardly human."

"Oh yes. Very human. The natural man bein' thwarted by the inhumanity of the unknown. Still preservin' faith in the human reason."

"I don't follow," Bubb grumbled. "Of course there has to be an inquest on the chief. But I have no objections to opening one on the boy's remains first, and I dare say the coroner won't mind."

"Thank you so much," Reggie murmured.

"It don't seem to me to matter which comes first," Bubb said. "What is the idea?"

"My poor Bubb! Some connection between the boy's bones and the chief constable's demise. Let us see who is interested in the evidence we're going to put in about the boy before we come to the man."

"Oh, I see. Do you want to be called as an expert witness?"

"Not at this stage. No. I may come in later. Your surgeon can say what I should say. You have the bones and the cameo here?"

"Yes sir. Do you want to see 'em again?"

"Please," said Reggie sweetly.

Bubb went out and returned with a deedbox and unlocked it.

Reggie inspected the contents. "Yes. Bones all present and correct," he murmured.

"Of course they are." Bubb was indignant.

"Of course," Reggie repeated. "As you say." He looked up at Bubb with narrowing eyes. "But where is the broken cameo?"

"The bits are there—in a cardboard case." Bubb came to the deedbox and turned the bones over. "God bless my soul!" he muttered. "It's gone."

"Superintendent Bubb is surprised?" Reggie's drawl was disagreeable.

"What do you mean?" Bubb flushed. "Are you saying you think—?"

"Thought it was a possibility."

"Possibility how?" Bubb spluttered. "Meaning I've made away with it? I take my oath I haven't seen the thing since the chief had the deedbox brought to him before he questioned Miss Brabazon."

"Oh yes. When last seen, passed to the chief constable. The one piece of evidence we had against the keyman in the whole confounded case, against the man who wanted us to put the boy's murder on Aston. After I pointed out the cameo was a fraud and disappointed the chief constable by warning him he couldn't use it against Aston, the cameo is removed, and the chief constable is removed. Accident? Suicide? Or murder? Very interestin' problem." Reggie contemplated Bubb with benign curiosity.

"What are you suggesting, Mr. Fortune?" Bubb was subdued but resentful.

"Dirty work, Bubb. Very dirty work. Nobody could have removed the cameo but the deceased chief, what?"

"There's no denying that," Bubb growled. "I'll stand for it, he had his reasons."

"My dear chap! Oh, my dear chap! So will I. What were they?"

"I won't have it he was anything but straight." Bubb was defiant.

"Then you do suspect foul play." Reggie smiled. "You said you didn't."

"No more I did," said Bubb. "But I grant you I do now. Unless I can find the cameo in his house."

"I should say you won't," Reggie murmured. "However. Not the real problem."

"What is then?"

"Oh, my Bubb! Why it was taken away."

"I'd like to know who you're pointing at." Bubb was truculent.

"Yes. Very natural of you." Reggie smiled. "The higher we go the fewer."

CHAPTER XIV *Evidence of a Poacher*

AT THIS STAGE in the case Reggie received comfort. He discovered that hams of singular merit are made in the black land of Durshire and that all their virtues improve by being grilled, which he considers unique in ham.

The disappearance of the cameo in the chief constable's demise was only a minor source of pleasure, gratifying though superfluous and inconvenient— proof of the soundness of his judgment. Some fellow had been working hard to muddle the case, a fellow who did not know quite enough but a very shrewd fellow, and a fellow who stuck at nothing. A fellow worth Mr. Fortune's while. Just the sort of fellow to do business with. And anything might arrive before it was done.

Not so very pleasant to be right after the event—having no notion about the future. Who was the fellow? The chief constable had known more than he chose or dared to tell. He was frightened of an investigation which led to anybody but old Aston. He expected it would hurt somebody he didn't want to hurt. Himself or a friend?

Probably a friend—or somebody who wasn't a friend but had a hold on him. Yes. He hadn't the brains or the courage to work the cameo trick. But when it was exposed he had his notion who did it. Probably he dealt with the fellow privately, and the fellow took his chances and wiped out him and the cameo.

Quite a good theory. The only theory. No other in sight. Leaving the original question—who was the fellow?—unanswered. Superintendent Bubb? The correct, indignant Bubb? He had every chance—except that he wasn't a hunting man. But the only man in the hunt he drew attention to was young Aston—and neither of the Astons could want to eliminate the faked cameo. It needn't have been a hunting man. Needn't have been a horseman at all. However. No sort of evidence against Bubb. Only that he was rather too good to be true.

The mind must remain open. Wide open. Might be anybody. Might even have been accident. And the cameo beguiled out of the defunct beforehand.

Thus Reggie had attained to impartial uncertainty as he smoked his after-breakfast pipe on the morning of the first inquest. The placid and benign face which he took to it owed much to the inspiration of the originality of the grilled ham. But he also enjoyed the sense of challenge and felt competent.

His chauffeur, who had contracted a dislike for the narrow and winding roads of Durshire, took the big car along with resentful caution and was surprised and annoyed to get no demand for speed.

What came to his angry ears was a murmur. "The willows are breaking color, bless 'em. There's celandine out and primroses. Look, Sam. Lent lilies!"

Sam hunched his back and pressed the accelerator.

They drove on from the bright banks and copses of the black land up to the gray green of the chalk ridge, which was still unsure of the coming of spring, where the short-stemmed buds would not open.

In the bleak village of Elstow they stopped before a hall of corrugated iron about which were cars and a little gazing crowd. Reggie went in and made his way to Superintendent Bubb, majestically important at a side table with satellites. Reggie hoped he didn't intrude. "Happy to see you, Mr. Fortune." Bubb spoke with condescension. "I didn't gather you would attend."

"You never know," Reggie murmured. "Just going to begin, same like Mr. Snodgrass."

Bubb signed him to silence. The coroner was entering.

Reggie turned and surveyed the hall with dreamy eyes. A jury of stolid country folk uncomfortable in Sunday clothes. Bubb had told the truth about one thing at least. His type was common. Most of them were dark and solid like him. Dress them differently, give them a different job, and they could pass for him or the banker Cope. One or two might have mixed with the tall blond race of which the Astons came. Not a man showed the fierce, redhaired Tracy strain.

Reggie's eyes passed to the people who had come to listen. Quite a crowd for a little place, but all plain country folk of the same make as the jury. Neither of the Astons was there, nor Tracy. So the hating families chose to have it understood that the inquest meant nothing to them. Not even a lawyer employed. Nobody could be seen who seemed to be anybody. Curiously incurious county, Durshire. Determined not to admit the existence of anything to disturb it. Same like the defunct chief constable.

Yes, there was somebody. That long, fat face at the back, silly and shrewd—the enigmatic, opulent Brown. And Bubb had said he was in London. Very energetic of Brown to come back for the inquest. Very interesting of him. Evidence of his anxiety about what might turn up about young Tracy's death confirmed.

He should have been soothed. Under the careful control of Bubb and the coroner the inquest ran a swift, inconclusive course. Leading questions kept General Duddon to the briefest evidence that he had found bones in the land-slip and taken them to the police. Bubb identified and related that he had dug up others and submitted them to the police surgeon, and the surgeon swore that they were the bones of an adolescent boy and had been in the ground some ten years.

Then Bubb told the coroner that the police could not take the matter further, and the coroner announced that he would adjourn sine die.

Reggie showed no attention to any of these things. He sat turned to contemplate the people in court, but with a languid, sleepy gaze as if they were not there. When the inquest was over, when they began to go out, when Bubb stood up and bustled, he remained in his chair.

"Well, there it is, Mr. Fortune," said Bubb. "As you were."

"You think so?" Reggie's eyes opened. "Come on." He took Bubb's arm and drew him along after the dissolving crowd to stop suddenly just before the door.

"What's the idea?" Bubb asked.

Reggie compressed his arm but did not answer. A drawling, sneering voice was heard from outside: "What's old Crowner mean by his sine die, George?"

"Eh, he means no telling when inquest will go on again, 'Lijah."

There came a cackle of a laugh. "No telling! Ay, ay, surely. That would be the word."

Reggie moved forward and directed Bubb's eyes to a little man limping away alone. "Do you know that fellow?"

Bubb snorted. "I should say I do. He's been in jail half-a-dozen times. The worst poacher this end of the county. What about him?"

Reggie turned back into the hall. "Oh, my Bubb! Didn't you hear what he said? Don't you notice anything? He was the only man in court amused at your discreet proceedings. The others were all solemnly satisfied. But Elijah the poacher grinned. And now we know why. Because there was no telling."

"You'll excuse me, Mr. Fortune," said Bubb severely. "Talk like that just means you're letting him pull your leg. I know his kind, and you don't. It's meat and drink to him to make game of the police and the magistrates. That's all he's after."

"You think so? Well, well. Study to improve. Quite a useful inquest. Why was our Mr. Brown there? You said he was in London."

"So he was. I didn't see him here." Bubb stared.

"No. You didn't see anything," said Reggie. "However. If at first you don't succeed, try, try, try again. One more inquest. Good-bye."

He went off to his car and gave his chauffeur another dose of irritation. "Drive in your own sweet way, Sam. Your natural twenty will suffice. To travel hopefully is better than to arrive. And we will admire the flowers that bloom in the spring. Because they have nothing to do with the case. And the elms are red, and the chaffinch sings on the orchard bough. Not very well. But he's a gay and cheery soul. And the violets ought to be out, Sam. Watch for a violet."

Sam put the rug over him with a certain ferocity.

Next morning, in Colsbury, the same discreet coroner presided over the inquest on the chief constable, and again Reggie took a seat at Bubb's table. The greasy courtroom was provided with permanent, traditional inconveniences instead of those of improvisation. The people there were more sophisticated, less uniform: a jury like thousands of other juries—an insignificant mixture—and the crowd included all sorts and conditions of men. The well-to-do of Durshire admitted an interest in the extinction of their chief constable.

Old Tracy had come with a black tie underneath his crimson countenance. No other sign of concern about him. He was talking to his neighbors with that blank poker stare which Reggie had remarked on their first meeting. Quite under control, in spite of drink and temper. Hardboiled gambler, Mr. Tracy—or he thought he was. People round him obviously of the same landowning class—some of his own square make, some more like the Astons. But neither the old nor the young Aston showed up.

At the solicitors' table Cope the banker sat with a man who probably was a solicitor, both of them frock-coated in old-fashioned full-dress mourning. They conferred with manners to match.

Reggie searched again for the Astons but failed to find either. Very shy people. Only a few country folk. The Aston countryside was not connecting the death of the chief constable with the bones in the landslip. Except one man. A brown, wizened face looked over shoulders, peering every way.

Reggie touched Bubb's shoulder and murmured, "Our Elijah assists," but Bubb brushed him aside.

Tracy's gamekeeper was in the box, stumbling through his story of finding the chief constable dead. The doctor who first saw the body and the police surgeon agreed that the cause of death was drowning, and they were of the opinion that the deceased was thrown from his horse and stunned as he fell into the water.

The hunt secretary gave evidence that the chief constable had been going well in the morning and had told him that he meant to get back to his office early. This solicitor related that he was an old and intimate friend and, with Mr. Cope, the chief constable's executor. The chief constable's health had always been good, and he had no embarrassments of any kind. Bubb added loyal confirmation, and the coroner thought that they had heard enough and delivered a funeral oration after which the jury handed him a verdict of accidental death and deepest sympathy.

"Yes. All according to plan. With flowers," Reggie murmured. "Now we'll get on, Bubb. Collect Elijah."

Bubb glowered at him. "What do you mean? It's finished."

"Your error. Your gross error. Only beginning."

"I'm responsible, thank you. And I'm satisfied."

"Yes. That's what's in the way," Reggie drawled.

"You—" Bubb began furiously and checked himself. "Are you suggesting I'm hushing things up?" he whispered.

"Who is?" Reggie asked.

Bubb started up and sent a sergeant after Elijah and turned on Reggie. "There you are; you can have him if you want him. I tell you, it's just asking him to play the fool with you, that's all. I know the little rat. Come on. He'll cheek you like hell. Don't blame me."

But the sergeant did not bring Elijah Hawke to the police station. He had gone there of himself. He was waiting when the angry Bubb marched in.

CHAPTER XV *Evidence of a Song*

ELIJAH STARTED UP from a bench, spat his chew of tobacco into the grate and came forward with a grin which showed gaps in his yellow teeth. "Good morning, Mr. Bubb. How's yourself?"

"Here again, Hawke!" Bubb was scornful. "What's the charge this time?"

"Don't bark like that. There ain't no bite to it. You will always get me wrong, Mr. Bubb. I don't bear no spite against you. I'm a lawful Christian man, I am. I just come round to do you a bit of good, which you need it cruel, s'elp me, you do. Here," he beckoned with a dirty finger. "I got some information for to lay."

Bubb strode past him into the chief constable's room, and Reggie followed. "There it is," Reggie smiled. "As you said. Inquests did produce something. In spite of Superintendent Bubb."

"I'm not going to stand for that talk, Mr. Fortune," Bubb exclaimed. "I haven't stopped any evidence."

"I hope not. But you didn't find it. And yet it's here. As expected."

"What do you mean by that?"

"I expected some of the country people could tell us a thing or two. I mentioned it. Very loud and clear."

"This fellow would tell the tale about anybody," Bubb answered. "He's just a bag of spleen."

"Doesn't love the police force? How sad."

Bubb rang the bell and ordered Hawke to be brought in. He came with a sidelong, shambling gait. He sat himself down uninvited and said, "Who's the new gent, Mr. Bubb?"

"None of your impudence," Bubb admonished him. "What have you come to me for?"

Elijah sucked his teeth. He was a little man with a narrow head and not much shoulder but broad across the middle. In his brown face, crinkled like a walnut, black eyes were deep-set—cunning, jeering eyes.

"You're of an old family, aren't you?" said Reggie.

There was a splutter of laughter. "He knows something, don't he, Mr. Bubb? That's right, mister. I was born under a hedge; my father come out of the ground; my get and breed was here before any. Black land, white land, it's ours by right; them as has it is no more nor grabbers."

"We don't want to hear any of that old guff," Bubb broke in.

69

"Don't want to hear!" Elijah snarled. "I believe you. No telling! Crowner shut up the first ruddy inquest with that, and now he makes it accident your old man was scragged. No telling! Oh no. Not for you. Now I come to give it you straight, Mr. Bubb. You rout out Squire Tracy."

"That's the lay, is it?" Bubb scoffed. "I thought so. The last stretch you did was for poaching his coverts."

"Yes. And he's a gent, ain't he? So you don't dare touch him. I tell you he's the fox that got the chickens, and your old man knows it in his coffin."

"You think so?" Reggie asked. "Why do you?"

"Stranger, ain't you?" Elijah sneered. "You're flummoxed. Look to Mr. Bubb. He ain't." For Bubb was looking wrath but not surprise. "Where did the old man die? On Tracy's land. Who found him? Tracy's ruddy keeper. And where was Squire Tracy all the time? Prowling round with his gun—which he hadn't ought to, the greedy stoat, with the close season here and all mating and breeding."

Bubb let off rage in a laugh. "So Mr. Tracy shot him! Though he wasn't shot. That's enough from you, my lad."

"Ain't you clever? I never said nothing about shot. Laid for and knocked off his horse, that's how it was done."

"Did you see it?" Reggie asked.

"I tell you no lies, I didn't. But you hear what I did see—and I wonder at Mr. Bubb he didn't see it too."

"What do you mean?" Bubb roared.

"Getting flustered now," Elijah grinned. "How did it happen the old man come by his death over this business of the boy's bones? Ain't you never asked Mr. Bubb that, guv'nor? I'll tell you. One morning way back Mr. Bubb drove out early for to see the landslip where the bones come out. Foggy, weren't it, Mr. Bubb? I've heard tell as you found some'at too, more than what old general did. There was another gent out and about earlier than what you was, in the fog by the cliffs. Didn't you never happen to see him going back as you came out? Down along by Squire Tracy's. And your old man, he was out to Tracy's that morning, wasn't he?"

"Don't you put up lies to me." Bubb scowled at him.

"No more I do. It's the truth as worries you."

"We're not getting very much," said Reggie mildly. "Elijah—you were saying—somebody was near the landslip before the superintendent. Who was it?"

"I tell you no lies. There was a gent. But in that there fog I never got near enough for to see him, and he went off back in a car."

"Pity. Any reason to think it was Mr. Tracy?"

"The car went that way."

"Oh yes. Might have been going anywhere. It's the way back to here, isn't it?"

"Ay, so it is," said Elijah, and his eyes twinkled malice at Bubb. "And a bit after, I see the old man coming away in his car from Squire Tracy's."

"Well, well. Not much of a story, Elijah. No real fact against Mr. Tracy. You notice that. What makes you say he was interested in the bones?"

Elijah grinned. "Eh, cunning! You know what. For sure he's sweating blood over 'em. That's why you had no telling. You know they be boy Tracy's bones sure enough. And you know Daddy Tracy give out his poor little boy was drownded and washed away out to sea never to come back no more—so Daddy could get his mother's money which was his'n, and no questions asked. Cruel hard on Daddy the old white land give up its dead. Eh, but his good friends stand by him. You won't have no telling."

"Oh, Elijah!" Reggie sighed. "Waiting and anxious to be told. Get on!"

Elijah leaned forward. "So I am telling you. It was his own dad put sonny into the cliff."

"Did you see it?" Reggie asked.

"I did not. Don't you try to trick me. You listen. That there morning boy Tracy was lost I was going round Tracy's land, and I see Squire Tracy and the boy at it hammer and tongs. Everybody knew they was like that; you ask Mr. Bubb—but no telling, no. And the boy cheeked his daddy and went off laughing and singing, away to the cliff, and after a bit old squire followed, and the boy was never seen no more. How was he killed? You know."

"I wonder," Reggie murmured. He was studying Elijah's spiteful face. "What was he singing?"

Elijah's low brow twisted. "I dunno the name of it." He licked his lips and whistled a squeaky, droning snatch which was not always a tune.

"Oh no. No." Reggie moaned.

"It went like that; I swear it did," Elijah said.

Bubb laughed. "Have you finished now? You've taken twelve years making up this tale. Can't you hand us any more?"

"There ain't no more. I don't tell no lies," Elijah said sullenly.

"Not you! Only a stew of slander. You mind your eye, my lad. By your own account you've concealed information from the police. If I believed a word of it, I'd have you in jail now. And if you go spreading this stuff that's where you'll land anyway. Be off with you."

Elijah made a scornful, improper gesture and shambled out.

Bubb turned to Reggie. "I told you so, didn't I? Just spite and playing the goat with us. Not a bit of evidence."

"That is what you said, yes. And he is a good hater. However. There were points, Bubb. He said somebody went to the landslip before you met me. We know that's true. He said your late chief went over to Tracy's about the same time. What do you know about that?"

"I don't believe a word of it," Bubb declared. "The chief never said anything to me of going there. It's just a lie to make scandal against Tracy."

"Yes, it could be. But if it was, why didn't he lie harder? Why not say it was Tracy he saw by the landslip? Very careful what he didn't say. He might have said he saw Tracy attack his son."

"Careful! I believe you," Bubb snorted. "Of course he is. He's a cunning, little, cowardly sneak."

"Oh, my Bubb! There is hate about," Reggie smiled. "Yes, he is inconvenient to the police. And not one of the world's great souls. Poor beggar. However. Try him out. Ring up Tracy and ask if the chief constable did visit him that jolly morning."

"All right." Bubb frowned and used the telephone. "Superintendent Bubb speaking. I want Mr. Tracy. …" With his hand over the receiver he turned to Reggie. "They say he's gone away, didn't say where or when he'd be coming back."

"Well, well," Reggie murmured. "Ask for Miss Tracy."

Bubb did so. "What? I see. … Thank you. Good-bye." He looked at Reggie. "She's not there either. She went off last Monday. They haven't got her address."

"Last Monday," Reggie said. "Day of chief constable's demise. I wonder. The Tracys go, and Elijah comes. Job of work for you, Bubb. If I were you, I should ask the Criminal Investigation Department to lend a hand."

"Thank you, sir. I can handle my own business," said Bubb.

"You think so? Well, well. One other point. Elijah's best point. The song the boy was singing on his way to die." Reggie whistled a snatch of a tune with a gay and romantic lilt.

"Why, that isn't what he gave us," Bubb objected.

"Not quite, no. Not a true ear, Elijah. But that's what he was trying for. And he didn't invent it. Song popular in school concerts.

> "'There was a ship came from the North Country,
> And the name of the ship was the Golden Vanity.' "

"Suppose the boy did sing it, what then?" Bubb asked. "It don't prove anything."

"Not yet, no. Lot of work to do." Reggie rose. "Good-bye."

When he went back to his hotel he found a letter for him.

DEAR MR. FORTUNE,

I had no chance of a word with you at Elstow yesterday. I was hoping to ask you to call on the wife and me when you come up to London again. We are in Regent's Gate and always very happy if you could spare time to look in.

Yours sincerely,

WM. BROWN.

CHAPTER XVI *Evidence of a Call*

Mr. FORTUNE CAME BACK to London by easy stages. He loitered among bud-
ding beech woods and in river meadows where cowslips glimmered through
the sheen of the grass. To such indulgence he is always prone, but he scorns
the allegations that he took the case lazily, was bewildered, did not know
what to do next.

His mind, according to his commentaries on the case, was made up that
further action by the enemy must be awaited, and he was right. That he did
not know how to deal with Superintendent Bubb he admits heartily, declar-
ing that it was then beyond human power, so safe has the world been made
for officials. He understood a good deal of the case already, but he had no
means of control—a state of consciousness inducing languor. He could not
foresee how the primeval savage forces would react to his pressure; he was
prepared for darker storms. He had not a notion of the end to which he would
bring them, but he had a placid, scientific confidence in his careful brain.

He spent some happy days in his laboratory, attending to the urgent needs
of the warts, until an afternoon when he put away his favourite culture with
a murmur which startled his assistant:

> *"There may be heaven, there must be hell.*
> *Meanwhile we do our work here. Well?"*

He departed and drove across the park to experiment upon Brown's invitation to call.

The Brown mansion in Regent's Gate was as blatant as the colossal concrete of the pile which they had put up on the white land of Durshire, but in
a grotesquely different way—an imitation of a French Renaissance palace.

Reggie was conducted to a Louis Quinze drawing room, sky-blue and rose-
pink and gold, unkindly discordant with the woman who sat there. Her dress
was green, and her hair was red, and she was, on the edge of a couch made
for limp repose, fiercely alert.

"Miss Tracy," Reggie murmured. "What a charming surprise!"

"How do you do? Mrs. Brown will be here in a moment," she said all in a
breath. "Didn't you know I was staying with her?"

"Brown hadn't mentioned it, no. Modest man. Not wantin' to boast of the
attractions of his house."

"Thank you. That is a neat compliment! You wouldn't have come if you'd expected to find me." The flecks of red in her green eyes glowed.

"How can you say so?" Reggie was plaintive. "Too subtle, Miss Tracy."

"You're quite simple, aren't you?"

"Oh yes. Yes. That is my strength. The natural man. Naturally delighted." He surveyed her with a gaze which passed in humble admiration from helmet of red hair to the flushed, delicate face and quick bosom. "Also natural you should resent it."

"I don't like being sneered at," she told him.

"But that hasn't been done. Nothing like it. Not by me. Is your father here?"

"No, he isn't," she cried, and her flush darkened. "What ever made you think so?"

"I tried to see him in Durshire, but he'd gone away. I thought he might have come here. Do you know where he is?"

"I don't know where he's gone. Most likely to Monte Carlo."

"Oh. Is that usual?"

"He's very fond of it," she said angrily. "What do you want him for?"

"Just a little talk about things," Reggie murmured. "However. Time enough." He hummed the tune, " 'There was a ship came from the North Country. And the name of the ship was the Golden Vanity.' " He gazed at her dreamily. If it meant anything to her she did not mean to let him know. "I hope you haven't been worried by all this nasty business in Durshire."

"Poor Mr. Seymour. It was dreadful," she said.

"Very sad, yes. Did you know him well?"

"Not well. I don't think we know anybody well. But he was always nice to me."

"Naturally." Reggie nodded, and Mrs. Brown came rustling in.

It had been charged against Mr. Fortune that he always fascinates ladies of mature years. Mrs. Brown gushed adulation which would have been sickly but for its insistent maternal tone, and that was uncomfortable.

So kind of him—everybody told her Mr. Fortune never went anywhere— and she didn't wonder; she couldn't think how he found time for all his work. He was doing great things in the hospitals, she heard. She thought that was just the finest thing a man could do—if she had had a son she would have wanted him to be a doctor. And what was Mr. Fortune doing specially just now? She would love to hear, and so would Alison.

"My dear lady!" said Reggie sadly. "The wart. The common wart."

But Mrs. Brown was not checked. It seemed to her so splendid for a clever man to set himself on troubles like that, just to make people more comfortable—gaining nothing by it. "Mr. Fortune ought to be very happy. Oughtn't he, Alison?"

"I'm sure he is," said Alison.

"You two would make a good pair, my dear." Mrs. Brown's crimson face shone upon her. "You don't care a bit about anything except doing what you think right. She's like that, Mr. Fortune."

"We are embarrassed," said Reggie. "Comparison not flattering to Miss Tracy. I was made quite a lot lower than the angels."

"That might be, Mr. Fortune," Alison answered. "Everybody says I was a little devil. I haven't grown up."

"Pride, pride." Reggie shook his head.

"You do talk, dearie," said Mrs. Brown affectionately. "Oh, here's the tea."

It was brought with the pomp of a butler and a footman, but it had an abundant solidity before which Reggie, though a tea-eater by nature and habit, quailed. Mrs. Brown plied him and wished William were there; William would show him how to make a tea. She couldn't think where William was—and her William came in. He did eat. He was very hearty. He chaffed Reggie's abstinence. He talked of eggs. And Reggie's nerve gave way.

"Must you really go?" Mrs. Brown protested. "We don't seem hardly to have seen you. Well, if you must! You are staying in London, aren't you? I can send you a card?"

"Please." Reggie bowed and fled.

Brown followed him out of the room. "I take it kind of you to accept my little invite, Mr. Fortune." The loud voice was hushed, but the long, fat face looked up into Reggie's, still beaming silly good will. "Could you spare me a minute or two?" He took Reggie's arm. "Just one or two things I couldn't hardly say to you before the ladies. Come in here, will you?"

Reggie was brought to a somber library which bore evidence of complete disuse and put into a chair. Brown perched on the cushioned fender, and his queer, long-distance, brooding gaze looked through Reggie and beyond.

"I reckon you haven't forgotten a bit o' talk I had with you at the ball."

"Oh no. No. I was interested."

"I saw you were. I said bringing out the truth of what really happened might do more harm than good."

"That was the substance. Yes. Meant for a warning. I have wondered why Mr. Brown didn't want me to investigate."

"I reckon you didn't wonder very long. You weren't surprised to see me at the inquest on that poor boy's bones, were you?"

"Interestin' question. Difficult question. Just a little surprised, Mr. Brown."

"H'm. You're the sort I understand," said Brown in a queer, quiet, thoughtful tone. "Well, you know what I mean. That boy—whoever he was, however he died—making out he was Miss Tracy's young brother, and somebody murdered him … it couldn't do any good to him, and it might smash up her life. I'm right, ain't I?"

"I don't know," Reggie answered slowly.

"Miss Tracy is going to marry young Aston. You've met her. She wants what she wants, that girl. And Giles Aston is mad for her. You can take it from me, he's straight. I trust him, and I've seen some men in my life. I put it to you: let 'em marry, and there's the end of the old hell of a mess down there."

"It could be," Reggie murmured.

"That's why I went down to hear how you'd work the inquest. If you don't mind my saying so, it was done most sensible."

"I don't mind, no."

"Should I be right in asking you if there's more to come?"

"You would not. But it doesn't matter. I couldn't answer. Nor can you. Nor these two. How much do they know?"

"I tell you straight: they don't know a thing—nor fear, neither."

"I wonder," Reggie murmured.

"You're hard," said Brown.

"Yes. My job. I'm for justice. Good-bye."

CHAPTER XVII *Evidence of a Wedding*

IT WAS A WEEK LATER that Reggie, in the beatitude of recumbency on the small of his back after dinner, read two letters.

The first was from France, from an inspector of the Sûreté Générale, but quite unofficial. It told him that one named Tracy and of the physique so mordantly sketched was since ten days at Monte Carlo and had been observed to play high without luck but always with a great phlegm. This gentleman was not recognized as a regular visitor, though no certitude. So, with great expectations and a thousand friendships, Dubois.

The second letter was in the official style. Superintendent Bubb begged to inform Mr. Fortune that in accordance with conclusions reached at their conference of the 12th inst. enquiries had been conducted into the statement made by Hawke concerning alleged movements of the late chief constable on the morning of the further excavations of the landslip. The result was to establish that the chief constable had not left his house till after breakfast at the usual hour. His car was not brought to the door till the regular time—approximately 8:45. Shortly after, he drove away alone. He did not arrive at police headquarters till approximately eleven, as far as could be ascertained. Mr. James Tracy's butler stated that he remembered the chief constable calling to see his master on some morning about the date in question but could not fix the day or hour. Mr. Tracy was not in and was looked for round the home farm, which took some short time. But he could not be found, and, being told so, the chief constable left at once. On calculating the distances and considering the roads, it was therefore clear that the chief constable could not have been near the landslip. Otherwise his car must have been observed by Mr. Fortune or Superintendent Bubb.

"Yes. That is so, my Bubb," Reggie murmured. "You might have observed him. He might have observed you. Or observed somebody else. The time and the place and the loved one altogether. Poor old chief. Well-meanin' man, did it all for the best. And according to Dubois the man Tracy is playing high but without luck. I wonder."

He slid still lower in his chair and meditated over a vision of the poker face of Tracy at the tables of Monte Carlo and seemed to see himself as the croupier watching the game—without interest, without power over its fortunes, only an instrument of the decisions of chance. "Not quite, no," he protested. "The bank always wins." That did not console him. "On the average, yes. Averages aren't life. On the average it's a lawful world. Everything happens because it has to. But it don't; in fact, it won't. They all go playing the individual deuce. Nasty, untidy, messy." Suffering from a sense of ignominy he went to bed.

A few days later he received the card of which Mrs. Brown had warned him. It far surpassed his expectations. Mr. and Mrs. William Brown asked Mr. Reginald Fortune to the wedding of Alison Tracy and Giles Aston. The existence of parents of the happy pair was ignored.

Reggie gazed at the card with a crooked smile. "You play high too, Mr. Brown. Yes. Lots of bold people in this case. I am not. Oh my hat, I am not. However. You be blowed. I will assist."

The church of St. Wilfrid's, to which he was bidden, was built in the richest fervor of last-century Gothic for the ritual then fashionable. Its interior looked like a compromise between the Albert Memorial and the lounge of a hotel deluxe.

Reggie came early and took a corner of obscurity with a clear line of sight. There was not much of a crowd. Rather a hotchpotch. Dowdy and gaudy. Must be friends of the Browns. Yes. There was Mrs. Brown—hen got up as a bird of paradise—fussing like a hen and ready to cry like a mother.

Neither of the Aston parents to be seen. Nor Tracy. So there wouldn't be a row. Well, that never was likely. Here and there a few people who might be Durshire gentry: people with a look of sport and tradition. Marriage not absolutely ignored by the society of Durshire.

Giles Aston marched up the church aisle. Handsome lad, even in his wedding garment. Knew it too. Making a good show of himself. The best man trailed along, superfluous. No nerves for him to soothe. Giles stopped and turned and looked back as if he owned the world, and it was all dirt to him except the girl who kept him waiting. Playing his part for all it was worth. The perfect bridegroom. Very rare.

He was not kept waiting long. Brown, in a frock coat—a sight not venerable—came in with Alison on his arm, came a little in front of her, as if she had to be led to the sacrifice. But she moved along the nave in quick time for a bride, her veiled head erect. The simplest of white gowns—and a gown which hid her. But for a glimpse of her red hair through the veil, might have been any woman. Well! Same like a lot of brides before marriage. Or after.

Only a couple of little girls for bridesmaids. Maidens of Durshire not thronging round Miss Tracy. However. Not evidence.

The service began. ... I, Giles and I, Alison ... Rather gracious voice, her voice—never felt that before—deep, full tones in it. ... Mr. and Mrs. Giles Aston were blessed and disappeared. ...

They came back down the aisle. Her bare hand laced its fingers with his.

He was perfectly the exultant bridegroom, intent on her alone, smiling down at her unveiled face. Her head was thrown back, her lips parted a little—but not in a smile; her eyes gazed right on unseeing, and her pale face was sad and stern.

"Desperate?" Reggie asked himself. "It could be. 'As when a woman, desperate and tender—' " And then his mind squirmed, for the organ was pouring into it the luscious waves of Lohengrin. He fled for air.

To the house in Regent's Gate he made his way on foot and slowly, filled with pity for himself but resolute. The discomfort of the natural man at a wedding he is apt to feel grievously, and he was prepared for it, but he had not expected that it would be complicated by an interest in the bride. He had classified Alison as a simple, insignificant savage. She compelled reconsideration of her possibilities. Another confusing factor in the confusion.

With a vague, sleepwalking manner he came into the reception. There were quite a lot of people in the showy rooms, and they were being very hearty to bride and bridegroom—with the Browns keeping them at it, relentlessly effusive.

Not another creature he knew. Here and there a face he might have seen in Durshire. Oh yes, that dapper old fellow with the flowing mustaches—he was at the chief constable's inquest. Who was the chap with the solid back he was talking to? Might be the baffling Bubb, by the shape. Of course he wasn't; he was Cope the banker. As Reggie slid toward him, he smiled and lifted a hand of greeting.

"How are you, Mr. Fortune? Do you know Lord Werne?"

The old fellow made a formal bow but had plenty to say: prim and elegant small talk with a certain acidity. Regretted that he had not met Mr. Fortune in Durshire; was glad that his visit had not exhausted his interest in the inhabitants; did not know whether he took rank as bride's friend or bridegroom's.

Reggie hoped that one might be both.

Speaking as the oldest inhabitant, Lord Werne never knew anybody who had succeeded in keeping friends with both families—unless it was Cope, the universal Cope—or poor dear Seymour, the unfortunate Seymour.

"That's too bad." Cope shook his head.

"I was not predicting that you would go the same way as the chief constable," said Lord Werne. "You can ride any horse I ever saw, Cope."

"I never knew a man so good he couldn't take a toss," Cope answered. "What I meant was, it's not fair to talk as if poor old Seymour had got himself into trouble with anyone."

"I agree," said Lord Werne. "The last man in the county. And I speak as one of the sufferers from the burglaries in his jurisdiction. But one must not tempt Mr. Fortune to give an opinion on our chief constable."

"You don't," Reggie murmured. "I haven't one. But I didn't know it was so difficult to be friends with both an Aston and a Tracy. There seem to be some Durshire people here at the wedding."

"Quite as many as you could expect," Cope nodded.

"Even more," said Lord Werne. "Curiosity is potent, Mr. Fortune. You cannot have appreciated that. There are also those who would be happy to offend both Tracy and Aston."

"Which is your class, sir?" Reggie asked.

"I am too old for those pleasant emotions, Mr. Fortune. I like to think that I assist at an end of the feud. I comfort myself with illusions."

"You're not such a cynic as you pretend," Cope said.

"I am obliged to you. You were always a man of faith."

"I'm a banker." Cope smiled.

Werne made him a bow. "And therefore all hope and charity too. I am only a gambler myself. I snatch the fleeting delight of wishing these children joy. It will be an amusing memory." He made his way to bride and bridegroom.

"That's an odd fish," said Cope. "He never lets you know what he's really thinking. I don't believe he knows himself most of the time. He only wants his laugh."

"You think so?" Reggie murmured. "Rather amiable of him to come and bless the young things. Same like you."

"Oh, he's always a genial old soul. I take no stock in these inherited family hates myself, not being of any family to matter. They're only a nuisance to everybody. This boy and girl—all that's left out of the Astons and Tracys eating one another up—the best thing they can do is to come together. I wish 'em luck."

"Rushing it a bit, aren't they?" Reggie asked.

"You mean the fathers are still a snag? I can't say no. Both the fathers have the devil of a temper, and this London wedding under the Browns' patronage is bound to make 'em mad. It's a sinful pity old Brown butted in. The marriage might have been arranged all right, if he hadn't been in such a hurry. I haven't found him a bad chap, but he is a born meddler, one of these get-rich-quick men who go riding over everybody to put through a job that takes their fancy."

"I have met 'em. Yes," said Reggie. "But why should this marriage take his fancy?"

"You're asking something." Cope's eyes twinkled. "I never thought I saw through William Brown. He don't strike me that way, Mr. Fortune."

"Faith not adequate," Reggie murmured. "Perhaps you're right."

Brown had observed their aloof conversation and was making his way to them and arrived boisterously, slapping each of them on the back. "How's it go? What do you say? Not a bad show. Very handsome of you to come up for it, Cope. And Mr. Fortune too. His lordship was saying to me you gave it a cachet. That was his word, sir, a cachet. I don't rightly know what it means, but he meant kind, and I feel it myself. Come and have a word with Mrs. Giles; they're just off. Looks fine, don't she? He's a lucky dog, eh?" Brown winked and grinned and pushed Reggie on and followed, telling Cope that they were going to Paris before they settled down. What ho!

Reggie's affection for Mr. Brown was not enhanced. But he found himself admitting that fine was the word for Alison as she stood by her husband. The fierceness of vigor had gone out of her and left a gracious dignity. She was pale; her face, cream white against the white of her dress, was wistful, patient and tender.

"Here's Mr. Fortune, my dear," Brown announced.

She smiled. "How kind of you to come," she said. "You are kind, aren't you?"

"I wanted to wish you happiness, Mrs. Aston." Reggie held her hand a moment.

And Cope was saying to her complacent husband: "All the best, old fellow. And for Alison. But the congratulations are for you, you know."

"I do," Giles laughed. "Thanks very much."

"Good luck, Aston," said Reggie and got away. He has always maintained that no man can be a bridegroom and keep the respect of his sex, but Giles Aston made him more uncomfortable than most.

When he had come back home, when he was spread with a pipe and a volume of Boswell to restore the dignity of his enervated mind, a telephone enquiry came. Mr. William Brown, said the parlormaid, had rung up to ask if he could find him at home. "My only aunt!" Reggie moaned. "Oh yes! Yes. Tell him to come along quick," and he turned the pages of Boswell with lost zest. " 'Why, sir, I am in the habit of getting others to do things for me,' " he read and murmured, "Yes. So is my Brown, Dr. Johnson. Nasty habit."

Brown bustled in. "Very glad I caught you, Mr. Fortune. I did hope to get a word with you at the reception, but on the whole I thought better not. It might have looked queer, and I didn't want anything to spoil the show for the young folks, and people might have talked. See what I mean?"

"No," said Reggie.

"Well, it's like this. That dear girl Alison's been staying with us, you know. And this morning among the letters that came for her there was a postcard the wife brought on to me because she thought it might be meant nasty and upset her. I can't make head or tail of it myself."

"Oh. Then why did Mrs. Brown think it might be nasty?"

"I'll show you. First of all it was addressed to Mrs. Giles Aston with three exclamation marks after. That's a nice thing. The girl wasn't yet married. Besides—the spite of the dashes! You'll agree with me; the wife did well not to let her have it. And then the message is just a mystery. It's a bit of print, but lots of the letters ain't English letters at all. There's *e* and *o* and *a* like writing, but the rest are foreign or signs or something."

Reggie took the card. The address was in block letters, the postmark Colsbury. On the back was pasted a cutting. He read aloud: "Tod epi gan peson—"

"You can read it right off!" Brown exclaimed.

"Yes. It's Greek. Some Greek verses." Reggie frowned at them.

"Well, what's the meaning of it?"

"Not nice. No. As you suspected. 'Blood of death which once has fallen dark at a man's feet, who can call it back by his charms?' " He looked up and examined Brown with a cold and intent stare.

"Here! Say that again," Brown demanded.

Reggie drawled out the grim words one by one. " 'Blood of death—once fallen dark—at a man's feet—who can call it back by his charms?' Suggest anything to you?"

Brown's big face was distorted as if he were making furious physical effort in a fight or a hard game. "Ruddy all, it suggests," he said thickly. "You know what. It was sent to jab into the girl her brother was murdered."

"Yes, that is indicated. However. Any reason to believe the girl could have read it, if you *had* given it her? Does she know Greek?"

"I shouldn't think so. But she'd have shown it to Giles."

"Does he read Greek?"

"Why, of course. He was at Oxford."

"Evidence not adequate." Reggie gave a small bleak smile. "But he might know it was Greek. He might have got a translation. Not a nice wedding present. As you were saying. Apparent purpose to remind bride and bridegroom bride's brother was murdered by bridegroom's people. Which is not yet proved. Which you told me I'd better not prove, Mr. Brown. I wondered why you were interested."

Brown had recovered his self-control. The bulging brow was smooth; the cheeks sagged into their usual fullness. "Did you really?" he said. "That's right. I did tell you straight; the scandal about young Tracy's vanishing didn't ought to be dragged up again. Why did I? Because I knew these two meant to make a match of it. Trying to make out now what really happened to the boy would only stir up all the blighted silly spite of the Astons and the Tracys and make hell for Alison and Giles. I thought you'd tumbled to that yourself, Mr. Fortune, the way you handled the inquest."

"Did you? Your error. Your gross error. So you believe that if the truth of the boy's death had come out it would have broken off this marriage. That means you believe the boy was murdered by his father or by Aston. Rather a responsibility arranging a marriage with a family murder for husband and wife to inherit."

Brown was not embarrassed. "Come now, you're just talking. There's no stuff in it. Where are we? I don't believe anything about how the boy died. There's no facts to be got—only a stink—and I don't go by that. Arranging the marriage! Nothing like it. You've seen 'em. They'd got to have each other, those two and be damned to the old folks. God bless 'em, I say. Ain't they right? They're going to live, and this marriage—it wipes out all the stupid hate and sets things going straight down there."

"You think so?" Reggie murmured. "Very benevolent. Very hopeful. When you hurried on the happy marriage did you ask the parents to assist?"

"No hurry by me," said Brown. "They knew about it."

"Oh yes. So I gathered. And refused consent."

"There was a row with both of them. That's why the wife offered Alison to have it up here. The parents were all invited."

"That was hopeful," Reggie drawled. "Any appearance of any parent? Any letters?"

"You can take it there wasn't."

"So they were married and lived happily ever after," said Reggie. "Having wiped out all the stupid hate." He took up the postcard and read once more. " 'Blood of death which once has fallen dark at a man's feet, who can call it back by his charms?' " His blue eyes stared cold and hard at Brown. "You're not asking me to hush this up?" His voice rose sharply.

"I thought you ought to know of it." Brown's brooding gaze met his unflinchingly. "Being a sort of threat or slander. I leave it to you."

Reggie stood up. "Yes. Thanks very much," he said. "A challenge. Good-bye."

When Brown was gone he went to a bookcase, took out a green-bound volume and compared the Greek verses on the postcard with its text, line by line. Then he put the card to his nose and smelled it assiduously.

CHAPTER XVIII *Evidence of a Dinner*

THE CHIEF of the Criminal Investigation Department came to dine with Mr. Fortune and was given a meal of contrasts. The food was of a heavier richness than Reggie is wont to desire. From caviar they proceeded by way of red mullet to duck with a burgundy sauce. Crepes in which clotted cream was tinctured with curacao were followed by angels-on-horseback. But Reggie's conversation was without substance: vague irony about German actresses, the last new flats and similar themes.

He passed the port. "You will drink that, I suppose," he lamented. "Gaudy taste. Irrational taste. The English mind at its worst, the cult of port. No restraint, no delicacy, no sense of harmony. Demanding a wine which does more than wine can." He poured himself claret. "Beauty is truth, truth beauty—and both are elimination. This is exquisite—to the pure in mind—but you won't have any." He held the glass up to the light. "Margaux '99," he said with reverence and drank. "You have my pity, Lomas."

"Yes, we are amused," said Lomas. "Just a little. I like your praise of restraint after this barbaric, rich feeding."

"My dear chap! Oh, my dear chap!" Reggie was shocked. "Barbaric! Conventional stomach, the official stomach. Not a dinner according to the rules. Rules were made for the weaker brethren. The mind needed fortifying. I told you so. I am not happy." He gave himself more claret and was silent.

"Can the mind still function, Reginald?" Lomas called him back to life.

"Not wholly, no. Much impeded by officials and confused by the superfluous. The same thing, did you say? Not quite, no. Officials who won't officiate. Unofficials who will." He gazed at Lomas with large reproachful eyes. "Reference, that Durshire business."

"I was afraid so." Lomas made a grimace. "You have an infernally inconvenient conscience."

"Yes, I have. Poor me. However. What are we for, Lomas? To make the world safe for the murderer? Ignominious profession. I don't like it."

Lomas sipped his port and lit a cigarette. "You have no evidence that there was a murderer."

"Not published, no. Not conclusive. All the same, one murderer or two at large. You know what came out at those hush-hush inquests. Now listen to what didn't." He told the story of the vanished cameo and the poacher. "There's the evidence. Consider your verdict."

"Deuced queer stuff," said Lomas. "These Durshire fellows are shy, both the dead chief constable and his living deputy. What did you make of this man Bubb?"

"I haven't the slightest idea," Reggie murmured.

"Your theory is the chief was murdered because he had a line on somebody over the cameo."

"Yes, that is indicated."

"I agree. You put it up to Bubb and he didn't take to it. Not too good. But on this theory we have to assume that somebody was faking false evidence to connect Aston with the boy's death. Which means that the boy wasn't murdered—or Aston didn't murder him."

"Possible inference. Not certain."

"My dear fellow, the obvious inference."

"Yes, I did think that. It could be. Quite a nice inference—as this case goes. However. More evidence emerged since the hush-hush inquests. Not merely emerged. Thrust on us. Same like the cameo. That's what I wanted you for." He told Lomas of the hasty marriage of Giles and Alison under the auspices of Brown.

"Brown?" Lomas enquired. "That's the captain of industry who told you to run away and play."

"Yes. The intruding big business. However. He's not so sure he wants me to stand out now. I don't presume to understand Mr. Brown. He dumped this on me."

Lomas was given the postcard, read the address "Mrs. Giles Aston!!!" with a contemptuous exclamation, "Common form," and turned the card over. "Damn, Greek."

"Not common form, no," Reggie purred.

"What's it mean?"

"Oh, my Lomas! What did you do at Cambridge?" Reggie smiled. "Lines from the late Aeschylus, his *Agamemnon*. 'Blood once fallen dark at a man's feet, who can call it back?' Affirming the good old creed that when families have a murder between 'em, there's no way of atonement; they've got to go on killing. Application to Mrs. Giles: how dare you marry the son of the man who killed your brother?"

"Sweet message." Lomas frowned. "Just the sort of message some kind soul would send the girl with all this family scandal about. But in Greek! She can't read Greek, I suppose?"

"Not likely, no. I should doubt if her young husband can."

"Why was Greek used then?"

"Interestin' question. Old Aston is a bit of a scholar. He keeps a range of classics in his den and he uses 'em." Reggie's eyelids drooped as he watched Lomas. "There you are. Aston the father is the only fellow in sight likely to think in Greek, and he's a cunning old fellow—remember the sham burglary—and he's had a row with his son, and he set his face against this marriage. Just the sort of fellow to think of sending the hated Tracy bride a Greek curse. Works very nice, don't it? So far. But the force of the curse is: that a murder stands between the Tracy bride and the Aston bridegroom; that old Aston murdered the Tracy boy—which may be true. But you wouldn't expect old Aston to brag about it—even in a nasty temper."

Lomas meditated. "I don't know," he said slowly. "A man who murdered a child out of hate of his family … when his own son married into the family, he might do anything to hurt."

"Not bad, Lomas." Reggie smiled. "Yes. I think old Aston is possessed with hate and fear of the Tracys. Sees himself a tragic fellow. Just the sort of fellow who might go blind. One of the possibilities. Persuasive possibility. But there are reasons against. Old Tracy is also a good hater. Tracy raged over the marriage. A curse on his daughter for marrying an Aston comes more reasonable from him. Don't give him away at all. Charges Aston with the murder. Remember the sham cameo. Somebody has already tried to put the murder on Aston by a trick with a classical touch and when that didn't work abolished the fake. Repetition suggestive. And this pretty little thing—" he tapped the postcard—"quite good. Not good enough, Lomas. You notice the Greek is not written but a cutting from a book."

"What of it? The most elementary trick," Lomas scoffed. "Did you expect him to sign his name?"

"No, I did not. Nor did I expect him to give me a hint what his name wasn't. You miss the point. Greek quotation from a difficult author. Implying that the sender was a fellow who knew his way about in Greek. Same like Aston. But the cutting is cut from the Loeb edition, which has the Greek on one page and an English translation opposite. That is not the sort of edition Aston uses. Why should he buy an edition with translation to get a cutting? No. The man who did this is a man who don't know Greek too well. Same like the fellow who didn't know cameos very well."

"Very neat, Reginald." Lomas smiled. "In your best form. But where are you going to? You've gone a long way to clear Aston. If there's a determined effort to manufacture false evidence of murder, the natural inference is there never was a murder."

"And the chief constable?" Reggie asked. "He just died obliging and convenient so the cameo should vanish. Quite natural, isn't it?"

"Confound you." Lomas made a grimace.

"My dear chap! Oh, my dear chap! Don't say that. Quite sufficiently confounded already."

Lomas studied him quizzically. "No, Reginald. I think not. Come along. What is the theory?"

"No theory. Only impotent rage. Too many people. Too many facts. Too many tricks. Too many possibilities. I have no doubt the boy Tracy was murdered. I don't know who did it. I have no doubt the chief constable was murdered. I don't know who did that. The obvious probability is old Aston killed the boy. No obvious reason for him to kill the chief constable. Who else? Old Tracy might have killed his son—greed and temper. When the unexpected bones turned up he might have tried to put the murder on Aston with the sham cameo. When the cameo didn't work, when the chief constable was getting interested in him, he might have wiped out the chief and the cameo. All that fits—and there's the poacher's story to back it. Tracy's a fierce brute, and he is a gambler. I should be surprised if he knows his way about in Greek. So he would want a translation to help him find a Greek curse." Reggie gazed at Lomas dreamily. "How does that strike the higher intelligence?"

"Quite good," said Lomas. "Quite plausible."

"Yes, I think so. By itself. But only by exclusion of other facts. Aston was worried about those cliffs where the bones lay. He did hustle down to look at the landslip which brought 'em out. He don't stick at a trifle of crime to help himself—remember the burglary. He has a turn of cleverness which runs to fake. No evidence that Tracy has. Moreover, there are other persons acting queer. Our late-lamented chief constable began by objectin' to any investigation of the boy's bones, went on to be quite ready and eager for a case against old Aston, became hot and bothered at proof that he had to look for somebody else and proceeded to look privily and by stealth, telling nobody what he was after—if you believe the faithful Bubb. And so he got himself wiped out. Whereupon Bubb took great pains to have his death written off as accidental, hated me for bringing on him the poacher's information against Tracy and is now doing his best to stamp it out. Very obstructive, the man Bubb."

"I agree." Lomas nodded. "The police work has been damnable. But you mustn't make too much of that, Reginald. These local police forces are apt to be scared of bigwigs."

"Yes, as you say. Which never happens in our great metropolis. No. Still another tiresome person. The benevolent Brown. Why does he take Giles and Alison under his opulent patronage, why does he hurry on the wedding? There's nothing nobler than a man of sentiment. Tellin' me to hush up the murder of Alison's brother so it shouldn't spoil love's young dream—quite nice and sentimental. But when the Greek postcard turns up Brown brings it round to me good and quick. Not desiring to have that hushed up. Well. He may be straight. Somebody in the confounded case might be. But I wonder if it's Mr. Brown. I should say there's more in our Brown's fat head than meets the eye."

"What could he be after?" Lomas frowned.

"My dear old thing! He's after the ambitions of Mr. Brown. He means to be somebody in Durshire. And he has his own ideas how to do it."

"Oh that!" Lomas shrugged. "No doubt. A new millionaire often wants to get the old families under his thumb."

"Yes. And that bein' thus, we want to know more about the old families and the thumb of Mr. Brown." Reggie finished his claret and lit a cigar. "Well?"

"Are you putting that up to me?" Lomas frowned.

"Yes. General case for enquiry. Strong case. Urgent case."

"I'm not to deny it," said Lomas. "This man Bubb has shirked his duty. So did the chief constable. But I have no authority over them. Unless the local police call us in we can't act. You know that."

"Over the official the gods themselves have no power. Yes, I know that is the official creed. But the world is not quite so evil as you believe. Sometimes a way does open round the monstrous official. As here. A postcard threatening a resident in London has been placed before you. Your job to investigate. Send a good man down to Durshire."

Lomas meditated. "That could be done," he said slowly. "But I see no use in it. There is nothing definite to work on."

"Oh, my Lomas! Lots of definite lines. Fuss about posting of the card. Small place, Colsbury. Small mail. Some intelligent post-office fellow may have noticed such a queer card, and what box it came from. Who was in Colsbury on the date of postmark? Tracy has been abroad. Had he got back? Brown's been up in London. Did he run down? Fuss about the cutting. Who has bought a Loeb Aeschylus? Fuss about the stuff it's stuck on with. Not gum. Paste. Holdtight paste. Who uses that?"

"Plenty to play with." Lomas shrugged. "If you expect any result, you're sanguine. But suppose there was, suppose we could prove who sent the card, we couldn't go any further. The threat is not definite enough to be criminal."

"Oh no. No. But a good man down there could make his playful enquiries, stir up everybody. Put fear into 'em. There should be reactions." Reggie lay back, blowing smoke rings, and murmured in a droning rhythm, "Tis an palin agkalesait epaeidon."

"What?" Lomas asked. "What is the jargon?"

"Sorry. Only the Greek. 'The blood that once has fallen dark, who can call it back by his charms?' That's a challenge, Lomas. Challenge to you and me. We'll take it up, please."

"My dear Reginald!" Lomas laughed. "Your confidence in your charms is touching. I do not expect to bring the dead to life myself."

"Nor do I. No. Any objection to save the living?"

Lomas shrugged. "Well, I agree, we can look into the postcard. If it *does* make this man Bubb uncomfortable, so much the better."

"Spoke very handsome." Reggie smiled. "Even in officials there is a force which makes for righteousness. Sometimes. The natural desire of one official to knock another out …"

So the forces of the moral law in Durshire were strengthened by Inspector Underwood, and Reggie returned to the study of the common wart. He has always maintained that disease is far more interesting than sin. His warts were peculiarly grateful and comforting, for he had to wait a long time till any new facts emerged about the sin of Durshire.

Underwood failed to trace the posting of the card or the buying of a Loeb Aeschylus in the town and convinced himself that Holdtight paste was not on sale there. Tracy had come back from Monte Carlo before the posting of the card, but in Colsbury nobody had seen him. Nor had Aston been seen there. Brown had come down to his place about the time the card was sent—but not to stay—and the day could not be fixed.

In all the investigations Bubb had been reasonably civil and helpful but made it plain that he thought them futile. He told Underwood that there was no sort of line on Tracy. He had asked Tracy straight about the chief constable's mysterious visit to him, and Tracy answered that he had not seen the chief and had no notion what he came for. In the opinion of Underwood Bubb was telling the truth, for he volunteered the further information that Tracy's temper was something cruel—worse than ever—and when Underwood suggested his daughter's marriage had got his back up, Bubb replied there might be more to it than that. The talk was Tracy had got his estate into a devil of a mess with gambling, and old Brown was after it, which would make him mad. The existence of such rumors Underwood confirmed, but could get no further.

It took a long time to obtain these valuable results. Underwood reported the return of Giles and Alison from their honeymoon and their settlement in the house of the agent of Brown's estate, done up for them very handsome. They seemed to be having no trouble. People were decent with them. Everything was all ordinary, except that their parents and they stood off from each other. Giles was doing a straight job as agent, but Brown kept coming down and fussing; particularly attentive to the lady, so much that it was being talked about.

The weeks went by but brought no more. Underwood's reports merged into arguments that he should be taken off a case which never would be a case. He was told to come back.

Lomas announced the decision to Mr. Fortune apologetically. "I'm afraid you'll be disappointed, Reginald. So am I. It did look like a chance. But there's nothing more to be done."

He was annoyed by Reggie's smile. "Oh no. Not by you. Not by the earnest Underwood. He's better away. Something attempted, nothing done has earned a night's repose."

"Pleasant dreams," said Lomas bitterly. "I *had* thought you took the case seriously."

"My dear old thing! I never dream. I'm always serious," said Reggie and sat down to write to General Duddon.

At the beginning of the next week he had an answer. General Duddon was so pleased to hear from him. It was extraordinary he should be asking whether anything new had happened down there. They had had a queer scare: a girl on Brown's estate complained that she had been shot at in the dusk.

Reggie rang up the general.

CHAPTER XIX *Evidence of a Club*

IN THE DUSK OF THE SAME DAY his car brought him to General Duddon's door.

The general trotted out and chattered welcome.

"Thanks very much." Reggie drew him into the house. "You haven't let anyone hear I was coming, have you?"

The general took that cue exuberantly, led the way into his study, drew the blinds, shut the door and then answered in jerks of high speed. Fortune could rely on him absolutely—he understood the value of secrecy—learned that in the service. Fortune couldn't have done better than come to his little place—not a soul would know he was there—and any assistance—only to say the word. Exceedingly glad Fortune was taking action—nasty affair with that girl—shocking affair. And the police, pah! Pack of lazy, muddling fools, if not worse. Eh what?

"No opinion," Reggie answered. "What are they doing?"

"Nothing, sir. Nothing. We have had them blundering round bullying the girl till she don't know whether she's in her senses or not, and our blockhead of a sergeant here told me he didn't believe she *was* fired at; if there was a shot anywhere, it wasn't meant for her."

"I wonder," Reggie murmured. "What is the theory? Who was the shot meant for?"

The general gave a cackling laugh. Surely Fortune didn't expect a sensible theory—knew the police too well for that. Only one object, evasion of duty—seen it with the poor boy's bones. And, not to speak ill of the dead, the chief constable was killed in shirking—Bubb and his incompetents keeping up the traditions of their miserable force—simply concerned to make out they need do nothing.

"Yes. Let us be charitable," said Reggie. "First police theory. The girl is unreliable: nerves or naughty desire to attract notice. It does happen. Is she that kind of girl?"

The general scoffed. No more nerves than a leg of mutton. Stolid, matter-of-fact village wench. The usual Durshire type.

"Oh. Like our Bubb," Reggie murmured.

"Ha, much the same," the general chuckled. "Not an idea in her head."

"Well, well. Second police theory. There was a shot somewhere near the girl. But not meant for her. How does the local knowledge take that? I am not a shooting man, by the grace of God, but this is summer time.

Do you shoot through the summer in these parts?"

The general shook his head. Ah no. Point well taken. But he must say rather a townsman's point. It really wouldn't do. Close season, of course, no game shooting. But fellows would be out after rabbits or pigeons or vermin. You might hear shots many an evening. Farmers and their sons and so on—to fill the pot or keep down pests. Favorite time, sunset in summer. All sorts of people took out a gun at the end of the day. Old Tracy was often shooting round his land. Of course he was a birdkiller. Hawks, owls, any creature that might hurt his precious pheasants, any rare bird, he was death on it.

"Is that so?" Reggie murmured. "Marked interest in birds in the Tracy family. Son Tracy was keen on rare eggs. Father Tracy shoots rare birds. Conflict of interest. Not makin' for family love. However. To return to the damsel. She would not be alarmed by the sound of a shot, shots bein' common. Why did she think this one was fired at her?"

The general told him she hadn't a doubt. The shot came out of a copse close by where she was, and she heard the pellets patter into the hedge behind her. She screamed, but nobody showed up, and she ran back home. She was sure there hadn't been anything for a man to fire at along the road but her.

"Not too good," said Reggie. "I seem to have heard of wild shooting before this. Sportsmen who blaze away at nothing, sportsmen who let fly across a public road—they do occur."

The general was annoyed. Fortune really must not argue like that; it had no weight at all. Of course there was careless, reckless shooting, a devil of a lot of it nowadays. Lucky to find a house party without a fellow more likely to hit you than the pheasants. But fellows bred to the gun, fellows out all the year round didn't play fool tricks. Making every allowance that Fortune had no experience of shooting, surprised to hear him talk so. Sounded as if he wanted the affair shelved.

"Same like your police?" Reggie smiled. "No, General, I'm not very like them. I believe the expert. Your expert knowledge of shootin' manners and customs humbly accepted. Now what have you given me? There was a shot at the girl from close quarters. Though fired by a fellow bred to the gun, it didn't hit her. And yet the fellow didn't fire again. Curious and interestin'. Not a very determined attempt to slay her. Or only an attempt to alarm her. Why? What is the local opinion? Has she a disgruntled swain?"

The general told him not to think of it. Face like a plate, figure like a sack—most respectable girl.

"Virtue its own reward. Sad world. However. It was in the dusk. The shooter might have taken the girl for somebody else. Who was out with a gun last night? The local gossips ought to know that."

"I may tell you that was the first question I asked," General Duddon squeaked.

"My dear General! The expert mind. Splendid. And what was the answer?"

"Nobody knows of anybody but two fellows, a farmer and his son, rabbiting. They were together; they weren't anywhere near the girl, and they're absolutely above suspicion."

"Oh General! Doesn't local gossip go beyond that? Sad lack of imagination in the locality. What about Father Tracy? You said he was often shooting round his land."

The general made a queer movement of head and throat like a bird swallowing. "I did not suggest any suspicion of Tracy, Mr. Fortune. There is no ground. It would be quite unfair."

"Wasn't thinking you'd been unfair." Reggie's eyelids drooped. "Didn't feel there was any ground. I was just wondering—have others talked about Tracy?"

"In this matter—" the general was embarrassed—"I—I believe I've heard his name mentioned, but I couldn't be sure. The fact is, there's always a bad word for the man."

"Voice of the people, voice of God. Sometimes."

The general snorted. "No sir, I can't allow that. It's not right."

"You think not?" Reggie smiled. "Not always rational, no. Let us still believe the world is. So we will use a map of it. Do you keep a large map?"

The general's mouth came open. "I don't follow," he complained. "Oh—oh, you mean the district. Certainly."

"Yes, that was the idea," Reggie murmured. "Not the whole world. Not involved, I hope. Though we are struggling with the forces which made it." He hummed the tune of that vulgar song, recalled to him by the first stages of the case:

> *"All the jungle folks have habits of their own.*
> *The worm may turn in quite the nicest way.*
> *But the elephant never forgets!"*

The general did not remember the disrespectful words but was pained by the tune's levity. "Now, now, let me show you," he said severely and spread out a map. "This is six inches to the mile, you see. I take it you want to know the lie of the land where the shot was fired. Very well. This is where we are, Fairseat, my place. Now just to the east, near the river, you notice a village marked Combe, only a few houses. That's where the girl lives. She was walking along this lane toward the village. There's the copse from which the shot was fired; that's the place."

"I see. Lonely place. Why was she there?"

"She'd been doing a day's washing at this farm on the hill, that's the home farm on Brown's estate. His house is up beyond by that headland, the Haunches."

"So the shot, if any, was fired from Brown's land?"

"No, no. Brown's doesn't reach down so far into the valley—not yet. His estate marches with Tracy's along here." The general's finger marked out a line. "Across the hills, Tracy takes in Giants' Graves—the pits in the chalk, you know—and his boundary comes down to the big combe; all the woodland thereabouts and the copse are his—"

"Well, well. Tracy owns site of alleged shot. Very interesting. And the alarmed damsel—who works for Brown—does she live on Tracy's estate?"

"Dear me, no. The village belongs to Brown. You see a building marked north of the village? That's where the boundary of the two estates comes down to the river. That's Combe House. Brown snapped it up out of Tracy's hands when it came on the market. Now he's had it rebuilt for young Aston to live in as his agent."

"Oh. The young folks are living there." Reggie bent closer over the map.

The general said it was a queer place to put the agent, on the edge of the estate, but of course Brown was out to get a good deal more than he'd got. Buy the county if he could. If he got a chunk of Tracy's land, the house would be central enough.

"As you say. Farsighted man, the man Brown." Reggie sat back. "Finished with map, General." He gazed at the general with large plaintive eyes.

The general's hospitality awoke into fussy energy. Reggie was pressed to drink, bustled away to his room, told he must be starving, urged to dine as he was. And the general fed him on whiting and chicken and the lightest sherry, and he was vaguely discursive.

Reggie went to bed early, and he has seldom got up earlier. In the first hour after dawn he left the sleeping house and made his way to the lane on which the girl had walked. Silvery, sunlit mist clothed hill and vale and river. There were no sounds but from an innumerable choir of birds and the faraway roar of the sea. He moved slowly along the lane, made out the copse, stood still and took bearings. Yes, a man could be hidden in that cover on the very edge of the lane. Shooting at anybody in it he must fire downward; his shot would go into the hedge on the far side. Reggie walked on scanning the dew-laden bushes and found some leaves torn, saw scratches on the twigs. He cut out of one of them a flattened pellet.

"Well, well. Shot verified," he murmured; "not by our Bubb." He calculated the line of the shot and climbed up to the copse and wandered about in it. After a while he saw a glimmer of brass on the ground and came upon an empty cartridge case and a cartridge which had not been fired. He picked them up and gazed at them with dislike. "I wonder," he moaned. "Careless sportsman—or far otherwise. Too much evidence. As usual. Not discovered by our Bubb. Also as usual." The two cartridges were wrapped in a handkerchief and put away, and he went on through the copse to the open hillside and stood watching the mist thin and clear in a flood of sunshine.

The river flashed out like a broken chain of pools where it wound its way to the sea between dark mud banks. Broad fields of ripening corn glowed bright. That was upstream; that was the rich black land, Tracy's land. Under the hillside, scrub pasture stretched to the river and seaward. The squat square tower of the village church rose just below him, and beyond he saw the white house into which Brown had put his pets, Alison and Giles. It stood under the hills where they came nearest to the river, like an outpost of the barren white land. Near by, a great combe overgrown with bracken and thicket rose to shoulders of chalk-bearing mounds of ancient war or burial, scarred with shadowy holes—the Giants' Graves of General Duddon's cherished tradition.

The clock in the church tower struck six. Reggie groaned sympathy with himself and made haste back to bed.

He was very late for breakfast and found the general peevish. "Must apologize for not waiting, Fortune—didn't like to disturb you—afraid you haven't slept well."

"What there was, was good," Reggie sighed. "Don't stir unavailin' regret." He took off the lid of a dish of eggs and bacon and put it on again hastily and ate toast. "Is that coffee? Thank you." He sipped it and concealed his anguish. "Well, well. Can you trust your servants—in the larger issues? I am not here. They don't know anything about me. Because I'm going to stay."

The general was excited. The night had brought counsel, what, what? Fortune had his theory, eh? Action in view?

"Not by me. No. I am the patient student. But you might take useful action—if you'd go into Colsbury, to your club, and get people talking: about this business, and who could have done it, and the police work's rotten, and you must have 'em shaken up or nobody's safe. Just gossip round and see how it is taken, especially by Tracy and Brown or their friends—if any. Would you mind?"

The general would not. He went off in a fuss of happy importance, and Reggie shut himself into the study and rang up the Criminal Investigation Department.

"Fortune speaking, Lomas. Have you had any communication from our Bubb? ... No, I thought not. Our Bubb is self-contained as ever. Would you be surprised to hear that on the withdrawal of the active Underwood things began to happen? ... Yes, I thought you would. Preserve absolute calm." Reggie told of the shot at the girl.

"Wait a minute," Lomas interrupted. "Where are you?"

"Between black land and white land. On the battlefield. But secret and incognito. Address, in care of General Duddon, Fairseat, Combe, Durshire. Colsbury 1203."

"What the devil took you down there?"

"My dear old thing! Marched on the sound of the guns. Reported by the watchful general. There isn't much misses General Duddon, whether he knows what it is or otherwise. On your wise withdrawal of Underwood, I asked him to let me know the sequel. Here you are."

"Damn, you said yourself there was nothing more Underwood could do."

"Oh yes. There wasn't. Removal of Underwood highly desirable. He hadn't got anywhere, only made it clear to all concerned that there were police ready and anxious to be a nuisance. Disturbing to the guilty mind, if a timid mind. But this isn't. The one thing certain about it, it's fierce, and it's playing big and deep. So on the disappearance of Underwood it went on with the game. As expected."

Lomas made an angry exclamation. "Do you mean to tell me you expected an attempt to shoot a village girl? What's the sense of it? What's the connection with the Tracy-Aston business? What—"

"You wouldn't listen," Reggie complained, and related his conversation with the general, his inspection of the lane, his discovery of the cartridges.

"Well—" Lomas answered slowly—"deuced queer stuff. This fellow Bubb is a blight. Something worse than incompetence. Determination to be incompetent. But do you pretend to draw any conclusions?"

"Not yet, no. Too much evidence."

"Good Gad!" Lomas exploded. "Too little, Reginald. You have nothing definite at all."

"Oh, my Lomas! Lots. Horrid definite, horrid significant. Unoffendin' irrelevant damsel shot at with intent. Why? Obvious reasonable answer because she was mistaken in the dusk for Alison, who was to be wiped out as per threat sent on her marriage. Who fired? Local feeling, as reported by the faithful general, puts it down to her father. Which fits very neatly into the obvious, reasonable suspicion that Tracy sent the threat. Tracy does prowl round his land with a gun, and the shot came from his land. And the determined failure of Bubb and his minions to find the staring evidence that it did so is in harmony with the omission of the late chief constable to deal with Tracy by straight police methods. All very nice. But why was the evidence left to stare? Why two cartridges in the copse? Very careless—or not so careless."

"Did you say this was definite?" Lomas laughed. "My dear Reginald, it gets you nowhere. Whether the shot was intentional or accidental, the man with the gun would be rattled when he saw that he'd just missed the girl. He wouldn't stop to pick up his cartridge case; he might very well drop another."

"Yes, it could be," Reggie admitted.

"Quite. So in fact you have only made out a general suspicion of Tracy, and that you had before."

"Oh, my Lomas! Fresh grounds. Curious and interestin' grounds. Worth investigation. I want the earnest Underwood to come down again and investigate."

"The devil you do! My dear fellow, we can't take action against Tracy on this."

"No. You can't. Don't want you to. But you must investigate. Your responsibility. Following on your official enquiry into a threatening letter there has been an attempt at murder in the vicinity of the woman threatened. It is the duty and the delight of the Criminal Investigation Department to find out why and stop this nasty game. Get on with it. Send Underwood down privily and by stealth and let him report to me."

For a little while no answer came. Then Lomas said, "You put it to me that Underwood's enquiries may have induced this affair."

"Failure of his enquiries," Reggie corrected. "One factor, yes. His departure was another."

"You agreed to that yourself," Lomas protested again.

"Oh yes. The right tactics. On failure of first attack. Recoil to allure the enemy. Who has been allured. Now come on."

"Always right, aren't you?" said Lomas.

"My only aunt!" Reggie moaned. "Not me, no. Continually ineffective, continually defeated. Hitherto complete failure to eliminate the deludin', irrelevant facts. But still retain faith in the power of the human reason; and therefore in your earnest detectives."

"Thank you," Lomas answered. "Well, there may be a case for further enquiry. I'll send Underwood down to confer with you tomorrow. But until he has authority from me there'll be no fresh action. Understood?"

"I heard you," said Reggie. "By first train. Goodbye."

He spent the morning in study of the large-scale map of the district, measuring distances between village and copse and Tracy's house and Aston's house and Brown's house and the house of Giles and Alison by road and across country, and made—which he hates—calculations. Through the afternoon he slept and was dreamy over a very late tea when General Duddon returned.

"Well, well," Reggie blinked at him. "How's the club? Anybody there?"

Having recovered from shock at seeing the teapot still in use the general told him that there were quite a number, much as usual. Hadn't seen old Aston or young Aston, but Tracy was in for a drink—or a dozen drinks—

fellow did put it down, no fellow could stand so much liquor in the morning. Looked like going all to pieces, losing his nerve, drinking by himself—bad sign that, rather marked. Old Brown came in, and Cope the banker fellow just after. Brown fastened on him, and they had a cocktail or so together. Tracy used to be hand and glove with Cope—two of the regular old stagers. Cope waved to him, but Tracy didn't see or wouldn't see, and old Brown took Cope along to lunch—civil to everybody in his slap-your-back way—hadn't a look for Tracy though. Brown and Cope lunched at the long table with other fellows; Tracy went into a corner by himself.

"You're very good, General," Reggie encouraged him. "I see it all. Who did you sit with?"

"Not with Tracy, my friend." The general made his wizened face express subtle wisdom. He went to the long table, sat next but one to Brown—by old Werne—

"My dear General! Good and better," Reggie approved. "Free talker, the Lord Werne."

"I had that in mind, sir," the general squeaked. "We did talk. Devilish hard to say what we didn't talk about."

"Yes, I should think so." Reggie contemplated the general affectionately. "Anything definite?"

"Oh, I handled him," the general cackled. "We beat up and down all over this business, and the other fellows chimed in. Werne hasn't a good word for our police: let off that he didn't mind corruption, but he objected to imbecility. Brown roared and said that had always been his line: you hold your own with a rogue but no managing fools. Some fellow put in he didn't believe the police were corrupt; no man could think that of the poor old chief. Most of them backed him, but Werne sneered in his silky way it was much pleasanter not to think. Then I turned them back to the shot at the girl. Most of 'em didn't believe there was a shot anywhere near her. If there was, it was some poacher fellow afraid to own up and give himself away—happened before—fellows make a set at Tracy's land—like Elijah Hawke."

"Oh, Elijah," Reggie murmured. "Who mentioned Elijah, General?"

"I couldn't tell you." The general stared. "Nothing in that. Notorious poaching rascal—been caught more than once by Tracy's men—his name naturally came up."

"Yes. As enemy of Tracy. Yes. Did you notice Tracy listening to this suggestion?"

"I kept an eye on Tracy, sir. I don't know how much he heard, but he was watching Brown the whole time."

"Well, well. And how did our Mr. Brown take the Elijah theory?"

The general shook his head. "Simply cut out. Got Cope talking about harvest prospects. I took it up, said it was a scandal our police couldn't make sure of anything—who was going to be an accidental death next?—that rather roused them. Eh, what? And old Werne came in very neat: great consolation to know in the next world that one had been killed by a poacher. They didn't like that—sort of thing that gets these old country families. Began to talk about appointing a chief constable from outside—couldn't have Bubb keep the job."

"My dear General." Reggie purred over him. "Magnificent. Beautifully discreet, beautifully effective."

"Not too bad, I hope," the general squeaked. "But you mustn't call it effective. They have no drive, these fellows. No guts, sir. They won't act, it isn't in 'em."

"You did though. Well, what about our Brown and our Tracy? Any sign of interest in a new chief constable?"

"Nothing to signify. Brown said something about we could do with one and went off. Tracy followed him out. Then the rest of 'em talked round and round."

"I see. Yes. Well, well. Would you mind if I miss dinner? I want to go over the place in the dusk same conditions as time of shot. Don't wait for me. Just have something cold left about."

The general protested, torn between hospitality and devotion to punctual meals, but was easily persuaded. "Great man for duty, aren't you, Fortune?"

"I am, yes," Reggie smiled. Among his sacrifices on duty's altar he reckons high his submission to the table of General Duddon. But the abnegation of dinner gave him no extra pain. Anything, hot or cold, from the general's kitchen tasted much the same.

CHAPTER XX *Evidence of a Church Clock*

THE SUN HAD GONE DOWN behind the chalk hills. Their eastern slopes lay in dark shadow. The combes which led from them to the valley gave up shape and color to a deepening gloom, while the sky in the west was still suffused with golden light which gleamed upon the tide flooding up the river and showed the first of the night mist, a silvery veil over mudbank and sodden pasture.

Reggie sat on the hillside, indistinguishable from the juniper bushes about him, close to the lane which led from the village to the hills—the lane on which the shot was fired. No one traversed it either way. No one was moving in the copse or anywhere near on Tracy's land. His opinion that the place was not frequented by the inhabitants in the evening on their regular lawful occasions was confirmed as the sun set, and the gleam faded from the river.

He heard a distant shot echo from the hills. Then the heavy air was still and silent again. The throb of a motorcar came faint to his ears, and he watched the roads in the valley, watched the village and the white house of Alison and Giles. But no car arrived; no car departed. The engine-throb stopped, and though he continued to watch village and house he did not hear it again. A few people moved to and fro in the village; someone was in the garden of the white house. He rose and made his way down through the darkening twilight to the lane, to the main road of the valley. The lane came into it on the landward side of the village, nearer the white house, and toward the house he turned.

There was no one in sight, not a sound of anyone. A high bank with a huge ancient hedge on it protected the road from the marshy pastures of the river below to the right. On his left was neither hedge nor fence, but the ground rose sharply in thickets of thorn and crabapple and gorse and bracken to a deep, dark combe which climbed the ridge.

The white house seemed to be close and then was out of sight again behind the thickets as the road swerved away to avoid the sharp rise by the combe's mouth. There he heard some movement above him, a dragging, crackling sound. He stood still, and the sound stopped. He waited a moment, peering into the gloom of the undergrowth, then thrust on through the bushes toward the place whence the sound had come. He heard movement again, movement to his left, behind him, turned to catch a glimpse of a man in the dark and a swinging stick. He dodged that and, shouting and stumbling, drove a blow at the man's body as he fell, felt a crash on his head and all the world whirling and gone.

When it came back to him it was black-dark and still as death, but it pricked him, and he ached. He was lying on his face in a clump of brambles. He rose unsteadily to his feet, and the darkness grew gray. No, it wasn't night yet; or night was over already. Where was he? What had he been doing? ... He remembered. He plunged away through the thicket and found the road again and stood listening, heard nothing but his own panting, choking breath, looked all about him. ... Still twilight, a bit darker but only twilight. ... Couldn't have been very long. ... Then he heard a shot—not very near—not aimed at him—couldn't be. But near enough—been quite near enough already.

He made for the white house at the best pace his aching head would let him raise.

As he lumbered along, the clock of the village church struck a half-hour. He looked at his watch. Quite right. Just half-past eight.

He gave a laugh which ended in a gasp. "Oh my head! I earned that!"

CHAPTER XXI *Evidence of the White House*

THERE WAS NO LIGHT in the front windows of the white house, but he found the door open. He knocked and rang, and a maid came along the hall and switched on the lights. Reggie remained in the shadow outside and asked for Mr. Giles Aston.

"He's not in, sir, he's not back yet." The maid was a young country girl.

"Sorry about that. Rather late, isn't he?"

"He is generally in before now, sir."

"Wonder what's kept him?"

"He didn't say anything, sir."

"When did he go out?"

"Same as usual, after lunch."

"Not been in since? Well, well. I'd like to speak to Mrs. Aston."

"She's out too, sir. She went out to meet Mr. Aston."

"Oh. When was that?"

"I couldn't tell you the time. Just a while back."

"Did she say she was going to meet him?"

"No sir. She didn't say anything, but I saw her going down to the road; she walks a bit to meet him regular when he's not in early."

"I'll wait for Mr. Aston." Reggie came into the hall.

"If you please, sir. Oh!" The light showed her his dirty face and clothes. "My goodness, have you had an accident?"

"Yes, a little damaged, yes. I should be better for washing."

"I'm sure." The maid was sympathetic. "This way, sir." She took him to a cloakroom. "Are you much hurt? Could I do anything? Could I bring you something?"

"It's all right. Don't worry." Reggie shut himself in and looked at himself in the mirror and felt about the bruise on his aching head. "Quite enough. Short stick, probably loaded hunting crop. Only one blow. Luck for Reginald. Not luck, no. Operator was in a hurry. I had put a shout in. Probably other reasons not to dally with me. He had all the luck that was going. I wonder." He brushed himself, washed face and hands and found his left hand stiff and the knuckles bruised. "Hit him somewhere. It was a body blow. Didn't get his solar plexus, confound him. Ribs—or something in pocket—something hard. Time about eight. And I came to by eight-thirty—just before a shot. Oh my Lord! What was done between? What was doing

103

when I butted in?" He shivered and drew a long breath. "God help me! I have something now. The first I've earned. But it's late, it's late."

He came out with a face so pale and drawn that the maid gasped at him. "Won't you just have a drop of whiskey, sir?"

Reggie shook his head and shuddered. "Mr. Aston not back? No. Is there a telephone? Thanks very much." He rang up General Duddon. "Fortune speaking. Bring your car to Giles Aston's house, will you? Bring a torch. That's all. Thanks." He turned to the maid. "Could there be soda water?" he asked.

He sat in a lounge drinking it. The siphon was empty before a car drove up to the side of the house, quick footsteps came to the door, and a man's voice called "Alison! Alison!"

Reggie went into the hall and met Giles Aston and said, "No. She's not here."

"What?" Giles stared at him. "Mr. Fortune! Have you been here long? Did you come to see my wife?"

"I did try, yes. Arriving just after half-past eight. But she'd gone out. The maid said she'd gone to meet you. Did she?"

"What the devil do you mean?" Giles flushed. "Of course I haven't met her. You heard me calling to her. I can't understand it. I can't think where she's got to."

The maid came to him in a flutter. "Oh sir, haven't you seen mistress? Whatever has happened to her?"

"Don't be a fool," Giles said fiercely. "Which way did she go?"

"Just like usual. Down to the road, toward the village. But that was an hour ago."

Giles turned on his heel and strode out, and Reggie followed close. "What are you thinking of doing?" he asked.

"Look for her, of course," Giles snarled.

"On the road to the village? Haven't you just come along that?"

"Yes, I have." Giles stood still on the doorstep and scowled at him. "I must have missed her somehow in the dark."

"You think so? You think she let your car go by without calling to you?"

"I can't make it out," Giles muttered.

"She wasn't on that road when I walked along. You didn't see her when you drove along. I don't think she's there now, Mr. Aston. Which way did you come?"

"Over the hills and down into the road just by the village."

"Oh yes. And she knew you would come that way?"

"Of course she did. She knew where I was this afternoon—over at the Ridge Farm meeting Brown there. She couldn't go wrong; there's no other way for a car."

"But you were later than she expected. So she went to meet you. Quite clear. Why were you later?"

"Damn it, what's that matter? Brown left me to fix up the details with old Reddy; we're buying his land. What's the use of all this? What are you getting at? Why did you come here?"

"There was a girl from the village shot at a few nights ago in the dusk," said Reggie. "Didn't that suggest anything to you?"

"My God!" Giles groaned. "Do you mean Alison—"

"I don't know," Reggie said slowly. "I didn't know she was in the habit of going alone to meet you when you were late. But you did."

"That shot—I never thought," Giles muttered. "You get a stray shot across a road every once in a while."

"Your wife thought no more of it than that?"

"No, that's what we both said when we heard of it."

"Oh. Do you often come back in the evening down that lane where the girl was shot at?"

"Not often, now and then. Why?"

"That didn't suggest anything to you—or your wife?"

Giles swallowed. "No, I tell you. Don't keep me talking here." He made off into the dark.

Reggie stood still looking after him for a moment then turned back into the hall and went to the telephone again. "Is that county police headquarters? Speaking for Mr. Giles Aston, Combe House, Combe. Mrs. Giles Aston went out before eight o'clock on foot and has disappeared. Please give orders for search at once. What? What are the police for? Get on to it." He rang off as he heard a car come to the door and reached it before General Duddon got out. "Thanks very much. Sorry to drag you here. Push off but go easy, will you?" The general let off a chatter of talk. Happy to come, of course; hoped nothing wrong. Devilish queer business on the road—nearly ran down a man blundering about as if he was drunk. Man howled at him had he seen a lady. Stopped, and it was young Aston—said Mrs. Aston had gone out and not come back. Told him seen nobody; off he went. What was it all about?

Reggie explained in the fewest words while the general sputtered, "Steady, slow, stop. Yes, about here. Torch, please." He got out of the car and swept the beam of the torch along the roadside. In the glistening dew on the bracken he made out where he had plunged through it and followed the trail. He came to bramble bushes which were crushed. He found his hat lying a little way off. "Yes. That's where I fell." He turned, swinging the torch about. Its beam revealed some trampling and scraping of the dead leaves under the trees, a flattening of grass and bracken here and there, no clear footprints. "We were busy," he drawled, and stood staring over the torchlight into the impenetrable black of the thicket beyond. "Oh my Lord! Nothing to do but wish for the day." He went back to the car. "I am finished. Take me home, please."

The general squeaked anxious sympathy. By all means—could see he was pretty well all in—must have been a damned near thing. Mustn't do any more; have a doctor—

"My dear fellow! Oh my dear fellow. I am a doctor." Reggie was plaintive. "The head is hard. Quite hard. Without and within. Yes, quite hard."

The general went on to splutter speculations of who had attacked him, and what had happened to the woman, and what must be done, and Reggie put back his head and shut his eyes.

When they came to the house he asked, "You want to do something? Go and rout out the village. In case the distraught husband hasn't thought of that. Somebody might find her. Somebody might have seen something. Don't bring me in. If anybody else does, all you know is: I've gone to bed. I have. Praying for the light."

CHAPTER XXII *Evidence of a Scarf*

WHEN HE WOKE, dusty rays of sunshine were coming between the bedroom curtains. Feeling qualmish and confused, he was slow in recovering full consciousness and memory. Then he rolled out of bed and made for General Duddon's room. The general was not there; his Spartan bed undisturbed.

Reggie went heavily away and shaved and bathed, a process which refreshed but made him aware of a weakness in knees and back and a gnawing emptiness of body and mind.

He descended; he foraged in the stern precision of larder and cupboard. The general's cook and her husband, the houseman, coming on duty at the regulation hour of six-fifteen were horrified by the sight of him—consuming coffee and sandwiches in the kitchen. They said so with disciplined indignation and were removing him and his food to the dining room when the general came back.

"What's all this? Be off with you," the general squeaked. "Early, aren't you, Fortune? Bad night, I'm afraid."

"Not me, no. I've slept." Reggie took him into the dining room after the scratch breakfast. "You haven't." The general's thin face was deep-lined, and his eyes sunken and red. "Any results?"

"I'm all right. Old soldier. But it's a bad business, Fortune. The woman's in the river."

Reggie's hand stopped with a sandwich on the way to his mouth. He moved as if pain stabbed him, and his round face hardened into a stare of cold rage. "Go on. Tell me," he said. "What's been done?"

"Ah, I don't know that—don't know how she got into the water. Couldn't be accident though; no reason to go near the river. Incredible that she would—unless she meant to drown herself—might have been suicide. This fool of a police sergeant wants to make out it was. I haven't a doubt there was foul play. Have you?"

Reggie gave a little miserable laugh. "Didn't ask for doubts," he said sharply. "Asked what was done—by you, by anybody."

"Sorry, Fortune. Don't wonder you're on edge. When I drove back to the village last night—would you believe it?—that fellow Giles hadn't told anybody, hadn't even got there. I went to the inn and routed out the men—couldn't make 'em understand for a bit—none of 'em had heard or seen anything out of the common. When they got the business into their heads they turned out like good chaps; I believe we had all the men in the place on the hunt."

"What was the feeling? Sympathy with the wife—or the husband?"

"I couldn't tell you. Both well liked, for anything I heard. When we ran into Giles on the road he behaved like a madman, but they were very decent with him. They are good men, these village chaps—don't want better stuff."

"Don't you?" Reggie snapped at him. "What was the feeling? No sign of suspicion of anyone?"

"I didn't hear a word." The general was annoyed. "I'm not a thought-reader, Fortune—don't suppose they had any thoughts. What the devil do you expect? Men out hunting for somebody lost keep their minds on the job. Surely you know that."

"I do. Yes. Thought not a common faculty. Well? What about the active and intelligent police? I telephoned them to come and assist. Did they?   "

The general made a scornful noise. "That lout of a sergeant in the village came along yapping—what were they up to?—when he heard; said he must go back to report and ask for instructions—pshaw! Then a police car came out from Colsbury with an inspector—fussed round asking for statements—the men wouldn't stand it. He got shouldered off, left talking—fastened on Aston—that was the last seen of the police. Men beat up and down over the pastures and the combe all night. Sometime after dawn a lad working along the river saw a scarf left by the tide, went through the mud and got it—green silk scarf—seen Mrs. Aston wearing one just like it—took it up to the house. Her maid recognized it, said she was wearing it last night. Got boats out to search the river—at it now."

Reggie listened to this, watching the general with intent, anxious eyes but eating and drinking fast. He gulped a last mouthful and stood up. "I want to see where the scarf was found," he said. "Can you show me? All right. Drive down in your car, and I'll follow in mine. Go ahead."

The big car closed up on the little car before they came to the road by the river. The general drove on past the white house and stopped. "Somewhere just here, Fortune," he said, and opened a gate in the hedge and struck across the marshy pasture. On the verge of the glistening black mud in which it ended a man stood. The mud stretched far, but the tide was still running out, and he shouted to boats drifting down with it. "This is the place," the general squeaked. "Just below where he is. He's been directing 'em. Hallo! Hallo! Have they found her?"

A bearded face turned, inspected them and answered, "Nowt, sir, nowt."

They came to him. His gray beard spat tobacco juice. His tired eyes gave them a melancholy stare. "Ay, ay. They ha' been up along and down along. Her be sunk in the mud, I reckon. The mud's quick and greedy. Her's not the first."

"Oh." Reggie watched the vanishing boats. "Like that. Nobody expects her to be found."

"There's never no telling, sir. The tide do run so tricky. Her might and then her mightn't. If so be as you do find 'em you finds 'em quick, or the mud has 'em and swallows 'em down."

"I see. Yes." Reggie murmured, and directed his eyes to the mudbank at their feet, to deep marks in it a little below high-water mark. "That's where the scarf was picked up?"

"Ay. Young Garge Wick, he found un there not three hour since, and us poked all about."

"Three hours. The tide was then on the ebb?"

"Near half ebb, sir."

"Thanks. And the lady went out and was lost round about eight o'clock last night. The tide was then coming in."

"You may say near half flood, sir." The old man looked at him with respect. "It's like her went into river lower down, her scarf being washed up here. So the lads worked all down along first. But nowt! Nowt! You can't be sure o' nothing with the eddies, though. Her might have gone in hereby or up along. All's tried. There's no more us can do now. But the lads will be out again next tide."

"Good fellows," Reggie said. "What do you think about it?"

The old man sucked his teeth. "It's hard for sure. A rare high young lady and coming kind. Her did ought to have lived happy with her man and bore his childer, if ever. But Aston and Tracy, Aston and Tracy, they was never made nor let to mingle; it's not in the way of things."

"She was coming kind," Reggie repeated. "She was happy?"

"I never heard no other," the old man said, and stumped away.

"Well, well," Reggie sighed. "He's done his bit. So have you, General, and more. Sorry. Food and sleep for you. Now I'll take over." He quelled the general's zealous protests and incoherent speculations. "Oh no. No. Not any use talking. Good-bye." The general yielded and trudged away.

Reggie walked slowly along the edge of the mudbank far down the river and, turning, wandered across and across the pasture before he returned to the road. Then he made for the thicket in which he had been stunned.

Daylight showed him nothing more than he had discovered by his torch in the dark: crushing of bushes, trampling of the earth, but no clear footmarks, no trail to follow.

When he emerged upon the road again he stood a moment looking at the white house. But his round face showed no sympathy with Giles Aston, no emotion, only a cold, calculating curiosity. He made haste to his car and drove away furiously.

CHAPTER XXIII *Evidence of Zeal*

Among the merits of Durshire Reggie is inclined to give first place to its ham, a ham of mellow subtlety. In proof of the singular virtue thereof he points out that, having consumed sandwiches of this ham in early, joyless hunger, he went on to make a second breakfast of it grilled and was thereafter in his best form.

Leaving, thus refilled, the coffee room of the Maid's Head in Colsbury, he drove to the station and met the first London train.

Inspector Underwood's discretion did not permit him to recognize Mr. Fortune till he was spoken to. Then he said, "This is a surprise, sir. Fancy meeting you."

"Yes. You nearly didn't," Reggie murmured. "Not in this world. However. You're here, and I'm here. We will study to remain. Having been violently disliked incognito, I resume my simple self to ask for further and better particulars of action. Come on."

Underwood was taken, with explanation on the way, to the post office. There they shut themselves together into a telephone booth and rang up the chief of the Criminal Investigation Department.

Lomas' part in the conversation was for some time exclamatory and profane. "Preserve absolute calm," Reggie exhorted him. "Now you have all facts up to date: girl shot at in vicinity of girl who had threatening letter referred to you; that girl now sunk without trace; your eminent expert, Reginald Fortune, knocked on head at time and in neighborhood of her disappearance. How do you like it so far as you've gone with it?"

"Devilish business," Lomas answered.

Reggie laughed without mirth. "Thank you for those kind words."

"What's your theory?"

"My dear chap! Oh, my dear chap! Futile question. Too many facts. As usual. Only one relevant question. What is the Criminal Investigation Department going to do with them?"

"You haven't been to the local police yet?"

"Not yet. No. Waiting for the reinforcement of our Underwood. I cling to life, Lomas."

"My dear Reginald!" Lomas exclaimed.

"That's all right. Professional risk. But I want the profession backing me. Understood?"

"Quite. You show grounds to suspect the local police of gross neglect of duty or connivance with criminal acts."

"Yes, I do. So glad you notice that. And then? You're instructing Underwood to pursue enquiries—wherever they take him?"

After a moment Lomas answered. "I agree. Carry on. I'll put it through."

As they drove away from the post office Underwood said, "Well, that gives us a free hand and a backing. I suppose you were working for that all along, Mr. Fortune. You did take your chances. Rather fine, if I may say so, not caring what happened to you so long as it got the case done thoroughly."

"My dear chap! Oh, my dear chap!" Reggie smiled. "Nothing like that, no. Offering a life to a killer in order to get him hanged—it has been done—but not by me. Self-sacrificin' heroism not my job. No intention to get knocked on the head. Painful surprise. And much resented."

Underwood laughed. "All right, sir. But I've worked with you before. I hope you won't go running any more risks like that down here."

They came to the police headquarters. A haughty inspector who told them that they could by no means see Superintendent Bubb was efficiently bullied till he retreated to announce them. He returned obsequious, and when he brought them to the vast and gloomy room of the chief of Durshire's police, Bubb started up and came to meet them. "Good morning, good morning, very glad to see you again." He grasped at hands which were not offered.

"Are you?" Reggie murmured. "That was not the idea of your inspector. Obstruction as usual."

"Now really, it isn't fair to say that," Bubb protested. "He only meant I was up to my eyes in work. We all are."

"You should be. Yes. So naturally you object to any assistance."

"I do not, Mr. Fortune. I should be very happy, as I always have been. You know I have. I've been relying on your advice from the first time you came here. When the poor chief died, you remember, I asked you down specially to get an opinion from you."

"Yes, I do remember. Very wise. I appreciated that. Led nowhere. Further enquiries suggested had no result."

"That wasn't my fault, I'm sure. The inspector will tell you, when he came down to investigate that queer, threatening letter he had every facility and cooperation from me. But he couldn't make anything of it. There's no denying we're up against some very cunning fellow."

"Oh yes. That is indicated, Bubb," Reggie said, watching him with closing eyes. "Bygones will not be bygones. However. You were doubtless about to ask what we came for now."

Bubb allowed his solemn face to show surprise, to smile. "You will have your joke, Mr. Fortune. No need to ask. That nasty business last night, of course. I only just heard you were down here. I take it you wired for the inspector to come along. I'm very glad you did."

"Happy to oblige. Why didn't you ask for him days ago? When the girl was shot at. He'd been investigating who sent a threatening letter to Mrs. Giles Aston. Shot fired at girl walking near Mrs. Aston's house. Yet you didn't mention it to us."

"Well, come now," Bubb protested. "We had no reason to think the girl was shot at."

"No, you avoided the reasons. You didn't find the pellets. You didn't find the cartridge cases. I did."

"What's this?" Bubb frowned. "There's always shooting. How can you be sure what a dose of shot or a cartridge case was meant for?"

"Interestin' point. However. Not the urgent point. What's become of Mrs. Giles Aston?"

"Haven't you heard?" Bubb exclaimed. "Her scarf's been found washed up on the riverbank."

"Yes. Wasn't found by your men. What did they do all night? Her disappearance was reported to you about nine o'clock. Did you go out then?"

"I can't take up everything myself, Mr. Fortune." Bubb was impressive. "A competent inspector was sent out at once, and I am satisfied he did all that was possible."

"Left the search to the village people. Quite satisfactory to you as chief of police. Well, well. Did your competent inspector discover that at the time of the woman's disappearance there was a murderous attack on Mr. Reginald Fortune?"

"God bless my soul!" Bubb exclaimed.

"You think so? Sanguine man. Blessing not deserved."

"But come now," Bubb stammered, "tell me. How was it? What happened?"

Reggie told him succinctly and enquired, "Didn't know that before? You *are* well-informed. Very thorough investigation. Only ignored everything."

"That's too bad, Mr. Fortune," Bubb complained. "Why didn't you telephone me you'd been attacked? I'd have come out myself, at once."

"Would you?" Reggie said sharply. "I did telephone the essential fact— woman's disappearance. You didn't come out for that. Why not? Where were you, Bubb?"

"I'd had a long day, Mr. Fortune," said Bubb with dignity. "I was at home. I must say I consider you should have let me know the whole facts straight away."

"Did you need telling?" Reggie drawled.

"How do you mean?"

"Your competent inspector came out to Giles Aston's house. They knew there that I was enquiring about the lady. They knew that I'd been knocked about. Didn't he mention me to you?"

"It's in his report you were there," Bubb scowled. "He didn't know anything about an attack."

"Didn't bother to ask after me. Zeal, all zeal, your police force. However. No matter. I had all the facts about my knock on the head—"

"What? Do you think you know who it was?" Bubb broke in.

Reggie smiled and was silent for a moment, then he asked, "Do you?"

"If I'd been on it at once I might." Bubb glared at him.

"I wonder," Reggie murmured. "You could have been on the woman's disappearance at once. You should have been. Do you think you know who made away with her, Bubb?"

"I don't take it for certain she *has* been made away with," Bubb announced with solemn importance.

Reggie's eyes narrowed. "One of the possibilities, yes," he said.

"Now that's putting it fair," said Bubb. "That's what I'd expect from you. You've always took everything into account, Mr. Fortune. Well, finding this scarf of the lady's washed up does make it pretty likely she went into the river. But that's no proof she was murdered. She might have drowned herself. Mr. Giles Aston told my inspector she hadn't been altogether happy. She was worried about the old family quarrels, being cut dead by her father—and his people too. Just what you'd expect. And besides what he said we've got hold of talk about high words between him and her. There you are. Young married woman bothered over relations and rows with her husband. Just the sort of conditions that give you suicide."

"They do. Yes," Reggie murmured. "Convenient conclusion. Brother's death, insoluble mystery. Death of chief constable, accidental. This woman, suicide. Rest and be thankful. Only she didn't commit suicide. She didn't drown herself."

"How can you be sure?" Bubb asked. "How can anybody?"

"You underestimate my humble capacity. Everybody's going to be quite sure. I happened to be here for this crime. So there was immediate investigation. It was half tide when she disappeared. She would have had to plunge through yards of mud to get to the water. Not a likely method of suicide. Also the bank has a strip of mud above high-water mark. She would have made footprints in that. I went along the river this morning. There were none. She may have been thrown in, alive or dead. A murderer might have obliterated footprints after the operation. But *she* couldn't, if she drowned herself. No. Nobody's going to get away with it as suicide, Bubb."

"There's no question of getting away with it," Bubb said loudly.

"I wouldn't say that. Somebody's trying hard. Somebody put her scarf in the water. Somebody wanted to wipe me out. That doesn't go with suicide, either. Which you didn't notice. I did."

"Well, of course, this evidence of yours is all against suicide." Bubb gave a judicial nod. "Subject to anything new turning up, suicide is washed out. I was only putting it as a possibility; like you said, there was more than one. What's your own idea, Mr. Fortune?"

"To investigate this case," Reggie dragged out the words, "with my friend Underwood."

Bubb's eyes met his in a stare of sullen defiance. "You'll please to understand I'm in charge," said Bubb.

"You have been, yes. And nothing's been done. Hence me—hence Underwood. Any objection will be received with interest."

Their eyes fought, and Bubb looked down. "It's not fair to say nothing has been done," he complained. "I've done everything possible. I am doing."

"Doing what?"

"I have Mr. Giles Aston and Mr. Brown due here now for further enquiries. You're very welcome to be present and ask anything you like."

"Thanks very much." Reggie gave a small contemptuous smile. "Giles and Brown. Why?"

"To verify their actions last night." Bubb was aggrieved. "That's very necessary. I may tell you Mr. Giles behaved strange and unsatisfactory when questioned—"

"Fancy that!" Reggie murmured.

"Yes, he did. And I want to know about the time he left Mr. Brown, and how they parted. There's a lot more to all this than you think for."

"I shouldn't say that," Reggie murmured. "However. First suggestion of Superintendent Bubb: the wife committed suicide. Second suggestion: her husband or his employer made away with her. Any reason for it?"

"You aren't keeping everything in mind, Mr. Fortune." Bubb recovered some of his assurance. "You know very well Mr. Brown made a pet of the lady and hurried on this marriage which the whole county wondered at. You might ask yourself: why did he? People are saying he wanted to do Tracy in the eye because he's after the Tracy estate, and Tracy won't sell. And there's another reason you'll hear anywhere: he wanted to get the lady for himself; marrying her to young Mr. Giles was just a convenience to have her in his hand. It's common talk he's been at her all the time, and Mr. Giles didn't half like it. There you are. Brown may have fixed up with her to bolt. Or he may have tried to do more to her than she'd stand for and had a blaze-up and killed her. Or Mr. Giles may have found out she was doing the dirty on him with Brown and done her in. You see? Any of those ways would account for her disappearance and the assault on you."

"Yes. As you say. Quite good. These are some of the possibilities. Not all. Why confine yourself to Giles and Brown? The wife has a father, the husband has a father. Both hating the marriage like mad. And with one mysterious death between 'em already. Not to mention your late lamented chief."

Reggie murmured the Greek verse of the postcard. "Tis an palin agkalesait epaeidon. 'Blood which once has fallen dark on the earth, who can call it back by his charms?' Some sweet soul sent that memorandum to the girl on her marriage. Sort of soul who didn't mean her to live happy ever after. Quite likely to take the requisite action. Why not send for the lovin' fathers, Bubb?"

"You suspect old Mr. Aston? Well, I grant you it might be him. I will send for him." Bubb started up and made for the door.

"One moment." Reggie stopped him. "Grant me Tracy too."

"Mr. Tracy!" Bubb frowned. "You don't think he'd murder his own daughter?"

"Well, well." Reggie gazed at him with round eyes. "This faith in paternal love is very touching, Bubb. Evidence of things not seen. Send for your Tracy, please. Somebody shot at a girl, who might have been his daughter, from Tracy's land, and Tracy does go out with a gun in the cool of the evening."

Bubb stood still, frowning. "If you ask me, Mr. Tracy never fired at that girl," he said slowly. "He's got a rare good eye. He wouldn't mistake one woman for another. Taking it from you she was shot at, that was somebody else, not him. Most likely a poacher. And if it was deliberate, most likely done to get Mr. Tracy into trouble."

"Oh. You say that." Reggie's eyebrows rose higher.

"I do. You see, you want to know the ways of the country, Mr. Fortune. I should say it was a poacher."

"Would you really?" Reggie's eyebrows came down again. He gave a chuckle. "Our old friend Elijah! However. Grant me Tracy first. Get on."

But before Bubb reached the door it was opened by the haughty inspector, and they went out together.

CHAPTER XXIV *Evidence of Business*

"You've put the wind up him all right," said Underwood.

"I wonder," Reggie murmured. "Full of happy thoughts, isn't he? Always was. Knows a lot, done a lot of brainwork. Ingenious and various in all the possible directions. Except one or two. Very suggestive, our Bubb. Especially in what he didn't suggest."

Bubb came back with brisk importance. "I've given instructions to send for old Mr. Aston and Mr. Tracy," he announced. "Mr. Giles Aston has been waiting sometime. We'll have him in now."

Giles thrust past the inspector announcing him and strode across the room. "What the devil do you bring me here for?" he roared.

"That's a queer way to talk," said Bubb. "I want to know what's become of your wife, Mr. Aston. Don't you?" Giles swore at him. "You control yourself, sir. Have you heard that the scarf she was wearing last night has been found washed up by the river?"

"Of course I have." Giles glared down at him. "I should have been out in the boats searching for her, if you hadn't dragged me here to play the fool."

"When you were asked about her disappearance last night you didn't suggest that she might have been drowned."

"No, I didn't. I never thought of it. She couldn't have fallen into the river."

"You say now it couldn't be accident. Last night you said some accident might have happened to her."

Giles made a choking exclamation. "I hoped—"

"You hoped. I see. Now I put it to you: had you any reason to think she might have drowned herself?"

Again Giles cursed him. "It's a crazy, dirty lie. She didn't drown herself. She was murdered."

"You have no doubt about that now? Very well. Who do you suspect?"

Giles stood silent, and his pale face betrayed a conflict of rage and misery.

"Come now. This is a very serious charge, Mr. Aston. Who are you thinking of as likely to murder your wife?"

"I'm not thinking of anybody," Giles muttered. "I haven't made a charge."

"That won't do, Mr. Aston. You tell me I have to take the case as murder. Who had a motive that you know of?"

Giles cried out, "Nobody, nobody in the world! Alison!"

"I see your feelings," said Bubb. "But I have my duty, Mr. Aston. I'm bound to ask you: had your father shown any ill will to this lady?"

"Shown nothing. They've never seen each other since we were married."

"That isn't exactly being on good terms with her. Have you said anything to him about her disappearance?"

Giles looked away. "No. I rang up this morning and told my mother."

"How did she take it?"

"I could hardly make her understand, she was so upset."

"She didn't bring your father to the telephone?"

Giles shook his head.

"I see," said Bubb. "Now I'd like to know about you and Mr. Brown."

"What?" Giles started and stared at him. "What do you mean?"

"Yes. Surprise very natural," Reggie murmured. "Surprisin' omission, Bubb. The lady also has a parent. Don't you want to know whether Tracy had shown any feeling for his daughter?"

"I was coming to that," Bubb protested angrily.

"He's never been near us; she never had a word from him that I know of," said Giles.

"Not exactly on good terms with her." Reggie went on, imitating Bubb's phrases. "Have you said anything to him about her disappearance?"

"I rang up," Giles answered. "They told me he wasn't in."

"Well, well." Reggie sighed. "Carry on, Bubb."

"Thank you." Bubb was sarcastic. "Now, Mr. Aston—you told the inspector you were kept late by Mr. Brown last night. That was on business, fixing a price for the Ridge Farm. You didn't leave there till about nine o'clock. He'd gone before. How long before?"

"An hour or so. I don't know. I had a lot of haggling over details."

"Mr. Brown's been what I might call a very good friend to you—and your lady?"

"Yes, he has." Giles flushed.

"Did you ever wonder why he was so particular kind? I mean to say, he's a newcomer; you and her were strangers to him a year ago."

"You know as well as I do," Giles answered in a hurry, "he's bought a lot of land; he's out to buy more. He wanted an agent who knew the country and the people—I suited him."

"Very well, I'm sure." Bubb was emphatic. "I have to put it to you: there is talk Mr. Brown was too attentive to your wife."

Giles flinched and stammered oaths.

"You mean to tell me you never heard of that before? Never thought of it? Never raised it with him or her?"

Giles exploded something about a filthy, lying fool, sprang forward fists up, and Bubb rang his bell and stood up ready for action.

"Oh no, no." Reggie came between them, and Underwood laid hands on Giles.

"I make allowance for you, Mr. Aston," said Bubb with dignity. "But you—"

Giles broke from Underwood and strode to the door, charged a policeman, who was answering the bell, into the doorpost and was gone.

"Symbolic drama," Reggie murmured. "By the police force."

Bubb told the bewildered policeman to show Mr. Aston out, and when the door was shut turned upon Reggie. "How do you mean, symbolic?"

"Showing their futility. Very well done."

"Futility!" Bubb exclaimed. "What more do you want? There was no use in detaining him. I'd got what I was after—made him give himself away good and well. *Didn't* I? He is mad jealous of Brown and his wife. Now we know the line to work on."

"I wonder." Reggie gazed at him with closing eyes. "However. What is your next scene?"

"Mr. Brown, of course. He ought to be here and in fine trim, kept waiting while—"

He was interrupted by the entry of the haughty inspector.

"Just the man I want. Have you got Mr. Brown?"

The inspector cleared his throat. "Mr. Brown had come, but when told the superintendent was engaged he refused to wait. Said he'd be over at the bank or the club, and they could let him know when the superintendent wouldn't waste his time."

Bubb snorted. "Send for the fellow at once."

"Yes sir." The inspector came closer. "Could I speak to you a minute?" Bubb nodded and took him out.

"We are not liked, Underwood," Reggie murmured.

"You don't aim to be," Underwood grinned.

"That was the idea. Yes. A felt threat. Fear is required. Percolatin' fear."

Bubb came back. "Not to intrude on official secrecy," Reggie drawled, "any objection to my ringin' up Tracy on your telephone?"

"I have no secrets about the case." Bubb frowned. "The inspector was quite right to report to me first. We do things in order here."

"What things?" Reggie asked.

"Give me a chance. I was just going to tell you. We haven't been able to get into touch with old Mr. Aston. His wife says he's out in his car—didn't tell her where he was going, or when he'd be back. Queer, isn't it?"

"It could be. Yes. Rather queer to evade my question about Tracy."

"I'm not evading," Bubb barked. "One thing at a time. We've been on to Mr. Tracy's house too. His butler says Mr. Tracy went out yesterday evening and hasn't been home since. He went out, as he often does, in the cool of the evening, taking his gun. They don't know what's become of him."

"Well, well." Reggie's eyes opened wide. "Another disappearance last night. Only just noticed by the alert police force."

Bubb made an angry exclamation. "How could we notice till we're informed? This is the first we've heard of it. Ring up Mr. Tracy's house yourself, if you want to. They'll tell you the same."

"Oh yes. I'm sure they will. Not an excuse for your failing to get told before. You knew at nine o'clock last night Tracy's daughter had disappeared. Though Tracy was known to be on bad terms with her, though a girl close by her house had been shot at from Tracy's woods, you didn't look up Tracy. You weren't going to till I came in this morning. Marked neglect of Tracy by Superintendent Bubb. Why?"

"I don't stand for that, Mr. Fortune," Bubb told him fiercely. "I had no reason to believe—"

"No. You wouldn't have," Reggie interrupted. "You never will have. Same like your late chief. However. Is anybody looking for the vanished Tracy now?"

"I'm having enquiries made; of course I am," Bubb growled. "And for Mr. Aston. Talk about neglect. You're neglecting him. You always have done."

"Me? Oh, my Bubb! Who raised the forgotten dead to ask for justice? Family of Aston can't complain of neglect from me."

"Um," Bubb grunted. "You have raised the devil, I grant you," and he searched Reggie's expressionless face with an angry, anxious stare.

The door opened. "Mr. William Brown, sir," said a constabulary voice.

"Who's the devil, Superintendent?" Brown waddled in. "Hallo! I'm very glad to see you, Mr. Fortune." His fat hand grabbed at Reggie's. "I am that. Foul business, ain't it?"

"Not nice, no," Reggie murmured.

"You haven't been forward to clear it up, Mr. Brown." Bubb asserted himself. "Why do you shirk enquiries?"

"That won't go, Bubb. Everybody knows where the shirk is." Brown sat down and turned to Reggie. "What can I do for you, Mr. Fortune?" The natural, queer contrast between his silly fat face and his grave eyes was obscured. He had made his face solemn.

"Been at the club?" Reggie asked.

"I have. Called at the bank, went on to the club."

"Seen anybody?"

"I saw Cope at the bank, several fellows in the club—old Aston, Lord Werne, one or two more."

"Oh. The elder Aston is there?"

"Not now he isn't. He popped off some time ago."

"After talk with you—or avoidin' it?"

"I needn't tell you, he don't love me. He cut out when I got there."

"Pity. Might have been instructive conversation. However. You had some with the other fellows, Cope and Werne and what not?"

"That's right." Brown looked through him with a brooding gaze. "I wanted to know if they could make anything of it. And I got told the girl's marriage was bound to go smash, and she wasn't the first child of Tracy's to disappear and so on. Useful, eh?"

"As you say. Leavin' it to you whether old Aston or old Tracy made away with her. And which did you bet on?"

"I don't bet unless I know something," said Brown.

"But you bet on the marriage," Reggie murmured.

"I did so." Brown was not embarrassed. "Knowing those two was made for each other, and they'd wash out all the old blasted mess, give 'em the chance. Why haven't they had it? That was up to you. What's the police for?"

"I wonder," Reggie murmured.

"My God! You may!" Brown spoke slowly. "You had warning enough. What's done? You don't know how the poor girl's been handled, nor where she is, and here's talk and talk."

"Ah," Bubb snorted. "You're very fond of the lady. I get that, Mr. Brown. When did you see her last?"

Brown swung round to face him and gave a brisk answer. "The day before yesterday, when the wife and me had tea with her."

"Your statement is: you didn't meet her yesterday." Bubb's tone was portentous. "You have no knowledge where she went to when she went out?"

"I only know what she told the maid—she went to meet her husband."

"Is that all? Mr. Giles Aston says you left him at the Ridge Farm. What time was that?"

"About half-past seven. I got home to dinner at eight."

"You went straight home?"

"Yes, I did. Go on." Brown turned to Reggie. "He wants somebody behind him with a bradawl. I thought you'd bring one."

"It's no good trying to dodge, Mr. Brown," Bubb barked. "You attend to me. I am informed that you and Mrs. Giles Aston have been too much to-gether—more than Mr. Giles liked." He leaned forward to watch Brown with a teasing sneer.

But Brown did not explode. The only change of expression in his fat face was that it showed more serious consideration of Bubb. "Who told you that tale?" he asked.

"I don't tell you my sources of information," Bubb scowled. "You know it's true."

"It's a dirty lie," said Brown quietly. "But you won't get away with it." He

turned to Reggie. "What matters is, who put it up? Did he fake it himself or
get it from Tracy or where?"

"We haven't seen Tracy today," Reggie answered.

As he was speaking, Bubb rapped the table and called out, "I'm dealing
with you, Mr. Brown. Would you be surprised to hear Mr. Giles Aston showed
us he resented your attentions to his wife?"

"I'm not surprised to hear anything from you. But that isn't true." Brown
turned to Reggie again. "He set himself to drive the boy mad, eh? Make a
note of that. He's working to muddle it all up and hide what's been done, and
who did it. Why?"

"Don't you be insolent," Bubb roared. "I warn you, you're—"

But Brown went on talking to Reggie. "There you are. Leave it to you. For
the love of God, get a move on."

"Thanks very much. There is movement." Reggie rose. "Good-bye."

Brown stood up and nodded to him and waddled away. "Yes, you can go
now," Bubb called out. "Go home and stay there. See?"

"I'm going to Giles Aston," said Brown over his shoulder. The door banged
behind him.

"Ah." Bubb frowned at Reggie. "You're right; we have enough of him to
work on. When a fellow gets accusing the police of faking a case against him
you know he's a wrong 'un."

"One of the possibilities, yes," Reggie murmured.

"Making out Mr. Tracy had got round me to put up false evidence!" Bubb
was righteously indignant. "You don't fall for that I should hope."

"No fall. No. Come on."

"What do you want to do?"

"I want to talk to the banker. I want to know why our Brown had to call on
Cope the banker this morning. Don't you, Bubb?"

"If you like," Bubb consented dubiously. "Rather waste of time to my
mind. It's what's become of Tracy I want to get on to."

"Do you? Secondary question. First question: what's become of the girl?
Nothing yet been done by Superintendent Bubb about either. However. No
time wasted by me. Come on."

It was still more than an hour short of noon when they reached the bank, a
nineteenth-century Greek temple in stucco. Mr. Cope was not there; Mr.
Cope had just gone across to his house. That lay back from the quiet square
in which the abbey church of Colsbury stood, with a walled garden about its
mellow, sedate, eighteenth-century red brick.

They were brought to a room which did violence to its light and graceful
design and white paneled walls by heavy furniture in mahogany and brown
leather. Cope came out of the easy chair, in which he was drinking sherry,
and preened himself all over: double-breasted broadcloth, high waistcoat

with leather strap to the watch pocket, tight trousers. "Morning, Bubb. Good morning, Mr. Fortune." His shrewd, genial eyes twinkled at Underwood, and Reggie made the introduction. "How do? Join me, won't you?" He felt the fox-tooth pin in his tie, poured sherry and sat them down round his writing table, a big table with the multifarious equipment of old-fashioned business: trays of this, that and the other, quill pens, paste pot, sealing wax and candles. "I suppose there's no need to ask why the police are up so early. That's a queer business about young Aston's wife. But what can I do for you?"

Reggie smelled the sherry, sipped and smelled again. "A noble wine," he murmured, and his round face was blissful as he gazed across the table at Cope. "Yes." He drank more than a sip and set the glass down and glanced at Bubb. "Your case."

"Rare good stuff," said Bubb, not at his ease. "It's like this, Mr. Cope. I've been seeing Mr. William Brown. I learn that he came in to talk to you before he'd talk to me. Now the question I have to put is: did he say anything to throw light on Mrs. Giles Aston's disappearance?"

"Sorry, Bubb. Not a blink. Unless it's any good to you that the old boy's rattled. If you ask me, I don't wonder. Devilish fine gal, and he was sweet on her."

"Yes, I know," Bubb answered. "But what was his object coming to you?"

"By the rules of the game, that's confidential. But it's damn all of a secret by now. He's after Tracy's land and always at me about it. I can't help him. You know Tracy. He wouldn't sell to God Almighty. And to old Brown—after Brown married his daughter to young Aston!" Cope laughed.

"I understand that all right," Bubb nodded. "What gets me is Mr. Brown talking to you about buying up Mr. Tracy on the morning after the lady vanished. Did he say anything particular about Mr. Tracy?"

"Particular, begad!" Cope chuckled. "No, he's not particular. He was rubbing it into me rather more than usual—Tracy had been a brute to his daughter, and trying to get out of me how Tracy's affairs stood, and so forth and so on."

"How do they stand?" Reggie murmured. "I suppose you couldn't tell anyone that."

Cope shook his head. "No sir. I could not. Even if I knew. But I don't. Tracy's very close."

"Oh yes. He hadn't said anything to you about going away?"

"Tracy? Good God, no. Why should he?"

"Old friends, aren't you?"

"All of that, Tracy being the lonely dog he is since he lost his boy. I've known him well for donkey's years, as well as anybody did except your poor old chief. But he wouldn't tell me if he was going away. Nor anybody. You know that, Bubb."

"I suppose not." Bubb nodded. "He didn't tell anybody when he went off after the chief died."

"So we heard, yes," Reggie murmured.

"But what is all this?" Cope asked. "Has he gone off?"

"Bafflin' question," Reggie answered.

"He went out last night, Mr. Cope," Bubb explained. "With his gun as usual. He's not been seen since."

"My God!" Cope sat back. "Last night—disappeared—like the girl—like his daughter!" He stared, frowning amazement.

"Yes. That is the evidence," Reggie murmured. "Went out in the cool of the evening. Say after six. Girl went out about eight. What's the time now?"

"What? What do you say?" Cope was startled. "The time?" He swung round to look at the eight-day clock against the wall. "Quarter past eleven. They've both been missing fifteen to twenty hours. Isn't there any clue to either of them?"

"Not yet, no," Reggie said. "There wasn't any clue where Tracy's son had gone for a dozen years. We had better get on, Bubb."

"The boy!" Cope exclaimed. "You mean it's—" He checked and lowered his voice. "You think they've gone the same way?"

"One of the possibilities, yes." Reggie stood up. "Thanks. Good-bye. Come on, Bubb." And Bubb grumbled that he was ready.

"Well, I wish you the best, whatever that is," said Cope and showed them out.

"There you are," said Bubb as they walked away. "He just confirmed what I said. Makes it look very nasty for Mr. Brown."

"As you expected, yes. Anything else occur to you?"

"Well, of course, when you put it to him old Mr. Aston might have done 'em both in he had to agree. So do I. Anybody would. But you could see he didn't think of that himself."

"Oh yes. That was indicated. However. Try everything. Any ideas from you, Underwood?"

"I should be getting over to Tracy's place, myself," Underwood answered.

"My dear chap! Oh, my dear chap," Reggie sighed. "We will. We are."

But before they were out of the square they were met by the inspector coming to bring Bubb the news that Tracy had been found dead, shot by his own gun.

"Who says so?" Reggie asked.

The inspector ignored him and told Bubb that Mr. Tracy's butler had just telephoned that the head keeper came on the master by Goat's Hill wood, lying dead—shot in the face—with his gun by him, both barrels fired, and said it must have been accidental.

"Once again!" Reggie gave a short, hard laugh. "Isn't that nice? Did the head keeper move the body?"

The inspector, still despising him, remarked to the glowering Bubb that that was all the information they had.

"Sent anyone to get any?" Reggie asked. "No, I see you haven't. Good. You have your uses. Come on, Underwood."

He took Underwood off at the double to his car.

"I might have been there already but for him," Bubb complained to his inspector.

"That's right, sir. Just hampers you."

"Too clever by half," Bubb growled. "Have you got on to our own doctor?"

"Waiting for your instructions, sir."

"God! Go to it," Bubb exclaimed. "Double."

CHAPTER XXV *Evidence of a Watch*

THE BIG CAR cut skating figures through the wayward traffic of Colsbury. When the road down the river opened before it, and it rushed into speed, Underwood drew breath and spoke. "You don't trust this superintendent, Mr. Fortune?"

"My dear chap! Oh, my dear chap!" Reggie was sunk low in his seat, gazing ahead with eyes half closed. "Trust nobody."

"But you think he isn't straight?"

"That is the provisional hypothesis," Reggie mumbled. "I don't know who is straight. Too many facts. Too many factors. I should say our Bubb is under the influence. Same like others." He glanced across the flat fields of ripening corn to the stark chalk hills in the distance and waved a languid hand. " 'That's how it all began, my dears, that's how it all began.' "

"I don't follow, sir."

"Black land and white land never agree. Proverb in these parts. People who hold the black land where things grow rich always being pushed off it to the barren white land by thrustful newcomers. From age to age. From the dark and early natives through our Astons and our Tracys to our Brown. And learning hate, one and all. Their duty and their delight."

Underwood thought it over. "A lot of bad blood about, that's clear," he said slowly. "But I can't see how your idea of things accounts for Bubb being crooked."

"Oh yes, it could," Reggie murmured. "I said under the influence." He slowed the car and swung it round a sharp right turn into a byroad which made across the black land toward the hills. It brought them from the glowing fields to a belt of pasture. On the seaward side the pasture was bounded by an endless flint wall within which the undulations of a park rose gently, broken by coverts and noble trees.

They came to an imposing entry, wide gates of elaborate wrought iron between stone posts, over each of which a vague heraldic quadruped sat on its haunches to hold up a shield emblazoned with arms. Reggie stopped and had to make the horn roar and roar again before an ancient man came out of the lodge and told him that this was the private entry; he should go round by the village.

"Police car," Underwood snapped. "Open up quick." One gate was slowly and reluctantly opened. "Very private, aren't they?" said Underwood as the car gathered speed again.

"Yes. That is indicated," Reggie answered. "Always was. I think our friend Bubb will go round by the village. But this is the shortest way."

"You have the map of the county in your head." Underwood looked at him with respectful curiosity, rather like an earnest dog.

"Yes. That is so," Reggie murmured. "Fundamental."

The drive curved this way and that, giving vistas of the park, and the fields in the valley below, and bare shoulders and wooded combes of the hills. It had been planned to hold the eye with this expanse of ownership that the ponderous magnificence of the owner's house should be revealed as a sudden, tremendous climax.

Underwood gazed up at the palatial masses of dark stone and exclaimed, "Lord! Some place."

"Shock to the decent eye. Yes. I am the king of the castle; get down, you dirty rascal. That was the idea. Swaggering over the black land which it owns. Scoffing at the white land beyond, where the underdogs were driven. Home of the Tracys. And there isn't a Tracy any more."

They reached the terrace upon which the great house stood. Every window that could be seen from one towered wing to the other was dark with shutter or blind. "Mourning quick and thorough," Reggie murmured as he turned the car into the courtyard and stopped at the pillared portico.

The great door stood open. A gray butler came hurrying to meet them on the threshold. "Detective inspector," Underwood introduced himself, "from police headquarters, bringing a doctor. Superintendent Bubb will be here presently. I want somebody to take us on at once to Mr. Tracy."

"If you please." The butler bustled away and came back with a lank, bent man whose face was brown and wrinkled as a walnut, whose mouth shut the tighter for lack of teeth. "Mr. Brember, the head keeper," the butler announced.

"You found the body." Reggie inspected him. "Did you move it?"

From under a jutting gray thatch of eyebrows Brember's eyes stared back, unflinching but wary. "I didn't lay a hand to him. No use. You want to go out to him? You'd best get in your car again. You can drive most of the way."

"Good. Come on." Reggie put him into the front seat, and they drove off. "Now tell us all about it."

"You'll turn down past the stables and on yonder up along." Brember pointed to a ribbon of cart track across the high ground of the park.

"Oh yes. I asked you to tell us what you know about it."

"There's nowt to tell," said Brember. "I don't know nowt."

"Oh. Why did you say he shot himself by accident?"

"I never did say it," Brember answered sharply.

"Well, well. Some error," Reggie murmured. "You don't think it was an accident?"

"I don't know how it was. I ha'n't seen no way to be sure how it was."

"Cautious fellow, Mr. Tracy—not a likely man to have an accident with his gun?"

After meditation Brember answered. "I would ha' said he was not."

"Some change in him lately?"

"None of us don't get no younger."

"Not the man he used to be? Well, well. Was it a new thing for him to potter round with a gun in the evening?"

"No. He's done it for years."

"Always alone?"

Again Brember meditated. "He used to take a man. He's got more lonely like, some while."

"Has he? Any regular round for these evening shoots?"

"Not as I knows on. He didn't like for to have us about where he'd be."

"As you were sayin'. And where you found his body—would you have expected him to be there?"

"I wouldn't have expected to find him nowheres in partic'lar."

"But you were a long time finding him. You looked in a lot of other places first."

"There's many a place he might have been," said Brember and then, with sudden violence, "No matter if it was a long time. He was dead last night."

"Sure about that?" Reggie murmured.

"How else could he be? He wouldn't stay out all night."

"You think not? Any reason for his coming to this particular place?"

"He'd be round about one wood or t'other. And here it is; look 'e. Steady now, you can't drive no further." Brember jumped out before the car stopped.

The cart road ceased at the gate in the wall of the park. On the other side was dense woodland: stalwart beeches, which had seen many a year, rising out of modern undergrowth, rhododendrons and laurels.

Cock pheasants exploded and whirred through the leaves as Brember opened the gate. He marched on by a narrow green cut through walls of bushes and said over his shoulder, "Goat's Hill wood. D'ye see? The hill's up along." On their left the slope was gentle; on the right it rose more sharply, but the grass track kept at the same level all the way to the wood's end. Through the sunlight beyond they looked across a combe between shoulders of hill thrust out from the whaleback ridge.

The combe sides bore clumps of bramble and gorse; its depths were hidden in thicket which narrowed at the upper end and died away upon a scarp of gray-green turf through which the chalk broke out here and there in little patches under the ancient mounds and scars along the summit.

It was not far from the summit to the mouth of the combe. Pools glinted from the sodden pasture below. The river could be seen in gleaming flood which curved about the blue films of smoke over the village and the square church tower. Boats moved on the water.

On the stile in the fence of the wood Reggie sat and contemplated this landscape with solemn wonder, as if he saw it for the first time.

But he was only seeing it from a new point. Down in that combe, in the thicket where it came upon the road, was the place where he had been struck, out of the plot in the dusk. Not half a mile away. And somewhere hard by, Tracy had been eliminated forever.

"Will you be coming now?" Brember was impatient. "He's up along a bit, master is."

"Is he?" Reggie looked up the combe. On that side, too, the hills were close. "Has he been here often lately?"

Brember's wrinkled face moved as if it was swallowing. "I don't know. No more than anywheres."

"Get on," Reggie cried and made haste after him.

Along the edge of the wood they went for some furlong uphill and then saw two men keeping guard over Tracy's body.

"Seen anybody since he was found?" Reggie called to them.

"Nay, not a soul since Mr. Brember went," he was answered.

Reggie stood still some way from the dead man and scanned the grass all round—rank grass of the black land—then wandered about looking down at it.

"You ha'n't done nothing?" Brember snarled at his men.

"Ha'n't touched 'un, Mr. Brember," they protested.

"Brember," Reggie looked over his shoulder, "is this the end of the black land?"

"What do you say?" Brember strode forward, and Reggie turned from the grass on which he had seen a white clot of crushed chalk and came to meet him, repeating the question.

Brember's shaggy brows drew together in a frown of puzzled interest. "Ay, near about," he answered slowly. "The wood's all black land and here beyond a bit, then up along you'd be on the white land. D'ye see? You got it right, sir."

"I see, yes." Reggie proceeded to the body and knelt down by it. ...

Tracy lay on his face. In the right temple was a dark hole from which blood had spread to the eye and across the brow and down the cheek. About the wound the flesh was scorched and spotted with brown flecks. A double-barreled shotgun lay beside him. On his back was a game bag.

Reggie gave the wound a long study. When that was done he slipped the strap of the game bag over head and shoulders and opened it. Brember came to look. It held one bird, a bird of gray-brown plumage with black hooked beak. "A goshawk, eh!" Brember grunted. "Them's rare. I ha'n't seen one this ten year. He'd be proud o' that shot."

"You think so?" Reggie sighed and turned the dead man over, and Brember drew back with a gasp.

Tracy's face was distorted by suffering or passion into a hideous look of madness. Reggie pored over the clothes, felt about the body and at last put a hand in the watch pocket. The gold watch which he took out had its glass cracked. There was a dent in the back of the case. He frowned at that, turned the watch over and then his eyes opened wide.

The watch had stopped. Its hands pointed to five minutes past nine.

He put it away and again examined clothes and shoes.

He was still at work when Bubb came bustling up with satellites. "Ah! You got here very quick, Mr. Fortune." Bubb panted wrath.

"Yes, that was required, Bubb." Reggie sat back on his heels and looked up with a smile which was not kindly. "You didn't notice it."

"Our own doctor will take charge now, if you please," Bubb roared at him.

"Oh yes." Reggie stood up and held out his hand to the embarrassed police doctor. "How do you do? Met over those earlier things, didn't we? This also has interest." He drew the doctor aside. "Well. I've finished for the time. Cause of death: shotgun wound. Gun fired close to his head; nitrocellulose powder; time: more than twelve hours ago, say yesterday evening. Provisionally, no clear indication whether suicide, accident or murder. On medical evidence. There you are. I shall want to see the post-mortem."

He came back to Brember. "That is Mr. Tracy's own gun?"

"For sure it is," Brember answered and pointed to two empty cartridge cases in the grass beside it. "And them's the cartridges he used. Twelve-bore Schultze."

"Yes. They would be." Reggie sighed and put them in his pocket.

"What do you mean?" Bubb was truculent.

Reggie did not answer. He was using his handkerchief to pick up the gun. He inspected breech and barrels and smelled them and laid the gun down again and looked at Bubb with closing eyes. "You might find fingerprints on this firearm," he drawled. "But I suppose you've thought of that? It will be required."

"I know my job, thank you," said Bubb furiously.

Reggie laughed and walked away and called to Underwood and spoke in his ear, and Underwood listened with the intent look of a startled, eager dog. Bubb scowled at them and approached. "All right," Reggie said aloud, "take my car." And Underwood strode off at speed.

"What's the idea, Mr. Fortune?" Bubb demanded.

"This interest is very gratifyin'," Reggie drawled. "He's going back. I'm going home to my General Duddon. Anything else you'd like to know?"

"I should like to hear what you make of it now."

"Speakin' medically—accident, suicide or murder. But you're a policeman, Bubb. Get on with it."

"You cut out, do you? Playing a hand of your own?"

"Not me, no." Reggie left him.

Underwood had vanished into the wood. Reggie wandered away up the combe, looking back often at the cluster of men about the body till he and they were hidden from each other by the curve of the wood.

CHAPTER XXVI *Evidence of Chalk*

IT WAS from the clod of chalk in the long grass by the body that Reggie had taken his line. He went a winding way between the clumps of gorse and bramble, scanning the ground, but he found no more chalk till the rank growth of the black land shrank into short, springy turf through which patches of chalk broke bare.

Wandering to this side and that he could see no track, no footmark. He stood still, biting his lip. He was upon the bare scarp which filled the head of the combe which rose in an easy slope to the shoulders of the hills on either side. He glanced at his watch and struck across on an upward slant, going fast.

But soon he stopped again and looked all round and looked back. He had crossed and climbed into sight of the full curve of the wood, of the place where Tracy's body had lain. Bubb and the cluster of men were gone. Down the combe he could see a glimpse of Giles Aston's white house, and the road in the valley, and the hill road emerging to meet it from the next combe to seaward—the road under the copse from which the village girl had been shot at, the road to the Ridge Farm in which Giles had delayed so late that his wife went out to meet him.

With a comprehensive, calculating survey Reggie assured himself that the road and the mouth of the combe, those dense, low trees in which he had fought and fallen, were less than half a mile away if a man went straight; the edge of the wood was much nearer. He went on up the slope at his best speed and once and again where the chalk came loose through the turf saw a man's broad footprints, pressed deep.

Over the rounded summit of the shoulder above him shadows and sunshine chased. The ancient mounds and cavities of Giants' Graves were veiled and displayed again.

Reggie crossed a circling bank and came upon the first of the graves—a hollow from which a pit was sunk, not for any creature's tomb but to mine for flints in the golden age when flint served for weapon and tool. About it gorse and brambles grew and straggled over it, and down the shaft deadwood and leaves were held up by living branches. He wandered to another pit and another and found them choked by a like unbroken growth.

As he moved toward the mounds on the summit he came into a deeper hollow. He was on the verge of one more pit there when something, someone, hurled him forward, and he fell headlong down into the dark.

The sides of the pit struck at him, caught at him; arms and legs were wrenched and scraped and torn. He lay in a dazed heap … discovered that he was choking … spat out chalk and blew a bleeding nose.

Far overhead there was a lozenge of light. More by instinct than thought he dragged himself away from it. Yes, that was right. Mustn't be under the shaft. Might have something thrown on top of him.

The point of light vanished. He was in utter darkness. He moved his limbs. Nothing broken, no. Shaken up. Strained a bit. Bruised. He stretched out a hand on either side and touched nothing. Shaft opened out at the bottom. It would.

He came slowly to his feet and struck a match and chalk loomed out of the dark overhead—chalk walls some way off. "White land!" he muttered. "Yes. Pushed off into the white land. Where you go when they have you beat."

CHAPTER XXVII *Evidence of Gas*

HE COUNTED HIS MATCHES and lighted another. That burned long enough to show him that he was in a central chamber more or less round. Out of the dome of the roof the shaft rose like a chimney. On all sides there were holes which seemed to lead into level passages.

Oh yes. The usual workings of the old flint mines. Galleries into which the fellows crawled, digging along the flint layer with their antler picks. He struck his third match. The ground beneath the shaft was covered with dead-wood and leaves. A shapeless bundle lay on them. Something in a sack. Feet stuck out of it, a woman's feet.

The match dropped dead. He felt for the sack and drew it away from the shaft. A choking, groaning sound came out of it. He dragged it into the shelter of one of the galleries and knelt down and used his penknife on the sacking.

Whoever threw him down the shaft was a devilish smart fellow. Whether he had divined that Mr. Fortune would come from Tracy's body to Giants' Graves, whether Mr. Fortune's arrival interrupted his plan to abolish the woman, he wouldn't be content to leave them with a chance of life. Something more must be tried.

While he groveled over the sack and plied the penknife on it he strained his ears to listen for sounds from overhead.

A cord was tied about the woman's legs, another cord round arms and body. He drew the sack away, over her moaning head. "I'm Mr. Fortune," he whispered. "Don't cry. Don't be afraid. You're Alison, aren't you?"

She writhed and moaned as his hands felt at her. "Oh, oh, it hurts. Don't. Yes, I'm Alison." The voice was hoarse and faint.

"I know. Brave girl. Hold on still. You'll win, my dear."

She broke out in groans of hysterical laughter.

Reggie crawled back into the central chamber, struck a fourth match, raked together the dry leaves and deadwood beneath the shaft and, sheltering the flame of a fifth match in cupped hands, put it to the base of the pile. The leaves glowed, kindled, and the wood above them broke out in smoky fire. He gathered the rubbish to it with hands and feet, and its flames leaped in the upward draught with surges of smoke shot with sparks of red tinder which caught on the bushes in the shaft and set them sputtering and crackling into flame.

The shaft was like a chimney on fire when something was flung down through the flame and murk, something like a jar. It fell with a thud and crash and through the acrid heat a pungent, bitter smell came upon him.

With desperate haste he raked all the fuel that he could reach to the spluttering fire and plunged back against the wall of the chamber.

No doubt about the smell. Gas. Bitter almonds. Hydrocyanic gas. Jar full of fumigating chemicals. Going strong. Devilish strong.

He groped for the entry of the gallery in which Alison lay and put his head into it. No gas there yet. He looked back at the smoky blaze beneath the shaft.

Good old fire. Holding out fine. Must be drawing the gas up fast. That's what he hadn't thought of, the devil. No. Not quite a match for Reginald. Though he had a great big pull. However. Might have another dose of dope to use. Get away from it while the going was good.

Reggie crawled along the gallery to Alison.

"Have to go on a bit." He straddled over her. "Make it as easy as I can. We're beating 'em, Alison. Now let me—" He turned her onto her face. "Raise yourself on your left arm. You can. That 'll do." He dragged her along the gallery, sniffing at the air which met them—a draft which smelled of earth but was cold and clean. "Yes. Quite all right. There. So." He moved her gently till she lay on her left side, propped up against the side of the gallery.

"Oh, don't, don't," she groaned. "Let me die."

"My dear," Reggie spoke close to her, "there's better than that."

"No, no!" She was shaken with sobs.

"Light ahead. Be brave yet." He crawled on through the gallery and in a few yards more saw a faint glimmer above. It came from another, smaller shaft, one of those over which the growth of brambles was unbroken. He stood beneath it, feeling the downward draught, listening. … After awhile he heard voices, among them a piercing gull-squawk—the unique voice of General Duddon.

"Thank God," he muttered and sent a roar up the shaft. "General! General! Here I am. Come along."

There was a scurry overhead. "Is that you, Fortune?" the general shrieked. "What the devil's doing? The big pit is blazing like hell."

"Brought the rope?" Reggie shouted. "I want a fellow down here quick."

The bulk of a lumpy lad was lowered through the bushes. "Smash 'em," Reggie exhorted him. "Beat 'em back. Make a clear run." The lad's arms and legs struck out earnestly, and daylight opened about him as he came.

He stood beside Reggie undoing the rope at his waist and grinned broadly. "Sir? What's to do?"

"Come on." Reggie crawled into the gallery again. "Slow. Don't butt me."

When he came again to Alison she was silent and still. He struck one last match to show the lad how she lay. "See?"

"Coo! Be she dead?" the lad gasped.

"Oh no. No." Reggie slid over her and turned. "You get round too. Take her under the left arm. Ease her all you can. Now."

So, supporting her beneath them as they crawled, they brought her along to the shaft.

"Duddon! Can you haul up two together?" Reggie called.

"My God!" the general squeaked, and deeper voices muttered, and then he cried, "All right, old fellow. Come on."

Reggie gathered up Alison to hold her erect while the lad tied them both into the rope, and so she was hauled up slowly, fended off from the sides of the shaft. They hung just below its mouth. Hands reached down at them and drew them over the edge till Reggie was prone on the turf with Alison above him.

The rope was loosed, and he laid her down beside him. Her eyes did not open. No sound came from her but the gasp of struggling breath. Reggie stood up. "Have you seen anyone about?" he asked.

"Not a soul." The general stared at his filth. "I saw the pit blazing before we got up, but there wasn't a creature near it."

"Pity." Reggie sighed. "However. You've done damn well. Thanks very much."

"I pushed off as soon as Underwood phoned your message—got hold of some fellows—brought 'em straight up here." The general chattered on. "We haven't seen anybody since we left the village—had our eyes open too. Who did you expect? What made you think the girl was down in Giants' Graves? What the devil set fire to the pit—"

"Oh, my dear chap!" Reggie cut him short. "One thing at a time. She's the one thing." He turned and looked down at Alison. Her bosom rose and fell in deep surges, but her eyes were closed and her face, livid beneath swollen bruises and smears of chalk, was drawn with pain.

"Begad, you're right." The general went off again at the same speed but in a lower key. "Poor child—had the devil of a time. What do you make of her? Is she badly injured? Better get her—"

It was not Reggie who stopped him, but Alison. She had opened her eyes. "Oh, the light!" she said hoarsely and put her hand to her brow and whimpered.

Reggie knelt down by her. "Back in the light, yes," he said gently. "I told you there was light ahead. Here it is. Safe now. Quite safe." While he talked his hands were busy about her. "Steady. You've come through. All over."

Her sunken, streaming eyes turned to look away from him this way and that; she shrank and jerked and tried to raise herself on her right arm and fell back with a groan.

"Mustn't do that, no. Quite quiet. Don't try to move. We'll do the moving. Put you to bed and make you comfortable. All going right." Reggie stood up. "What's the transport you brought, General?"

"I have my car—the lads came up in the carrier's van—will that do? Get her home at once, what? Run her down there in five minutes."

Alison gave a hoarse cry. "No, no. Not home."

"What's that?" the general squeaked.

Reggie bent over her. "All right. I'm looking after you. Don't worry. No more fear." She broke out into sobbing laughter. "General!" he spoke loudly. "Your place is nearest. Go on and tell your people to get a bed ready—there's a good fellow."

The general gave him a sharp, frowning glance and a nod and then squeaked out, "Mrs. Grey will make her comfortable—very happy." He trotted off to his car.

Reggie looked down at Alison. "There you are. That's the way."

She turned her head from him; her quivering mouth opened and shut without a sound.

"Now then—" Reggie spoke to the little circle of village folk whose grave eyes met his with a stolid, knowing stare "—easy with her." His voice fell. "It's up to us. You see? Gentle it."

They laid her in the van, and, at a walking pace, she was driven away to General Duddon's house.

CHAPTER XXVIII *Evidence of Interest*

CLEAN, BUT WITH SOME BRUISES swelling iridescent on his pallid face, Reggie came stiffly down General Duddon's stairs, escorting the village doctor to the door.

"Thanks very much. Don't mind my saying you did that uncommon well. You'll get the nurse here quick, won't you?"

"You can depend on me, Mr. Fortune. Pray look after yourself, sir."

"My dear chap! I will." Reggie gave a twisted smile. "Good-bye."

He limped into the study, and the general, springing up to thrust upon him the most comfortable of its severe chairs, twittered solicitude. "There, there, you have had a devil of a time, Fortune—ought to be in bed yourself. Is that all right for you? Really, you ought not to take these risks—I know, I know a fellow does. Blame myself—shouldn't have let you. How is the poor child? Is she coming through?"

"Could there be tea?" Reggie was plaintive. "A lot of tea?"

The general swore at himself and rang the bell. "Too bad of me. What do you think of her? What do you make of it? How the devil did it happen? Do you see your way at all?"

"Not to the end, no. However. Confusin' facts are bein' eliminated."

"What, what? Eliminated?—more of a devilish confusion than ever—" The general broke off as his man brought in the usual frugal tea of the house.

"Oh." Reggie sat up and gazed at it with melancholy eyes. "Would you mind? Toast—buttered toast? A dish?"

The general squeaked orders and suggestions.

"No, no. There will also be dinner," Reggie sighed. "Lot of milk, please. And sugar. Three lumps. Thanks." He drank; he ate bread and butter. "Well, well. The lady—speakin' medically, she will come through. Some concussion. Right shoulder dislocated, and collarbone broken. Body heavily bruised. Severe shock and exhaustion. However. Your doctor's quite good. Fracture and dislocation all right. She's now sleeping off slight anesthetic. Your Mrs. Grey is with her. Nurse coming along for the night. So that is that. More tea, please."

"Poor girl—damned brute!" the general squeaked. "Does she know who it was?"

"No statement. Not fit to make a statement." Reggie took the last of the bread and butter.

"But she did though—" The general's little gaunt face sharpened. "She said she wouldn't go home—points against her wretched husband, doesn't it?"

"You noticed that? Yes. Natural inference."

"I suppose you didn't get a glimpse of the fellow yourself?"

"Of the operator? No. My error. My grave error. Neither last night nor today. Resourceful fellow. Determined fellow. Took points off me twice. As in our former games. However. Not points enough to win. I am still extant. Though he had trumps he didn't ought to. He has underestimated Reginald. Ah—" It was a gurgle of delight at the arrival of the buttered toast. "Thanks so much." He spoke fervently, and the stern manservant relaxed to smile.

As soon as they were alone again the general let off another shrill volley. "What do you say—talking about today—you asked if we saw anybody up at Giants' Graves? Do you mean you were attacked there too? And the fire— you—"

"My dear General," Reggie interrupted with his mouth full. "This interest is very kind. I will talk. If you let me. In order. Lady first. She was going to meet her dilatory husband last night; she was knocked on the head and re-moved from the road to the thicket in the copse. The operator was then inter-rupted by my arrival. Stunned me, too, before I was effective. Tied the un-conscious girl in a sack and went up the combe with her to bury her alive in Giants' Graves. Leavin' no trace of identity except that he's a hefty man. Nothing out of the way. Less than half a mile to carry her, uphill but easy. However. Man of some vigor. Several of 'em about."

"Bury her alive!" the general squeaked. "My God, Fortune, just like her brother, isn't it? The boy in the crack in the cliff—the girl in the pit—"

"Yes. Strikin' similarity. By chance or design. I wonder. And this morning her father was found dead, not far from where she was stunned, not far from where she was buried. Striking accumulation of disasters in the Tracy fam-ily."

"You believe old Aston—" The general subdued his shrill voice to a whis-per. "Can't deny it—everything points to him—" the general made a gri-mace of horror—"working out that old hate—damnable."

"Not nice, no. Father Aston would do. Big fellow, still fit. Has a motive. Has a dubious past. Certainty not yet established. Is there still tea?" He drank it; he looked under drooping eyelids at the general. "There was another pos-sibility," he said plaintively. "Tempting possibility. Father Tracy. There were tales he hated his son. We know he hated his daughter. Somebody did shoot at a girl who was walking near his daughter's house in the cool of the evening same like his daughter did last night when knocked on the head. Father Tracy used to wander round with a gun at that time o' day, frequent and common. Subsequent to the livin' burial of his daughter, Father Tracy lay shot, and, medically speaking, he might have shot himself. As if having done his daughter in he had nothing left to live for. Suicide following murder quite common in our fair island story." He drank up his tea; he lay back and took out pouch and pipe. "All this bein' thus offers strong temptation to infer Tracy was the operator. There were other facts pointin' to the same inference." He filled his pipe with slow, delicate care. "Strikin' impressive facts," he murmured. "I hit the operator a body blow. Tracy's watch had been hit. Glass cracked. Case dented. As from useful punch. And my knuckles did make contact with something hard. Very curious fact, the watch."

"But wait, wait," the general broke in. "I don't follow this. You were attacked again today up at Giants' Graves. Tracy was dead then. That couldn't have been Tracy."

"As you say." Reggie lit his pipe. "Does not go with the watch. Which is also curious. Provides decisive evidence of interest in the death of the girl and me by another party." He blew smoke rings. "I am bein' a nuisance. Which is grateful and comforting. But the operator of today is a resourceful fellow." He smoked on, and his eyes closed. "I wonder if he expected to meet me up there. I should like to know his opinion of me. I don't think he did. His error. I think he was still underestimating Reginald."

"Why," the general squeaked, "why, what do you suppose he went to Giants' Graves for?"

"Oh, my dear General! To make sure the girl should be dead before I found her there. Taking a chance I might have seen him. He didn't think I should be so quick. He hadn't considered the relations of black land and white land."

"I don't follow you at all." The general was peevish.

"My dear fellow! Black land and white land, always at strife. Same like you said in the beginning. Tracy was shot on black land, but there was white land on the grass by him—clod of chalk from a shoe. No sign of chalk on Tracy's soles. Though he might have brought it. Anyway, he or another operator had come down from the chalk. That's why I went up. The operator today, the operator who flung me down the pit had gone there to give Alison a dose of poison gas."

"My God, that's devilish—devilish," the general gasped. "But how—how could a man get hold of a gas bomb? It's not possible."

"Oh, General! Bomb not required. A jar suffices. Gas warfare is not confined to the military. Commonly waged by gardeners and fruit growers and what not. On insects and vermin. The plan was to fumigate Alison with one of the usual prescriptions—oil of vitriol and potassium cyanide, as used in greenhouses for red spider and so on. Liberates hydrocyanic gas. The operator brought up a jar of vitriol and water, put the cyanide in and threw it down for us. Very neat. However. Again underestimating Reginald. I thought something would be flung at us. That's why I lit my fire quick. Not quick enough to frighten him off by attracting the public. Which was the idea. But in time to draw up the gas in the draught. So it worked all right. I wonder what he thought when he saw the smoke coming up. Interestin' problem for him. Deeply interestin'. Hallo!"

Reggie sat up with a jerk. A car had stopped at the door; the bell was rung. "More evidence of interest," he smiled.

A man's voice was heard demanding Mrs. Aston. "Oh. The anxious husband," Reggie murmured. He rose and went out into the hall. Giles Aston cut short an angry outburst at the general's manservant and turned on him. "You've brought my wife here, I'm told. Why wasn't she taken to her own house?"

"Well, well." Reggie gazed at him. "So that is your first question. The answer is, for her own sake, Mr. Aston. She's suffered a great deal; she was exhausted and distressed. Happy to tell you that she should recover."

"I want to see her." Giles was truculent.

"Yes. I appreciate your interest. You can't see her now. She's asleep after anesthetic and shock. As soon as she's fit to talk to you I'll see that you're told."

"I'm going to see her." Giles scowled at him.

"Not now. No. Don't make a noise."

"Has she said anything? Has she told you how it happened?"

"Oh no. No. Not yet."

"Do you know?"

"Natural question. There isn't an answer. You'd better go home, Mr. Aston."

Giles took a step forward. His body menaced; his sunken, red eyes challenged.

Reggie stood fast. "Don't bother to thank me," he murmured. "Good-bye."

Giles made a wordless noise and swung on his heel and strode to the door. But there he stopped. Another car was drawing up. Out of it came the amplitude of Mrs. Brown.

"Oh, Giles, my dear," she panted, "is it true? She's been found? She's alive?"

"Yes, she is—so they say," Giles muttered.

"So they say!" she repeated. "Oh, my dear, haven't you seen her?"

Reggie came forward. "It's quite true, Mrs. Brown," he smiled. "Very kind of you to be interested."

"Lor', Mr. Fortune, don't talk like that." She was hurt. "The poor dear! She's like a daughter to Brown and me."

"Mr. Brown is not with you?" Reggie murmured.

"Brown's in Colsbury. I've only just heard. Is that right she was found in Giants' Graves? What's been done to her? How is she?"

"You've heard quite correctly. Some unkind person put her in one of the pits. She was only found just in time."

"Does she know who did it?"

"She hasn't told me yet."

"Oh, my goodness! What a dreadful thing. Can't I see her, Mr. Fortune? The poor darling!"

"Not a nice business, no. Your interest is so kind. But nobody can see her now."

Mrs. Brown's full red face puckered in distressful anxiety. "You have had the doctor, haven't you?"

"Oh yes. He can't tell you any more than I have, Mrs. Brown. Good-bye." Reggie went in and shut the door on them.

He returned to the study and the general and lowered himself carefully into his chair again. "Lots of interest in the lady," he murmured. His round face was divested of any expression.

"You were hard with 'em, Fortune." The general spoke in an apprehensive whisper. "I suppose you think— No right to ask you. Sorry."

"Doesn't matter. It could be. The rigor of the game. We give nothing away. Not any more."

While he spoke the telephone rang. The general answered. "This is General Duddon's house. General Duddon speaking. ... Yes, Mr. Fortune is here. Hold on." He passed the receiver to Reggie and announced with awe: "The chief of the Criminal Investigation Department."

"Well, well. More interest," Reggie smiled, and the general's discretion sent him pattering out. "Yes, Fortune speaking, Lomas. In spite of earnest efforts to stop his innocent mouth. Has Underwood got through to you? ... Yes, I think so. ... Rejoicin' in your approval. However. Subsequent rapid developments." Reggie related his journey to Giants' Graves, his overthrow into the pit, the finding of Alison and the gas attack. "My dear chap! Bless your kind heart, I'm quite all right. Only annoyed. ... Oh no. It don't give any new line. The line Underwood is on is the right line. The only line. ... What? Yes, Underwood should have two or three men quick. ... That is gratifyin'. ..."

Again a car arrived at the house. The voice of Superintendent Bubb was heard demanding Mr. Fortune.

"Here is the Bubb," Reggie spoke into the telephone. "Fierce and furious. Good-bye." He raised his voice to call. "Wantin' me, Bubb? Come on in." With a small benign smile he met Bubb's vehement entry. "I thought you'd be interested too."

"What's this I hear, Mr. Fortune?" Bubb glowered at him.

"I haven't the slightest idea," Reggie murmured. "You hear such a lot."

"It's reported to me you found the woman down in Giants' Graves, and she's alive. Is that right?"

"Do you mind?" Reggie asked.

"Mind! Of course I don't mind. I'm very glad. What I want to know is why didn't you tell me? I don't like your way of doing business."

"Yes. I have gathered that. You should do it yourself. Where were you when I went to Giants' Graves?"

"I was carrying out my duty with Mr. Tracy. As you know."

"Not me. No. Quite obscure what you were doing. Except neglectin' to act on the evidence."

"What evidence?" Bubb barked.

"Don't be noisy. Plain connection between Tracy's body and Giants' Graves. Black land and white land. Chalk, Bubb."

"You mean to tell me there was a trail?" Bubb said slowly.

"Yes. Which you avoided and vanished."

"I didn't see it. Why didn't you show it to me?" The words tumbled over each other.

Reggie laughed. "I've shown you things to act on before."

"That's not fair, Mr. Fortune. You ought—"

"To have let the woman die?"

"You've no right to talk so. I'd have gone with you straight."

"I wonder. Somebody did go there, Bubb. Somebody tumbled me down the pit on top of her."

"My God! Who was it?"

"Oh. That isn't one of the things you know?"

"How should I?"

"You know such a lot."

"First I've heard of this. You say you were attacked again?"

"Yes. Somebody don't love me, Bubb. Not only threw me down the pit but put down a dose of gas on top of the woman and me to finish us off. Somebody is finding me a nuisance. Hydrocyanic gas. Ever heard of it?"

"Gas! Poison gas, you mean. Nobody could get hold of the stuff. I can't believe it."

"That is comfortin'. What Bubb can't believe isn't evidence. But it happened. The evidence is safe in the pit. Not to be obliterated."

"You're telling me somebody had poison gas ready for you?"

"For her. So she shouldn't be found. I should say I was unexpected. Wouldn't you, Bubb? I was being troublesome. But continually underrated. You hadn't noticed that?"

"I don't know what you mean. I don't hold with your way of working alone. You say you were chucked down the pit. Did you see who did it?"

"Oh no. No. Very well done. Like last night."

"There you are. That's what comes of going on your own. If you'd taken me it wouldn't have happened."

"No. It wouldn't. Not this way. But something seemed to say to me Superintendent Bubb wouldn't have gone quick. He doesn't."

"You've no right to say so."

"Oh, my Bubb! However. I am not wholly on my own."

"You mean Underwood. Was he with you?"

"No. Other urgent business. Conferring with the Criminal Investigation Department. You may like to know the public prosecutor is taking on."

"Is he! That makes no difference to me. I do my duty. Now then. What about the woman? What's her story?"

Reggie sat silent, smiling at him.

"What has she told you?" Bubb leaned forward.

"You are interested," Reggie murmured.

"Of course I am. Come on; who does she say did it?"

"She hasn't said."

"Where is she? I want to see her."

"So I gather. You won't."

"You mean she's not able to speak? Won't she come round? Is she going to make a die of it?"

"Well, well." Reggie's eyelids drooped. "What humane anxiety. No, she's not going to die, Bubb. Not now. But she won't tell us who did it yet awhile. Up to you."

Bubb made a queer gasping noise and flung himself back. "My God, you're a cruel, cold hand."

"Me?" Reggie laughed.

"What do you think I can do? I've nothing to go on."

"Where did you go?"

"I told you; I've been with Mr. Tracy's body and the doctor. He says suicide or accident, one or the other. And there's no fingerprints on the gun but Tracy's."

"No. There wouldn't be. And so, having accidentally suicided, Tracy sent his ghost back to finish killing his daughter and do me in. Good story."

"Well, of course he didn't," Bubb muttered. "The thing's been faked very clever. Like it was with Tracy's son."

"Oh yes. Like it was with the chief constable. Tracy was suspected of that too."

"So was old Aston," Bubb growled. "Of both."

"Not by me," Reggie murmured. "Not of your chief. However. Evidence not investigated." He took from his pocket two cardboard boxes. "Exhibit A: cartridges found by Tracy's gun today. Exhibit B: cartridges found where the village girl was shot at. All twelve-bore Schultze powder. But cartridge fired on the girl was not from Tracy's gun. Mark from striker hole different. You see? So we infer that the operator who shot at her was not Tracy."

"Didn't I always say so?" Bubb exclaimed. "Mr. Tracy had too good an eye to make a mistake like that. I said it was done to get him into trouble."

"You did. Yes. You said it was our old friend Elijah. What have you done about that?"

Bubb glowered at him. "I haven't had time. You're right, though, I grant you. You do miss nothing, Mr. Fortune. I'll be on to him, don't you fear." He started up. "He's the fellow. We'll have him quick."

"What a change!" Reggie murmured. "Good-bye. Oh, by the way. Have you a greenhouse, Bubb?"

"A greenhouse?" Bubb exclaimed. "Why?"

"Just wondered."

"I have a little one for tomatoes. What about it?"

"Nothing. Good-bye. You're in a hurry."

Bubb's flushed face seemed to swell; he choked down some sound and strode out.

CHAPTER XXIX

Evidence of the Oldest Inhabitant

IN THE MORNING, after breakfast, two men from the Criminal Investigation Department called upon Mr. Fortune; they were dirty and the worse for wear, but complacent.

They presented to him the portions into which a big earthenware jar had broken and a sack. They informed him that he could take it no one had been down the big pit since the fire there.

"I thought not. No. Operator now rather impeded." Reggie smelled at the bits of the jar, which had still a bitter odor, and in one of which lay some dark, viscous fluid. "As expected. Commercial sulphuric acid with a cyanide. That goes to the analyst, Sergeant. Ask Inspector Underwood to pursue enquiries who's been buying vitriol and cyanide for fumigation. And where that sack came from."

"Very good, sir." The sergeant coughed. "If I may say so, it's not too hopeful. The sack has no mark of origin. It's had potatoes or some roots in it; most likely it was pinched off a farm shed. And about fumigating chemicals, they needn't have been bought down here at all."

"Yes. That is so. However. I think somebody here has been buying 'em."

Reggie went upstairs again to talk to Alison's nurse. While he was with her he beheld the arrival of a car which surprised him—a big and high car painted orange color, a car which had been the noblest work of man twenty years ago and still was as resplendent as if it had just left the factory.

Out of it came a dapper old man from whose mouth white mustaches were flowing, from whose breast pocket gleamed an orange silk handkerchief.

"Well, well!" said Reggie. "Not the art which hides art."

"It's Lord Werne," the nurse told him with reverence.

"That's what I meant," Reggie murmured.

As he went downstairs he heard Werne's prim voice enquiring after Mrs. Giles Aston and the general's manservant declining to know anything about her. "Good morning. Very kind of you to come, Lord Werne." Reggie conducted him to the study. "People are being kind."

"You feel ironical?" Werne answered. "I am not to complain. Kindliness has not been conspicuous in the county. But you may permit me an old man's

145

curiosity. How is the lady?"

"Not a bad night. The expectation is she'll come through."

"I take leave to thank you, Mr. Fortune." Werne bowed.

"So kind," Reggie murmured and waited for him to say something else.

Werne took his time. "It is perhaps improbable that I could assist you in any way," he said slowly. "But I wished you to know that you may rely upon the support of persons of influence if your work is obstructed here."

"Thanks very much. You expect that?"

"I repose upon your judgment, Mr. Fortune. Permit me to recall to you the wedding of these young people. When we met then, I said something of my pleasure in finding your interest in the county was not exhausted."

"You did, yes. You were rather enigmatic. Havin' thus told me there was work for the police you also said you hoped the marriage was the end of the feud and wished 'em joy. Are you still hoping and wishing?"

"In what is left of my heart." Werne made a flourish. "It is agreeable to talk with you, Mr. Fortune. You have a nice apprehension. I think I need not remind you that when I spoke of the old hatred between the Tracys and Astons I added that there were those who hated both."

"Oh yes. Also enigmatic. You gave no names."

Werne spread out his lean old hands and smiled sadly. "Do you find people so definite, so obvious? What was in my mind was the atmosphere, the tone, the customary ancient feelings of the community. I know them as the oldest inhabitant. There are these particular family hostilities; there are also general traditions. Some of our people, sprung from the soil, love the Tracys and the Astons no better than Tracys and Astons have loved one another."

"Yes, I did see that was your point." Reggie's eyelids drooped. "Any particular reason for making it again now?"

"I am not to advise you, Mr. Fortune. I only put such knowledge as I have at your service. It has appeared to me that the futility of our police work might be accounted for by this state of feeling."

"Oh. Meaning the police were quite happy for Astons and Tracys to eat one another up—hated both lordly families impartial. Meaning our Superintendent Bubb, sprung from the soil, inherits a tradition of 'down-with-the-gentry'."

The waxen, fastidious expression of Werne's face quivered into puckers of distaste. "That meaning is not to be found in my words, Mr. Fortune, or in my intention. You surprise me. Permit me to say you disappoint me. I deplore your demand for a definite charge which the facts do not justify."

"Did you happen to think you were bein' helpful?" Reggie complained. "Nobody here dares to be definite. That's why you go on from crime to crime. I'm going to ask you one or two questions, Lord Werne. Here's the first. Your Superintendent Bubb told me that Mr. Brown has been too attentive to Mrs. Giles Aston, and Giles was jealous. Do you believe that?"

Werne's distaste was more deeply marked. "I do not, sir."

"Thank you. Second question: Where did Bubb get it from? Have you heard it from anybody else?"

"I have heard such gossip," Werne answered, biting the words. "I have heard Cope facetious about it. It is a disgusting absurdity."

"Oh! Mr. Cope the banker. Knows Brown well, doesn't he?"

"In the way of business, I should suppose. Pray understand that Cope jeered at the story. He is a coarse fellow but shrewd."

"I see. Not believed by Mr. Cope. Only by your Superintendent Bubb. Well, third question: Could you tell me anything about the financial position of Tracy?"

"You may conceive that I do not seek to inform myself of Tracy's private affairs—" said Werne and stopped.

"Thanks very much." Reggie smiled.

Then Werne went on: "I can only tell you what is common report—that Tracy had been speculating lately and with disastrous loss."

"Well, well," Reggie murmured. "How do people know these things? Brown was playing fast and loose with Mrs. Giles, but that's a disgustin' absurdity. Tracy had come a cropper in speculation, but that isn't absurd. Why did he go speculating just now?"

"I fear he was always a gambler," said Werne.

"Yes, I've heard that before. But which was the new motive for going blind? That his daughter married into the hated Aston family? That Brown wanted to buy his estate? Very convenient for Mr. Brown to have him crash."

"I do not follow you," Werne answered. "It is impossible that Tracy's actions should have been dictated by Brown."

"You think so?" Reggie murmured. "Fourth question, Lord Werne: Did you tell Brown you were coming to talk to me about the case?"

"I did not, sir," Werne answered quickly.

"Well, well." Reggie watched him with closing eyes. "Does he know your opinion of Bubb, and the scandal about Mrs. Giles and Tracy's finances?"

"My opinions are my own—" said Werne with incisive emphasis and interrupted himself. "Pray understand me. I did talk over the case with Brown yesterday. He suggested to me that I should lay before you such knowledge as I had, such conclusions as I had reached. I did not inform him what I intended. I do not take instructions from Mr. Brown. On consideration I decided that I might be of some assistance to you."

"Oh yes. You have been. Yes. Farsighted fellow, Brown. Thanks very much."

Werne did not choose to take that for sarcasm, nor ask what it meant. He made a little bow. "You have a subtlety, Mr. Fortune," he said and stood up. "If I can serve you, command me." He took a ceremonious leave.

Reggie watched the imposing old car drive him away. "Not the art which conceals art," he murmured once more. "No. Not meant to. I wonder."

He lighted a pipe and went out into the garden and smoked there, contemplating its rigid discipline with dreamy melancholy.

After a while the general's car fussed up the drive. Reggie went to meet it. "Well, did you reassure the anxious husband?"

"I found him at home, Fortune. Looks dead to the world—worn out—absolutely. I told him his wife was making good progress—as you said. He took it like a knockout, and when he came to began gibbering that he must see her at once. I told him she wouldn't be able to see anyone today—doctor's orders; then he damned my eyes and flopped again. Don't know what to make of it—"

"No. Nor does he. 'Perplexed in the extreme,' our Giles."

"What's that, what's that?" the general squeaked. " 'Perplexed in the extreme'—out of *Othello*, isn't it? 'Being wrought perplexed in the extreme'—mad with jealousy, murdered Desdemona. My God, Fortune, you believe that?"

"You're so literal. Our Alison hasn't been murdered. Lots of perplexities for our Giles. How did you leave him?"

"He left me. I told him what you said—you'd ring him up tomorrow morning, if he could see her then. He just flung himself out—don't know where he went."

"Don't worry. Our Giles is provided for. And others. Just run me into Colsbury, will you? I could bear to see my car again."

The general was delighted. But before Reggie drove back in his beloved car he visited one of Colsbury's minor taverns and there conferred with Inspector Underwood who did most of the talking, who suffered from excitement and impatience.

"Preserve absolute calm," Reggie admonished him. "Did you happen to think you saw your way to the end? You don't. We're not going to strike till we have 'em all where we want 'em. I won't leave anything behind this time. Finish, my friend."

CHAPTER XXX *Evidence of a Lie*

IT WAS EARLY on the next day when Reggie came into Alison's room. "I think we're doing very well, Mr. Fortune," said the nurse.

"Looks like it, yes." Reggie sat down by the bedside. "What do you say, Mrs. Aston?"

Her face was wan and shrunken, all brow and eyes, below a flood of red hair. The full brow was lined; the eyes gazed at him wide and dark.

"Thank you. I'm quite all right," she said.

"That's the spirit. You're going to be. How's the pain?"

"There isn't any now."

"Oh. As good as that?"

"Really, it's nothing. I slept beautifully. I shall soon be able to get up, shan't I?"

"You want to? Yes. Quite soon. Well, well." Reggie gave the nurse a glance, and she went out. "You're a brave woman, Mrs. Aston."

"Why do you say that?"

"The way you've taken it. The way you've fought through."

"I haven't done anything," she said. "I've only just lain here. You've done everything. Oh, I ought to thank you. You have been so kind."

"I've only been doin' my job. I rather liked it. But you can believe I shall be kind. I want you to tell me how it all happened."

"I don't know!" she cried, and the lines on her brow deepened. "But I don't know!" The dark eyes flickered and looked away and stared fear at him.

"Let's go over it. You went out to look for your husband because he was late—"

"Yes, I did; I've often done that, just along the road."

"I know. And on the road somebody knocked you down. You remember that?"

"No, I don't remember anything."

"Oh. You were hit on the head. You were stunned."

"I suppose so," she said faintly. "I don't remember anything from just walking till I came to myself in that—that sack and the dark. And then it was like years."

"Yes. I was slow. Yes."

"Don't! Don't!"

149

"Sorry. I was going to ask, you didn't see who hit you?"

"Of course I didn't! I shouldn't have let him. I should have fought."

"Gave you no chance? I see. But you must have thought about it since. Who do you think did it?"

"I don't know. I can't think. There isn't anybody," she panted.

"There isn't anybody who's had a quarrel with you?"

"Who do you mean?"

"Your husband has been very anxious to hear whether you'd told me anything about anybody."

"Well, of course he would be," she cried.

"Yes. Very natural. Has there been any trouble between you and him?"

"Ah!" She raised herself with a gasp of pain and excitement. "That's not true! That's not true! Why do you say it?"

"I'm sorry. It has been said."

"Everything's said—everything beastly and ghastly and horrible." She was quivering. "Don't believe it. It wasn't Giles. I'm sure it wasn't."

"But you didn't see the man," Reggie murmured.

She fell back on the pillow. "You don't think it was Giles?" she moaned. "It wasn't! It wasn't! The man wasn't like him in the least." Under Reggie's steady compassionate eyes she began to stammer. "He—he—wasn't—wasn't so tall—so big. I'm sure."

"You would be. Yes. No more questions. Only one. Do you feel up to seeing Giles? You could, for a minute. Just a minute."

"He's here?" she asked, and Reggie nodded. "Of course I want to see him."

"All right. You mustn't talk," Reggie said.

"Talk!" She gave a little miserable laugh.

"I'm in charge, you know," Reggie said and went out.

Giles was sitting on the edge of a chair in the study while the general chattered trivialities at him. He started up as Reggie opened the door. "Yes. You can have a minute with her," Reggie said. "Gently. She's said she doesn't know who tried to kill her."

"She doesn't!" Giles exclaimed.

"She said she couldn't think."

Giles strode upon him. "I want to see her alone."

"For one minute. Yes. You are not to ask her about it."

Giles stood glaring into Reggie's expressionless face. "What do you mean?" he whispered. "You believe you know, do you?"

"Are you going to see her?" Reggie answered.

Giles drew back with an incoherent mutter. Reggie made a gesture and turned and went upstairs again, and Giles stumbled after him. "Quiet," Reggie said over his shoulder. He opened the door of Alison's room.

Giles pushed past him, calling, "Alison!"

She gave no answer; she lay still but for the surge and fall of her bosom. The wide eyes gazed at him, dim and pitiful; her pale face was puckered with distress.

He knelt down beside her and pressed his head against her body. She stirred; she flinched; then her left arm moved feebly, came across, and she laid her hand on his head.

Reggie left them. When he opened the door again he heard her voice, faint. "I don't know, Giles. I don't know anything." Giles was looking at her hungrily, fiercely intent.

"Time for you to go, Aston," Reggie said.

Giles leaned forward and kissed her, forcing her face down into the pillow, sprang up and was gone. As Reggie came into the room she turned from him, moaning, and shut her eyes upon tears.

"Yes. But tomorrow's another day," Reggie said gently. "There will be tomorrow."

He crossed to the window and looked out. Giles was already driving away. His car vanished. When it came into sight again on the road it was not going back home but up to the hills.

Reggie went out and made haste to his own car. He drove to Colsbury and drove furiously.

CHAPTER XXXI

Evidence of a Poacher Resumed

INSPECTOR UNDERWOOD sat in the landlady's parlor of his inn filling his fountain pen when she opened the door. "Oh, my dear chap!" Reggie protested over her buxom shoulder. "The time for literature has not come."

"Mr. Lomas will want a report, sir."

"Forget it. No material yet. If ever. The lady has spoken. She didn't see who hit her. She can't think who did. It's all a horrid lie her husband was jealous. So she did see the fellow who hit her. And he wasn't her husband. Not a bit like. Not so tall. Not so big. She's quite sure."

Underwood frowned. "She does know then? She's lying hard to cover up. That don't go well." A puzzled, enquiring gaze consulted Reggie.

"Lying, yes. Gallant lies. She is brave, poor girl. Knows? I don't think so. I should say she don't know what it is she's trying to cover. However. Our Giles has the wind up. Very high. Rattled off to Brown's place or father's place. You have them fixed?"

"Absolutely. And I've been round myself asking Cope about old Aston, like you said. Cope was sticky but civil and willing to oblige. Told me Aston was an impossible sort of fellow. Nobody really knew him nowadays. Gave me to understand, without saying so, that Aston's affairs are about desperate."

"Oh yes. As expected. However. What about our Bubb?"

"He's on the jump." Underwood gave a grim chuckle. "Comes round about every hour to ask what we are doing, if you please."

"What's *he* doing?"

"Search me. Running about and yapping."

"Not communicative? Well, well. Come on. We will go and commune with our Bubb."

They entered the gloom of the vaulted chamber which enshrined the brain of the Durshire police.

"Well? What have you gentlemen got to tell me?" Bubb demanded.

"Why so fierce, Bubb? Beautiful are our feet upon the mountains. Good news for Superintendent Bubb. Mrs. Giles Aston don't know who hit her. She didn't see him."

"Oh, didn't she! What do you call that good news for?"

"Thought you'd be relieved."

"Of course she'd say she don't know. She wouldn't give him away."

"Meaning who?" Reggie murmured.

"Whichever of 'em it was—her husband, or his father, or old Brown—it's hell for her, anyway."

"Oh. Limiting the possibilities to them?"

"Who else is there? Say it was her own father. She wouldn't want to put it on him."

"I wasn't saying so. However. What are you doing in the great war, Bubb?"

"I'm tracing all their movements. And if you want to know, I find old Mr. Aston was out and about along the time she was attacked."

"Oh yes. It could be. I thought you'd concentrate on him. You have your uses, Bubb. However. The lady is saying that the operator wasn't tall. That won't do for either Aston."

"Of course she'd keep the Astons out," Bubb grunted. "It'd do for old Brown. It'd do for her father."

"As you say. Yes. However. You had another bright idea. What about our old friend Elijah? Have your active and intelligent investigations brought in Elijah our poacher?"

Bubb scowled. "Yes, they have. I'm holding Elijah Hawke for further enquiries."

"My Bubb! What zeal! Why?"

"I may tell you, he couldn't give any account of himself at the relevant time."

"Well, well! That was convenient. So our Elijah becomes one of the suspected persons. How gratifying! Any visible cause for Elijah to attempt murder on Alison Aston?"

"She's a Tracy. You know very well Elijah Hawke has a raw grudge against all the Tracys. I told you that."

"You did. Yes. However. He was willing and eager to talk before. Won't he talk now?"

"Not a word. He told me flat to start with he wouldn't answer any questions, and he stuck to it."

"I wonder," Reggie murmured. "Perhaps you didn't get to the right question, Bubb."

"What do you mean?" Bubb demanded.

"Why he wouldn't answer Superintendent Bubb. Have him in, please."

"I did ask him that." Bubb was loud and indignant. "And he only grinned at me."

"Oh, Bubb! How could he? Come on. I want him."

"All right, if you like," Bubb muttered. "Try it yourself. It's asking him to make a fool of you."

"I've heard you say that before," Reggie murmured. "Have you forgotten? When our Elijah came to give information all on his own. And you didn't want me to listen."

"I have not forgotten," Bubb retorted. "Nor I don't take it back. If you remember, Mr. Fortune, his story was Mr. Tracy murdered his son and murdered the chief too. Much you've made of that!"

"Not much, no. But that wasn't his story. He was very careful. He showed cause to suspect Tracy. If that's what he has in his head now, why wouldn't he tell you?"

"God, I don't know." Bubb was angry. "He's a dirty little rat."

"I want him," said Reggie, and Bubb made an angry exclamation and rang his bell and gave orders to bring Hawke up. "Thanks very much. I should like to know what's happened to him."

"Nothing's happened to him," Bubb exclaimed. "What do you mean? He's been treated quite right."

"Why so touchy, Bubb? I didn't suggest he was being tortured. The point is different. When Elijah came to the police station spontaneous after your late chief's demise, he was full of talk. Now you've brought him in for enquiries about Tracy, he's dumb."

"Don't that show he was in it?" Bubb demanded.

Elijah was led in by a sergeant. He stopped short and leered at Bubb, and his brown crinkled face emitted a snarl. "What's the game? Don't you try no more tricks with me."

The sergeant told him to shut his mouth and speak when he was spoken to.

"Lie down, Fido," Elijah answered and turned the quid in his cheek and chewed for a moment while his deep-set eyes looked from Bubb to Underwood and Reggie. "Blimy, Bubb." He chuckled. "This here's the gent what was bothering about how your old man come by his death. So you got him on you again. That's spit in your eye."

Bubb sent the sergeant out with a brusque gesture and told Elijah to behave himself.

Elijah winked at Reggie. "Keep it quiet, see?" He shambled across the room. "So you wasn't done with old Bubb after that, guv'nor. You are a fret."

"Yes. I didn't find you helpful over the chief constable's death," said Reggie. "Your story was Tracy had a hand in that. What's your story about Tracy's death?"

"Here! That ain't taking me right. I never said as Tracy corpsed the chief. What I said I stands to. I told you Tracy and the coppers was all mixed for to hide things. And that's God's truth. Ain't it, Bubb?" Elijah showed his yellow, broken teeth.

Bubb told him he would not help himself by lying.

"Help my foot. I don't need no help."

"Don't you?" Reggie sighed. "You were complaining the superintendent played tricks on you."

"That's right. Ain't he told you? I lay he ain't. He has me locked up, so I shouldn't let out what I know."

Bubb gave a contemptuous laugh. "There's the sort of stuff he'll hand you, Mr. Fortune."

"Nor you can't deny it, Bubb. Where was I when you come, guv'nor? In the blinking cells. And for why? Bubb has me brought here and asks me what do I know about Squire Tracy having his head blown off."

Underwood took out a notebook.

"That's the way. Write it down, mate." Elijah shifted his quid with a gurgle. "Then I says to old Bubb, you don't get out like that. Come inquest, I'll tell Crowner. And Bubb, he curses like mad he'll put it on to me and has me shoved down in the cells again."

"There's an old lag's story," Bubb snorted. "You were detained because you couldn't give any account of your actions. As you know."

Elijah was watching Underwood's pencil. He jerked an impudent thumb toward Bubb. "Hear him! More to come, mate. I said I wouldn't tell ruddy nothing to him. I'd speak open when I spoke."

"Oh. Why refuse information to the police?" Reggie asked.

"Per-lice!" Elijah guffawed. "Him! He's blinking fine perlice. Ruddy keeper poaching for hisself. I tell you straight, guv'nor, you're here to know who corpsed Squire Tracy, ain't you? Then you go after old Bubb, that's what you got to do. Write it down, mate."

"You lying little rat," Bubb roared. "Where were you when Tracy was killed?"

Elijah sucked his quid and smacked his lips. "Likes it, don't he?" he grinned. "Now you see why he tried for to stop my mouth."

"Not yet, no," said Reggie. "Nothing's come out of it yet that is evidence."

"You wait. I tell you no lies. It ain't only that night. I goes out reg'lar, as you might say." He gave a knowing leer. "Nowt but rabbiting, guv'nor. There ain't nobbut conies yet awhile. Now you listen. More 'n one night lately there's been one of them little two-seat cars round where Tracy's coverts go up to the hills."

Underwood looked up from his notebook. "Number?" he asked. "Make of car? Color?"

"I don't know nothing about makes. Nor I didn't get the ruddy number. Dark color. See? I tell you no lies. I shied off the blinking car. For why? I wasn't going to work with perlice about. But it was a car just like what old Bubb has." He showed his teeth in a dog's menacing grin at Bubb. "Eh?"

"Go on," Bubb sneered. "This is great stuff. You were up to no good; you saw a car and funked; you don't know anything about cars, but you know it was mine!"

"I seed you, Bubb," said Elijah.

"That's what you've been thinking up, is it?" Bubb leaned forward, scowling. "You—"

"Where did you see him?" Reggie interrupted. "When?"

Elijah nodded at Bubb's fury and turned. "More 'n one night, guv'nor, I see a bloke the spit of him round the hills and the spinneys down the combe. The night Tracy was corpsed, there he was lurking down behind Goat's Hill. There you are. That's what I got to say when inquest comes."

"Yes. You have. Yes. Are you going to swear it was Superintendent Bubb?"

"I'll swear it was the very spit of him, s'elp me God, I will," Elijah said slowly. "And I never did the dirty on any man."

Bubb exploded upon him. "Didn't you! We know you, you rat. Never a dirty, silly trick you didn't play to cover your jobs. You've done for yourself this time. You own to it you were there when Mr. Tracy was killed. That's good enough."

"Ah, go to hell and fry yourself," said Elijah coolly. "I didn't own to nothing like it. What I says is: I see you, like I did the night the lass was shot at down in combe. On the night Tracy was corpsed me and my mate see you going down along by the Goat's Hill covert, and we cut away. There's for you, Bubb."

"Name of mate?" Reggie asked sharply.

"Don't you worry. Everybody knows him. Bill Penn to Elstow. He'll tell you the same."

Bubb broke into a roar of laughter. "That's a good witness. Penn did time with you for your last job, didn't he?"

"Anything else you want to say, Elijah?" Reggie asked.

"That's the whole of it." Elijah shifted his quid and chewed.

Bubb rang his bell and told the sergeant who answered to take the fellow away.

"Here, guv'nor," Elijah turned to Reggie. "Do you stand for that?"

"Out with him," Bubb roared.

"Go easy," Reggie said. "The gentleman's a witness. You have no charge against him. Remember that."

"He's held for enquiries," Bubb said loudly. "And he will be."

Elijah spat out his quid to splash on Bubb. "That for you," he chuckled and let the sergeant hustle him away.

Reggie gazed at Bubb's furious cleansing of himself. "No, you don't look well," he murmured. "Are you thinking you can rub this out? Your error."

"I handle my cases my own way, Mr. Fortune. Get that into your head."

"I have. That's why I came." Reggie looked at his watch and started up. "Good-bye."

"Where are you off to?"

"I'm going to Elstow."

"What, to get onto this other rascal, Penn? I'm with you."

Reggie laughed, and Underwood and he were first at the door.

When they reached the outer office they found one of Underwood's men in an altercation with Bubb's haughty inspector. "What's the trouble?" Underwood struck in.

"I've been kept out here; he wouldn't let me come in to you," the man answered.

"Is that by your orders?" Underwood turned on Bubb.

"There's general orders I'm not to be disturbed in conference," Bubb retorted. "I didn't ask you to come here."

Reggie laughed. "You are doing yourself proud. Come on, Underwood." They took the man with them and walked away in close conversation to the quiet side street where Reggie's car was parked.

Before they reached it the man turned back to the market place. In the bustle of business there another joined him but dropped behind when he went on to the quiet shade of the square about the church.

Reggie drove Underwood off, on the road to Elstow, and as soon as it widened and straightened out the big car shot into speed.

Even so, they had gone some three miles before they saw a two-seater in front of them. They gained, they closed upon it and passed. Underwood watched it keenly. "Bubb driving," he spoke to Reggie's ear. "Longman ten, dark blue." He gave a grim chuckle. "That goes just right with the poacher's evidence. No wonder Bubb blew up."

"Yes. Elijah was awkward," said Reggie.

"What a case!" Underwood exclaimed. "They have mucked it up among 'em."

"As you say." Reggie sank lower in his seat as the car rushed up the long climb to the white land of Elstow Manor. "So help us God!"

CHAPTER XXXII *Evidence of a Greenhouse*

THE CAR SLOWED along the wall of Aston's park and turned in through the gateless arch of the ruinous gatehouse.

When they had gone some way across the park a man rose from a hollow in the treeless turf, nodded, pointed them on and sank down again out of sight.

"Young Aston's still there," Underwood said.

"So I gather. Good chaps, your chaps. However. He would be. Things are getting calculable."

"You feel certain now, sir?"

Reggie gave a little queer laugh. "Feelin' in charge. At last. And without excuses."

The mellow, gracious form of the old house was near; its curved casements flashed back the sun in their eyes. Just above the slopes of the ragged garden Reggie stopped a moment for Underwood to get out and drove on alone to the courtyard and the porch.

Underwood strode away by a grass-grown path to the range of glass in a sunbathed hollow. There was no one to challenge him. The glasshouses had been opulently planned for vines and fruit and exotic flowers and forcing. Most of them stood empty in squalid decay.

From one to another Underwood passed with searching eyes. The house which had a dismal show of dead orchids, the house in which unpruned shrubs were half wild, half dying, the house in which a few alpine plants still lingered in miserable life among a range of pots did not delay him. When he came to another where a few tomato plants were fruiting he went in and searched under the staging but came out empty handed.

Beyond it was a house overgrown by a vine which bore a few puny clusters of grapes. He opened the door and, stooping under the loose branches, peered about. The leaves had been much eaten. Little red spiders scurried to and fro.

From behind the door he picked up a high-shouldered dark bottle and a brown cardboard box with a red label: "Poison. Potass. Cyanide." He pulled out the stopper of the bottle and smelled the sulphurous liquid within, looked at the white stuff in the box. "Ugh, the devil," he muttered and strode off with them.

Before he was back upon the drive he saw a small car coming toward the house—Bubb's car. Bubb saw him and stopped and sprang out and made for him. "What have you been doing down there?"

"Looking at the greenhouses. Have you got a greenhouse, Mr. Bubb?"

"I don't want any impudence from you."

"You're very touchy. Mr. Fortune asked you, you remember."

"I don't remember all the fool questions he's asked. What do you mean by it? What if I have?"

"It's interesting. I found some stuff that's used for fumigating greenhouses put in one of these here."

"Damn you, talk sense. Suppose you did? What's that got to do with anything?"

"Come now, Mr. Bubb." Underwood grinned. "You're not expecting me to believe you don't know that the chap who got Mr. Fortune into the pit dropped a dose of poison gas down on 'em."

"Mr. Fortune told me so. I know that," Bubb spluttered. "He never said a word about the gas being made with insect-killer stuff. I never heard it could be. If he had that in his mind, why didn't he tell me straight?"

"It might be because the authorities don't care so much for the way you use information," said Underwood.

"I'll report that, my man," Bubb snarled.

"They will be wanting reports on this case," said Underwood. "Well, here's the stuff, Mr. Bubb. Vitriol and potass. cyanide. Deadly, I'm told, on insects and others. Makes prussic acid in a gas, you know. Do you use it in your greenhouse?"

"I don't. I never heard of it, I tell you," Bubb answered in a breath and then stopped for a struggle of thought. "Look here." He prodded Underwood. "You say you found these goods in a greenhouse here. Well, don't you see what that means? God, I always thought it was old Aston. Now we've got proof. Come on up to the house. The old fox, he's for it now."

"I didn't know you had a line on Mr. Aston," said Underwood. "You haven't done much with it so far. What brought you out here all of a sudden? That poacher accusing you? I thought you were going to check up on his mate. How about that?"

"Nothing about it," Bubb told him. "I don't fall for your tricks. Mr. Fortune gave me to understand he was going to talk to Penn. When I saw he didn't take the turn to the village I drove on after you here to find out what the real game was."

"You are worried, aren't you?" Underwood grinned. "I don't wonder." And he walked on toward the house.

"What do you mean?" Bubb caught him up. "What do you mean by that, I say?"

"You know best, Mr. Bubb."

"Where is Mr. Fortune?" Bubb demanded and saw the big car standing empty. "Gone inside, has he?" The sound of voices came from an open window upstairs. He tried the door, found it unlocked and strode in.

CHAPTER XXXIII *Evidence of a Wife*

REGGIE BROUGHT HIS CAR slowly round the moss-grown gravel of the courtyard to the porch in a curve of exact precision.

From a window in the shadow of the porch's pillared canopy a face looked
out at him—white, grotesquely distorted by the uneven old glass.

He stepped into the porch, and as he came to the gray oak door it was
opened, and Giles stood against it, holding it. "What do you want here?" The
words were spoken in an angry, excited whisper; the haggard white face
came close, its eyes miserable and desperate.

"And you?" Reggie asked. He looked beyond Giles into the dappled sunshine and shadow of the big bare hall.

Giles's mother sat there, bent and huddled in a shawl, staring at them. She
brushed back wisps of gray hair from her eyes; she stood up slowly and
swayed and grasped at the chair back. "Giles! Oh, Giles," she called. "Let
him—let him—"

"Please." Reggie put his hand on Giles's arm, and Giles fell back and went
to his mother, and Reggie followed. "I'm sorry, Mrs. Aston, I have to," he
said gently, but his round face showed neither pity nor kindness. "When I
was here before—about your burglary—Mr. Aston took me to your wainscot
parlor. Do you remember?" She bent her head. "Yes. He explained it was
made for the privacy of the master and mistress of the house. Could we go
there again? Privacy would be better."

"Yes, oh yes," she gasped. "Come!"

"You're not going to talk to my mother alone," Giles cried.

"Giles—Giles, please." She put out her hands to him.

"No, Mother. I won't have that." He thrust her away. "This is for me now;
you know it's got to be."

She shuddered, and all her body trembled. "Oh, Giles," she moaned. "Oh!
You can hear, then. Yes. He must, Mr. Fortune."

Reggie bit his lip. "I see. Well. Make it so. But I want to go to that wainscot parlor again, Mrs. Aston."

"If you please," she said faintly and tottered away to the staircase.

"What do you want to go there for?" Giles growled at Reggie.

"You're doing no good to anybody," said Reggie. "She'd help you if she
could."

"Help!" Giles groaned. "Oh my God!"

160

His mother gave a faint cry. Reggie made haste after her up the stairs and put his hand to her arm, but she shrank from it to stumble on alone.

They came to the dark paneled room, and she sank down in the first chair she met, a chair by the writing table. The sunlight came through the open window to show her shrunken like a cripple and her haggard face mottled purple through the tears upon its lines and wrinkles.

Reggie looked at the shiny oil painting of her husband above her—the colored fashion plate of a fine fellow in riding clothes with buttonhole. "Your husband's not in the house, Mrs. Aston?" he asked, and she shook her head.

He turned upon Giles. "What did you come for?"

"To see him," Giles growled. "I'm waiting for him. You know why."

"I wonder," Reggie murmured. "Why isn't he here, Mrs. Aston?"

"He's gone to Colsbury. He had to see Mr. Cope."

"Oh yes. His banker. Any urgent reason?"

The clasped hands, holding the shawl at her bosom, twisted. "I don't know," she said. "There was a telephone message."

"Mr. Aston didn't tell you what about?"

She shook her head. "It would be money. I don't know about money."

"Well, well." Reggie turned away to the bookcase and looked at its vellum-bound rows of college prizes and spoke to her over his shoulder. "Has your husband said anything to you about Tracy's death?"

"He said it was terrible; he said it was like fate," she answered as if she were repeating a lesson.

"Fate. You think so?" Reggie took one of the white books from the shelf and turned the pages. "Was that before he heard of the attack on Tracy's daughter, your son's wife?"

There was a catch in her breath, and she shook with coughing. Still Reggie did not look at her; he was glancing from page to page, his face hidden. She raised herself panting and tried to see it. Giles frowned at her and from her to Reggie. "Before—no, after," she stammered. She put her hand to her head. "What am I saying? Let me think. We heard first Alison was lost—just talk—we didn't believe it. Then the next day they were talking in the village that Mr. Tracy had shot himself. That was when my husband said it was like fate."

"Oh. And then you heard Alison had been found in Giants' Graves alive. What did he say then?"

"We didn't hear till quite late, till the evening," she said faintly. "I don't know what we said, we were so glad."

Reggie made no answer. He had stopped turning the pages. He was reading. Giles strode to him. "What is this book? What are you doing with it?"

"Your father's Aeschylus," Reggie murmured. "The play I'm looking at is the *Agamemnon*. I was finding a quotation." He showed Giles a page on which there were one or two notes written in a minute, academic hand. "Here it is." He pointed to some lines and read in a solemn drone: "Tod epi gan peson hapax thanasimon propar andros melan haima tis an palin agkalesait epaeidon.' " He turned and looked at Mrs. Aston. "Do you know it?"

"It's Greek, isn't it?" She stared bewildered fear. "I don't know any Greek."

Reggie swung round upon Giles. "And you?"

"I don't understand a word. I haven't looked at a Greek book since I left school."

"Those lines were sent on a postcard to Alison when she was staying with Brown in London to marry you."

"She never showed them to me."

"She never saw them. Brown gave the card to the police. Suggestin' it might not be nice. It wasn't. It means: 'Blood that once has fallen dark with death before man's feet, who can call it back by his charms?' Addressed to Mrs. Giles Aston. Message on her marriage. Suggestin' there was a curse on both your houses. Suggestin' a threat."

"Brown didn't tell me!" Giles muttered.

His mother gave a cry. "It wasn't, it wasn't! Giles, your father wouldn't; he never thought like that, Giles." She held out a hand that shook.

His white face worked; he gulped; he looked at Reggie with wretched appeal. "You're saying he sent it?"

"No. I haven't said that. But somebody sent it. Somebody who didn't like your marrying Alison. Somebody who meant to have things remembered." He turned again to Mrs. Aston. "Where was your husband the evening that Alison was attacked, the evening that Tracy was shot?"

"He was here with me," she gasped. "Giles, I told you so. He was. You can ask the servants. I told you. He didn't go out at all."

Reggie watched her without a sign of feeling. "There was another child of Tracy's went into a hole in the ground. Twelve years ago. You remember that day. Where was your husband then?" Her swollen red eyes opened wide to stare horror. She shook her head; her hands plucked at her bosom. "The boy came singing up to your cliffs here," Reggie went on quietly. "Like this:

" 'There was a ship came from the North Country,
And the name of the ship was the Golden Vanity.' "

He spoke the words to a hum of the tune.

She screamed, "It was me, it was me! I was so angry. He'd been told not to come. I scolded him; I pushed him—and he fell, he fell, oh, down into the cliff and then—oh—" She huddled herself together moaning and sobbing.

"Mother!" Giles called out and sprang at her and took her in his arms. "You didn't! You couldn't! You weren't here. You know you weren't. When

Charles Tracy was lost you were away with me at Bayford."

"Not that day, no, Giles," she sobbed. "It was me."

"My dear. You mustn't," Giles groaned.

Heavy steps sounded on the stairs, along the corridor. Bubb and Underwood came into the room together. "So here you are, Mr. Fortune," Bubb exclaimed. "What's all this?"

Reggie swung round. "You!" The word came with cold fury. "Take him out, Underwood. You know what he's wanted for."

"I like that! Who do you think you are?" Bubb roared.

"Come on." Underwood gripped him and, between them, Bubb was thrust out.

Reggie stood with his back to the shut door. "Giles," he said gently, "it wasn't like that. Nothing like that. She doesn't know. Nor do you. You can be kind. Good-bye."

CHAPTER XXXIV *Evidence of a Detective*

BUBB STOOD IN THE CORRIDOR abusing Underwood when Reggie came out. "Now then, Mr. Fortune." He took a stride forward to be checked by Underwood's hand on him. "You keep your hands off me. You're assaulting your superior officer in the execution of his duty—"

"Your duty!" Reggie murmured.

"Yes, get that in your head. I hold you responsible, Mr. Fortune. You incited him. Setting discipline aside, that's a criminal offense."

Reggie gave a little sharp laugh. "I ordered him, Bubb. I am responsible. Come on, I want you."

Between them they compelled Bubb, resisting more by threats than force, onto the stairs. "What do you think you're doing? I heard that woman say it was her. You won't be able to hush that up."

Again Reggie laughed. "Hushing up is finished, Bubb. Come on."

Bubb was urged downstairs. "You get this. I'm here to question Mrs. Aston, and you're preventing me by force."

"No. That's not going to be the story. You've had days to question Mrs. Aston. You shirked it till you knew I'd come here. Then you tried to confuse the case. As ever. Not any more, Bubb." They reached the hall, and Reggie turned to Underwood. "Did you find the chemicals?"

"Yes sir, in one of the greenhouses under a vine," Underwood answered briskly.

"What do you know about that, Bubb?"

"Ah!" Bubb drew away and confronted him with a sneer. "Silly, tricky way you have of working. That fixes it on old Aston, don't it?"

"You think so? I suppose you've been hunting for the fellow who kept vitriol and cyanide handy."

"I've had it in mind; of course I have."

"Have you? Looked in all the greenhouses except Aston's, of course. Yet you didn't come here till we came. By the way, what about Elijah's mate? Does he agree with Elijah that Mr. Bubb was lurking round Goat's Hill when Tracy was shot?"

"I haven't been to him yet. I came after you."

"Well, well. Not wantin' confirmation of Elijah's evidence. Your error. Wantin' to interfere with me. Your gross error."

"Interfere with nothing. My God, that's a bit o' brass. You're doing the interfering. I ask you straight: what was it the woman owned up to, saying it was her?"

Reggie smiled. "No, Bubb, you're not helping yourself. She didn't put the chemicals in the greenhouse. She didn't shoot Tracy. Nor did she throw Mrs. Giles and me into the pit."

"Well, of course she didn't—she couldn't. But she *did* say it was her; you can't deny it. That means she knows it was her husband. Didn't I always tell you old Aston was the man? You know it. Now then. Why are you trying to keep me from putting her through it?"

"Because you have to be put through it, Bubb. Come on. We're going to take you back to Colsbury."

"The hell you are! Don't you think it!"

"Oh yes. You didn't know this house has been watched day and night. By a detective officer."

Bubb's jaw fell. "What if it has?"

"Late last night he saw a man going round by the glasshouses. It wasn't Mr. Aston. It was a man your size, your make. Same like Elijah saw. Unfortunately, he got away then. However. Come on."

"You—you—" Bubb stammered. "You dare to put it on me I brought that stuff here? It's a fake; it's a lie."

"Oh no. We don't fake, Bubb. Having no need. Come along." They closed upon him and urged him along to the door.

"What's the idea? What do you want to do?" Bubb muttered, letting himself be pushed on.

"Confront you with Mr. Aston," Reggie told him.

"He's in Colsbury, is he? You know where he is?"

"Yes. Not much we don't know now."

"All right. I'm willing. Old Aston! I want him myself. Go on. I've got my own car."

"Damn your little car," Reggie cried. "You've wasted too much time already. In with him, Underwood." The door was slammed upon Bubb; the car rushed away.

CHAPTER XXXV *Evidence of Temper*

FROM THE PORCH of the abbey church of Colsbury a man came briskly and crossed the quiet square to the gate in a garden wall.

He had a good pair of shoulders; he was otherwise indistinguishably ordinary. At the gate he stopped, looking across a lawn with a round rose-bed to an ample red-brick house.

In front of its doorstep stood another man of the like ordinary figure and clothes. The door was open. From the doorstep Aston towered over the man below, his gaunt, handsome face looking blind and dazed in the glare of the sun. Behind him, showing him out, was Cope.

The man spoke to them. "Mr. Francis Aston, I believe? And Mr. Cope? I am Sergeant Quett of the Criminal Investigation Department. I have orders to make some enquiries of you gentlemen. If you please." He pointed them back into the house.

Aston turned on Cope. "You—you knew he was coming. You arranged it?"

Cope laughed. "Not I, my friend. I had no idea the police wanted to talk to you. How did you know Mr. Aston was here, Sergeant?"

"We should be better in the house, shouldn't we?" said Sergeant Quett mildly and glanced back at the man by the gate. "You see?"

"Were you thinking of resisting the police, Aston?" Cope smiled. "I suppose not. Come along in, Sergeant."

"Thank you, sir." Sergeant Quett shepherded Aston in front of him, and Cope shut the door and led the way briskly, but Aston lagged with shuffling feet and bowed head.

Cope was waiting for them in his white room. He moved to the heavy sideboard. "Glass of sherry, Sergeant?"

"No thank you, Mr. Cope. Not on duty."

"Stern fellow. Sit down. Sherry, Aston?"

Aston did not answer. He was watching Quett with a queer woebegone stare—like a stunned martyr, sort of suffering king, said Quett afterward.

"Take a seat, sir," Quett remonstrated. "I have to ask you a few questions." He drew out a notebook. "We'll have it quite at your leisure, Mr. Aston. You have no need to hurry." He wrote a line or two and considered the result with his head on one side. "Now would you tell me first why you came here this morning?"

"I came to see Mr. Cope. He telephoned that he wanted to see me," Aston answered in a flat, lifeless voice.

Quett's pencil moved slowly, rather as if he were drawing than writing shorthand. When he was satisfied with the effect he turned mild eyes on Cope, who had given himself a glass of the rejected sherry and sat at his writing table, sipping with relish. "Would you confirm this, sir?"

"Certainly. I telephoned to Mr. Aston this morning and asked him to come and have a business talk."

Again Quett made a painstaking note. "When you say business, do you mean money matters?"

"Yes, Sergeant," Cope smiled. "I happen to be a banker."

"Just so," Quett nodded. "Am I to understand Mr. Aston banks with you?"

"If you want to know anything about Mr. Aston's affairs you must ask him."

"Quite correct, sir," Quett agreed respectfully. "Well now, Mr. Aston, is this right? Mr. Cope asked you to see him on business, and you came for that purpose, he being your banker?"

"Yes, go on," Aston muttered.

Quett labored over his notebook and then looked up—looked from Cope's shrewd, amused attention to the limp woe of Aston. "Was there any particular reason why the business between you gentlemen got urgent this morning?"

Cope shook his head. "I don't answer questions about the affairs of people who bank with me, Sergeant. You should know that's against the rules."

"There's no rule against my asking Mr. Aston," said Quett. "If you please, sir." He looked at Aston.

"I have an overdraft," Aston answered.

Once more Quett made a prolonged note. "Do I understand that your affairs are embarrassed, and Mr. Cope was pressing you?"

"Yes. Go on," Aston muttered.

"My dear fellow, you're making too much of it," said Cope kindly.

"That was what you had to say to Mr. Aston?" Quett asked.

"Well, Aston?" Cope smiled at him. "I think we could put it that we went over your position. Nothing unusual in that, Sergeant. Mr. Aston has banked with my house all his life—and his father before him."

"I see. Quite an old family connection." Quett labored with his notebook a long time and then spent some more time studying it.

"What are you doing?" Aston cried. "What are you keeping me for?"

"I'm sorry, sir. I have to consider things." Quett continued to consider them still further before he asked, "Do you tell me this talk between you was all about your financial difficulties, and nothing was said on any other matter?"

"You're tying yourself in a knot," said Cope sharply. "There are no financial difficulties. Have you finished?"

"Well no, sir." Quett was apologetic. "I couldn't report that I've got it clear, could I? You and Mr. Aston don't exactly agree in your statements." While he spoke a car came purring to a stop, and the doorbell rang. "If you just listen to my note," he went on, "you'll see what I mean." He ran his pencil slowly down the pages. "Oh yes, here it is. Mr. Aston being asked—"

Neither Aston nor Cope was listening to him. They strained to hear a conversation outside in the hall: protest from a servant that Mr. Cope was engaged, gentlemen being with him on business, and a brisk answer, "Oh yes. As arranged. This is the same business. Don't bother. We know the way, don't we, Bubb?"

The door opened to admit Underwood and Reggie with Bubb, red and uncomfortable, behind them.

Cope stood up. "Good morning, Mr. Fortune. Ah, Bubb." As he acknowledged the presence of the embarrassed Bubb through his shrewd, genial composure came a disagreeable smile. "You're in a sudden hurry, my friend. And something less than civil." The tone was threatening. "I don't care for it. You've never had any difficulty in seeing me when you asked for my help."

Bubb scowled at him, redder than ever. "I'm not asking your help, Mr. Cope. Nothing like it. I came here because you had Mr. Aston with you."

"Temper, temper," Reggie murmured. "Why so cross with each other?"

"I *do* find our superintendent's methods strange, Mr. Fortune," Cope answered.

"So I see. Yes. However. Not his methods. My methods."

"Oh, I beg his pardon," Cope said. "Have you superseded Mr. Bubb?"

"Well, well. Why should you think that?" Reggie's voice rose in plaintive surprise.

"I gather that I am indiscreet." Cope turned. "I had better leave you with him and Mr. Aston."

"No. Don't go. No." Reggie wandered across the room to lounge against the mantelpiece behind him.

"At your service," said Cope and sat down again at his writing table, half-turned toward Reggie. "What can I do for you?"

Reggie surveyed his amused attention and Aston's dumb, dazed misery with dreamy eyes. "I wonder," he murmured.

Bubb drew up a chair opposite Aston. "Now, sir," he began truculently.

"Not like that," Reggie interrupted. "Carry on, Underwood."

Underwood sat at Bubb's elbow and turned to Quett. "How far had you got, Sergeant?"

CHAPTER XXXVI *Evidence of a Likeness*

SERGEANT QUETT licked his lips and spoke as if he were reciting what he had learned by heart: "On seeing Mr. Aston being shown out of this house by Mr. Cope, I approached the house and informed them I had orders to make enquiries of them—"

"By the way, who was giving orders?" Cope interrupted.

"Superintendent Bubb wanted to join your conference," said Reggie.

"The deuce he did!" Cope gave a knowing chuckle.

"Any objection from you, Mr. Cope?" Bubb demanded.

"None in the world. I was only amused at your relations with these gentlemen from Scotland Yard."

"We do try to please," Reggie murmured.

Underwood nodded at Quett. "Go on, Sergeant."

Quett continued his recitation: "In reply to my questions, both gentlemen agreed that Mr. Aston came here because Mr. Cope telephoned to see him on business. I then asked why the business got urgent this morning, and their replies did not agree—Mr. Aston saying his affairs were embarrassed and Mr. Cope pressing him, Mr. Cope saying there were no financial difficulties. All this took some time, and I have obtained no definite answer whether they discussed any other matter."

"Ah!" Bubb exclaimed. "That's what I want to know."

"What are you thinking of, Bubb?" Cope asked, but Aston sat still and dumb, looking down at the floor.

"Go on, Sergeant," Underwood said sharply.

"Yes sir. I was still working on this contradiction between the two gentlemen—" a complacent smile passed over Quett's face—"but they were impatient. Mr. Aston asked why he was being kept, and Mr. Cope was wanting to know if I had finished, which I had not, when Mr. Fortune and you arrived."

"You'd taken such a devil of a time with your enquiries," Cope laughed.

"I suppose he had," Reggie agreed. "What is the time now, Mr. Cope?"

Cope swung round to look at the grandfather clock in the corner. "There you are. A quarter to eleven."

"Oh yes. You go by that. I remember." Reggie contemplated him with closing eyes. "Yes, Mr. Aston was with you before ten, what?"

The answer came from Quett. "Close on ten, sir."

"You've done very well, Sergeant." Reggie's praise was cordial.

"Oh I see," Cope laughed. "This talk was dragged out to keep Mr. Aston here. You're very subtle."

Aston started and showed for a moment a face of hopeless misery.

"Not subtle, no," Reggie protested. "Careful and industrious. Quite a lot of pains been taken."

"We are wasting time now." Bubb asserted himself. "Give me your attention, Mr. Aston, if you please. Would you be surprised to hear that a jar of poison gas was flung down on your daughter-in-law in Giants' Graves?"

Aston jerked up his head and stared amazement.

"Oh, you are surprised?" Bubb sneered. "How do you account for the fact that materials for to make this poison gas—hydrocyanic gas—were found in your vinery?"

Aston made an inarticulate exclamation and groaned, "It's not true; it can't be."

"It is true, Mr. Aston," said Reggie quietly. "It's not the whole truth. A man was seen near your vinery in the night, who wasn't you. Any idea who that could be?"

Aston shook his head. His mouth came open and could not shut again; the wretchedness of his face was frozen into stupefaction.

"Not in the habit of fumigating your glasshouses?" Reggie asked. "No. Lot of red spiders in the vinery. You have a greenhouse, haven't you, Bubb?"

"You know I have." Bubb was scowling at him. "I told you I never heard of this stuff."

"You did, yes," Reggie murmured. "Has Mr. Cope any glass?"

Bubb sat back breathing hard and looked sideways at Cope. "I dare say. I suppose so."

"What's the embarrassment, Bubb?" Cope laughed. "My gardener has a forcing house. I don't ask him how he manages it. This—what d'ye call it—hydrocyanic fumigation means nothing to me. I know nothing about gardening."

"Misspent life," Reggie sighed. "However. The evidence remains: somebody who wasn't Mr. Aston visited his vinery by dark and stealth. Somebody who was rather like Bubb." He gazed from Bubb to Cope. "You are like one another, you two." He turned to Bubb. "Do you remember, I took you for Mr. Cope when I first met you? You explained that you both came of village folk. People who were here on the black land and white land before the Astons and the Tracys pushed in." His eyes were dreamy. "Yes. That is fundamental."

Bubb and Cope were staring at him and from him at each other, and their full, dark faces were diversified in changing expressions of surprise, and distrust, and enmity and fear. Cope began to laugh. "Begad, am I like that?" he exclaimed with a gesture toward Bubb's gloomy horror. "I hope not. It's the first I've heard of it."

"Oh. Really?" Reggie murmured. "What do you say, Bubb?"

"There *is* a likeness, of course," Bubb said loudly. "No use his denying it."

"You flatter yourself," Cope sneered at him. "Nobody who knew me would mistake me for you, thank God. No one ever died conveniently because I wanted his job."

"Referring to the death of the late chief constable?" Reggie asked.

"I am, Mr. Fortune. You may be interested to hear that our friend Bubb has written me urgent letters on that subject. He wished me to use my influence to dispel the unkind suspicions of Lord Werne and others which delayed his appointment. I have not been able to oblige him."

"Well, well. Fancy that!" said Reggie. "Did you share those suspicions?"

Cope shrugged. "I have no more evidence than others."

"But Bubb thought you would help him. You've been hunting in couples?"

"That's not true, Mr. Fortune," Bubb roared.

"You're very noisy," said Cope. "No, Mr. Fortune, I have never had any relations with the man but in giving him some small help. Because he was in my debt he presumed to think I should push him on to a post of higher salary in which he could pay it off. I was not prepared to do that."

"I see. You had a hold on Bubb. Thanks very much. That's helpful."

"He has no hold on me to matter," Bubb broke out again. "It's a trifle what I owe him now, Mr. Fortune. Less than a hundred pound. Let's have this business out. He says I stood to gain by the poor chief's death. All right. What could I gain by killing Mr. Tracy, or his daughter or you? That's done me a lot of good, hasn't it? Now then, Mr. Cope. Just you answer me this. I have evidence that a man your size and make was seen on Goat's Hill when Mr. Tracy was shot. Where were you at that time, eh?"

Cope laughed. "Now I understand. This is why I am so devilish like you. It won't do, Bubb. You've schooled Mr. Fortune cleverly. But you can't produce a man who saw you to swear that it was me."

"Can't I?" Bubb growled. "I asked you where you were at the time?"

"In this room, my friend."

"Ah, you say you have an alibi?"

"Yes, thanks. And you?" Cope sneered.

"I'm all right," Bubb told him loudly.

"As you were with the chief constable!" Cope retorted, and Bubb called him a liar, and they stared at each other—alike in their truculent defiance.

CHAPTER XXXVII *Evidence of Another Watch*

REGGIE CONTEMPLATED THEM with cold curiosity. "You don't get anywhere," he complained. "You're wastin' time." He looked at the grandfather clock. "Is that right, Mr. Cope?"

"What?" Cope turned from Bubb to him. "The clock? Yes, absolutely. You have wasted a devil of a lot of time. Are you finished?"

"Not quite. Do you know Greek?"

"Me? Good God, no," Cope laughed. "Not a word. I came straight from school into the bank. Why?"

"I thought you didn't." Reggie droned out the verse: " 'Tis an palin agkalesait epaeidon.' Means nothing to you?"

Aston had raised his bowed head with a groan and looked piteously at Reggie. "Jargon to me," said Cope. "But there you are. Ask Aston. He is a prize classic."

"Oh yes. We know what it means, he and I," Reggie answered slowly, and Aston's face was hidden again, and he gulped and shook. "But when it came into this case it had been sent to Alison on her marriage."

A cry of pain or fear came from Aston; he turned to Reggie gasping something inarticulate.

"He *does* seem to understand you," said Cope.

"Not yet. No. It came cut out of an Aeschylus which had a translation opposite. That wasn't done by a scholar. He wouldn't need the translation to find the lines he wanted. Mr. Aston knows his Aeschylus well." Reggie gave him a grave, searching glance. "Don't you?" And again he murmured, " 'Tis an palin agkalesait epaeidon.' "

"Oh God!" Aston groaned.

"Not askin' you," said Reggie and turned to Cope. " 'Who can call it back by his charms?' That's the translation, you know."

"Call what?" Cope answered. "You say it was sent to Alison Tracy when she married young Aston."

"Yes, that is so. But not by Giles Aston's father. 'Who can call it back?' The answer is, I can. I'm going to."

Aston gave a start as if he were trying to stand up but failed and sat half-erect, gaping.

"Why do you torture the poor devil?" said Cope. "You mean Tracy sent it."

"Tracy," Reggie murmured. "You think so? What for?"

"To remind the girl there was her brother's death between her and the Astons."

"Oh. You *do* know that the verses sent her referred to a death. Though you don't know any Greek."

Cope gave an angry laugh. "I know what you've told me. Call it back by charms, you said. What the devil could that mean but something about a death?"

For the first time Reggie moved from his stand by the hearth and came to the writing table and at Cope's elbow surveyed its multifarious equipment, while Cope looked, with a frown and a sneer, from the table to his expressionless face. He reached across Cope and took up the paste pot and lifted the brush and smelled it. "Yes. Holdtight paste. Good old stuff. Distinctive smell, hasn't it, Underwood?" He gave a little twisted smile.

"You're right, sir." Underwood nodded.

"What's this hocus-pocus for?" Cope exclaimed.

Reggie turned away and wandered back to the hearth while Cope swung round to watch him.

"You don't do me justice, Mr. Cope," Reggie said plaintively. "You never have. However. Study to improve. The threat to Alison was stuck on a post-card with Holdtight paste, which nobody concerned uses except you. Small point. But crucial point."

"Damned nonsense," Cope told him contemptuously. "Thousands of shops keep the stuff. The thing could have been stuck on anywhere."

"Oh yes. That is so. I didn't say the paste was conclusive. But it was crucial. Gave us a line, didn't it, Underwood?"

"It did so." Underwood grinned.

"Are you making a charge against me?" Cope demanded.

"You are being asked to give an account of suspicious circumstances," Reggie drawled. "You deny sending to Alison a threat that her marriage would end unhappily. You say that at the time she was attacked, and I was attacked, and her father was murdered you were here. You say that you know nothing about cyanide fumigation. Do you stand by all those denials?"

"Of course I do."

"All right. Where were you from eleven till three o'clock on the day after the attack on Alison?"

"Part of the time in the bank, part here. I came here for lunch."

"A long lunch?" Reggie drawled.

"Much as usual. An hour or so."

"Oh. You didn't notice the time by your reliable clock." Reggie nodded at it.

"I've no recollection. From about one to two."

"You didn't look at your watch?"

"No doubt I did. I can't remember now. Those times are practically accurate."

"You think so?" Reggie smiled. "Time is the decisive factor." He glanced at Quett who was taking notes with an easy speed quite unlike his first labors. "Well now. As Bubb was tellin' you, we have evidence that a man like you, using a dark two-seater car, was out in the dusk wandering about the edge of Tracy's coverts when that village girl was shot at near Alison's house, when Alison was attacked, when Tracy was murdered."

"A man like me." Cope laughed. "A man like Bubb, you mean, and his car could be taken for mine by any fool or any rogue."

"That won't do," said Bubb with fierce satisfaction. "My car wasn't out that night nor any night lately, nor me neither."

"You would have an alibi—and a fool or a rogue for a witness," Cope retorted.

"Both of you claim alibis. Yes. You are alike, and your cars are alike. However."

"What the devil could I gain by shooting a village girl?" Cope demanded. "It's a crazy suggestion. What have I to gain by attacking Alison or murdering her father? The whole thing is impossible."

"You say you had no grudge against Alison, none against Tracy, no reason to contrive the death of either of 'em?"

"None in the world. What could I have?"

"Oh, hadn't you!" Bubb roared. "I suppose Tracy hadn't got troublesome? He didn't know too much about you? You hadn't made ducks and drakes of his estate, like you have with others, eh, Mr. Aston?"

"Well, well. You are opening out, Bubb," Reggie murmured. "Why keep all this till now?"

"Why indeed!" Cope laughed. "Devilish close he's been. You had him here with me the other day. Not a word of it. He was licking your boots and mine. Now you've driven him into a corner he's crazy to save his neck. He has to put his damned murders onto someone else, so he leads you to me and trumps up these lies. You—"

"I've done a lot of leading, haven't I, Mr. Fortune?" Bubb broke in with an anxious appeal.

"You won't find Mr. Aston backs your tricks," Cope said. He turned to Aston and flung at him a gesture of impatient command. "Have I ever done you any harm?"

"I haven't said that." Aston spoke feebly. "I never said so."

"There you are." Cope laughed triumph.

"Very fine. He daren't speak, that's all," Bubb retorted. "It don't let you out. You can't put it on me I had anything against Tracy's daughter. *I* never ran after her since she was a kid. She never turned *me* down. I haven't been after the Tracy land all my life."

"Filthy brute, isn't he?" Cope spoke to Reggie with a flick of his hand at Bubb. "The first you've heard of the girl's name being coupled with mine, I'll swear. Or anybody else."

Bubb broke out in spiteful laughter. "You won't get away with that; I'll find plenty."

"Will you?" Reggie asked. "Rather late, Bubb. Pity you didn't think of that before."

"Well. I never thought he was such a devil till he did these jobs," Bubb protested. "How should I? The old chief always trusted him. You know it was like that yourself."

"Oh yes. Lots of simple faith. You were sayin', Mr. Cope—you conceived yourself to have a hold on Superintendent Bubb."

"Nothing of the sort." Cope frowned. "He was in my debt in the ordinary way."

"As others are—or were. Very convenient. Yes. However. About your car. Do you say your car wasn't out when the girl was shot at, when Alison was attacked, when Tracy was murdered?"

"I do. I was here, and my car was in the garage."

"And the next day in the afternoon when I was thrown into Giants' Graves and the poison gas after me? Your car was seen out then."

"I wasn't out till four or five. Then I heard a rumor Tracy was dead and drove over to ask. No doubt I was seen."

"And last night?" Reggie drawled.

Cope had no answer ready. He shook his head. "I don't follow," he said at last. "What about last night? Nothing happened," he frowned. "I didn't take the car out."

"Oh." Reggie drew out the sound. "You hadn't noticed your house was watched? No. You wouldn't. Our fellows do that fairly well. You drove away just after midnight. You came back about one in the morning. Mr. Aston's house was also watched. And someone just like you was seen to go to the glasshouses and go away again. Any explanation?"

Cope turned on Bubb. "You used my own car that time, did you?"

"No, that's got you." Bubb gave a sputter of laughter. "It was you planted that stuff."

"I never heard till now there was such stuff—nor that it was used. But you knew. You thought you'd put it on Aston. Now you're trying to put it on me."

"Evidence not quite what we could wish, no," Reggie murmured. "About the attack on Alison and me, Mr. Cope. All my regrets. I didn't see the fellow clear. But I did hit him. Round about the short ribs. When I examined Tracy's body, I found his watch had been hit, stopped, case dented, glass cracked."

"What about it?" Cope exclaimed with a stare of blank surprise. "Good God! Do you mean to say it was Tracy you hit—Tracy! It was Tracy tried to murder her and then—then what— Then he shot himself?"

"That was indicated. Yes. However. When Tracy was dead and cold somebody tripped me up into the pit of Giants' Graves where Alison had been flung. Somebody threw a pot of poison gas down on us. It wasn't Tracy, Mr. Cope. You see that? Yes. I don't think Tracy shot at the village girl. He had a good eye still. I don't think he'd take a girl for his daughter who was somebody else. No certainty. That little effort may have been a miscarriage. But I should say it was made to suggest that Tracy was out for his daughter's blood. Thus ascribing his daughter's disappearance, when brought off, to him. Quite clever. Rather too clever. Because it attracted expert attention to the enterprise. My attention. Well, I came down without advertising my presence. And the enterprise was continued. A fellow who didn't use a gun caught Alison in the twilight and stunned her and put her in a sack. But I was present. He managed to knock me out too, though I got home on his ribs. Complication for him. He couldn't deal with us both. He dealt with her. Went off up the combe and dropped her into Giants' Graves. Was that intended? I wonder. He may have meant to drop her in the river, where he subsequently put her scarf. Clever touch that. Not quite clever enough. Didn't work with the state of the tide, and the foreshore, and the time and all." Reggie sighed. "I have been much underrated. However. He dropped her into Giants' Graves leavin' me unconscious. Then he had to get away. And Tracy was out shooting round the covert under the hill. Tracy saw him. He saw Tracy. Very awkward. They weren't loving each other. I wonder? Did Tracy ask him what the devil he was doing? Doesn't matter. He couldn't leave Tracy alive to say he'd been there. It was awkward. Tracy's habit of taking a gun out in the evening was the basis of the plan to put Alison's death down to Tracy's account. And in that the plan broke down. Ironic fate. Tracy was there to give evidence against him. Nothing to do but wipe Tracy out too. So Tracy was shot with his own gun. Quite neat. Just like suicide. Very neat. Father, desperate mad, made away with his hated daughter and himself. It might have worked. What do you think, Bubb? Yes, it might have worked. Only there was the watch, that watch I hit. The murderer knew I'd put his watch out of action. He was bothered. But still clever. He set Tracy's watch to five past nine. Then he hit it like his own was hit. Do you see now?"

"I'm damned if I do," said Cope. "Why the devil should he put the watch on?"

Over Reggie's face came a small happy smile. "I didn't say he put it on," Reggie murmured and was silent, and through the silence came the sounds of heavy, choking breath from Cope and Bubb and Aston. "You know he did, though. Thank you. Yes, he did, as you say. Your error. His error. I hit him, and he hit me soon after eight. I came to before half-past. Then I heard the shot that killed Tracy. There wasn't another shot, Cope. But Tracy's watch was stopped at five past nine. By which time his murderer could be back home. With alibi. Very ingenious. Bad luck on him I came to so soon. Do you remember, the day after the murder I asked you the time? You didn't look at your watch. I've asked you twice this morning. And still you wouldn't bring out your watch."

"There's a clock in the room." Cope glared at him. "If you want to see my watch, here it is." He pulled at the leather guard and drew out a small gold half hunter.

"You wear a lady's watch now?"

"My mother's, if you want to know."

"Didn't care to buy another at the moment? Quite natural. Where's the one you usually wear? The watch you were wearing the night Alison was attacked?"

"That's right, Mr. Fortune, that's right," Bubb exploded. "His watch is a big, old, gold repeater. Everybody knows it that knows him."

Cope slipped the little watch back into his pocket and laughed and opened a drawer of his writing table.

CHAPTER XXXVIII *Evidence of a Revolver*

THE WHITE ROOM WAS SILENT, every man watching Cope bent over his half-open drawer.

"Some people know a lot, Mr. Fortune." He spoke slowly.

"Yes. That is so. However. Doesn't matter. I know more," Reggie murmured.

Cope chuckled. "They have kept quiet about it, haven't they? You know their reasons now."

"Very well done," said Reggie. "But that sort of thing is all over."

"Is it?" Cope looked up, looked at Bubb and from Bubb to Aston's wretchedness, and smiled. "My congratulations."

"Oh yes. Finished. Were you going to produce your watch?"

Cope sat back, his hand still in the drawer.

"Well?" Reggie asked. "Where is the watch? You won't show it? You won't tell me? As you please. That 'll do. All clear."

"You're damned clever, aren't you?" Cope snarled. "You think you can put this on me? Where did it begin? Not with me, by God! Who killed young Tracy? What do you know about that?" He pointed at Aston, bent and cowering before him.

"No thanks, Cope," Reggie shook his head. "Nothing about it. We have all we want now."

"The hell you have!" Cope shouted and sprang up with a revolver in his hand, and, as Underwood and Bubb jumped at him, he fired into Aston's face and fired again.

They crashed down with him; Quett came to help. They had him beneath them on the floor, and he screamed at a grip on his elbow and let the revolver slip from his hand.

Swearing and spitting, he struggled while his arms were forced together above his head, and handcuffs snapped on the wrists.

"Have him up now," Underwood panted, and they dragged him to his feet and hustled him on.

He flung himself against them this way and that; he twisted round and looked back.

Aston had slid from the chair where he sat and lay on his side. Reggie was stooping over him.

"Go to it, you devil," Cope shouted, and his face, red and sweating and bruised, twisted in a wide grin. "You won't get him off. I have you beat."

"It's you that's beat," Bubb told him. "Out with you."

Cope was forced out, laughing loud.

The sound of his laughter died away. Reggie knelt beside Aston. He lay still, his tall form crumpled—bent at neck and back and knee as he had sat, as he had fallen. In the wrinkles of his brow between the eyes was a small hole from which blood was coming, a hole which grew wider beneath the shattered bone. His eyes had closed; the haggard face was frozen in the misery which distorted it while he lived.

Reggie stood up slowly. "Yes. My job," he said to the dead man, looking down at him with solemn eyes. "I did as I could, Aston."

He walked away to the window to the sunlight and shivered and breathed deep. ...

Bubb came back in a thudding hurry. "Mr. Fortune, is he dead?"

"Oh yes." Reggie spoke without turning. "Dead before you went."

"Poor old gentleman!" Bubb gave the dead body a look of respectful sorrow. "Too bad. Just when we'd got him cleared at last. That devil Cope! The gall of him. I lay he's been behind all the Aston-Tracy business from the start."

"You think so? Pity you didn't think so before."

"How could I? It hadn't worked out. He's been so deep; he never showed up at all. Now you can see—he's been after the Tracy estate all the time. That's the motive right through. Murder the boy, go after the girl, and then, when she turned him down and married Giles Aston, he planned to wipe her out and ruin the lot of 'em. My God, we've got him now! I'm sorry he managed to do old Aston in, though. I never thought of that, no more than you. But that's settled his own hash anyway. Shows what a nasty brute he is. I lay he got old Aston here to frighten the poor old man into thinking we were after him and drive him on to something mad. Hanging's too good for the devil."

"You may be right," Reggie murmured. "However. Try it. Good-bye."

CHAPTER XXXIX *Evidence of the Astons*

REGGIE DROVE OUT AGAIN to the house of the Astons. He had to wait long before the door was opened to him. An old and dishevelled womanservant snapped at him before he spoke. Master was out, and mistress was ill, and he couldn't see anybody.

"Tell Mr. Giles Aston Mr. Fortune has news for him." Reggie walked past her into the hall.

She toiled upstairs, and in a moment Giles came plunging down and ran at Reggie with a breathless whisper. "What is it now? What have you come for?"

"How is she?" Reggie asked.

"I don't know. The doctor talks about nervous shock. She's hardly conscious, I think. Fortune, you don't believe what she said?"

"Oh no. That never happened. Nothing like that. I told you so."

"When she says anything it's only to ask where my father is. Do you know? Has anything—anything—" Giles stammered, and his voice failed before Reggie's intent, compassionate eyes.

"My dear chap! Something has happened to him," Reggie said gently. "But there's nothing against him, never can be. Our friend Bubb has caught the fellow who murdered Tracy, fellow who tried to murder your Alison. It was Cope. Your father was with Cope when the evidence was forced out of him, and Cope got a pistol and shot. Your father was killed. There's no doubt now that Cope had tried to put everything on him—Charles Tracy's death and all."

"Cope!" Giles muttered. "Are you telling the truth?"

"Oh, my dear chap!" Reggie smiled sadly. "It's proved Cope murdered Tracy. Evidence conclusive and overwhelming. He tried to murder Alison and me and then planted his poison-gas chemicals on your father. Evidence of that also conclusive. We can't prove he murdered the chief constable. But I have no doubt he did, no doubt the chief had caught him out over that fake cameo which was planted in the landslip. Did you ever hear of that? Planted to connect your father with Charles Tracy's death. No doubt Cope planted it. Is that enough?"

"Cope!" Giles repeated. "Did he mean to shoot my father?"

"Oh yes. Yes," Reggie said. "Last effort."

"Your fellows couldn't stop him?"

"Not quick enough, no. They did their best. Desperate beast, Cope. All over in a minute."

Giles stood looking away from Reggie across the hall, shaken by a storm of emotions. "My father!" he said. "God forgive me! I thought—"

"My dear chap!" Reggie held his arm for a moment.

"Why did my mother say she did it?"

"Don't you understand now? She was afraid I meant to accuse your father. She didn't know."

"Why did my father go in to see Cope this morning?"

"Cope called him in for urgent business. Your father thought that meant money. Cope's had claws into him a long time, what?"

"Sucked his blood," Giles muttered.

"Not a nice man, Cope, no. You see now? Cope knew we were close on the truth. So he dragged your father in for another effort to make us suspect him. When that didn't work—killed him as he killed Tracy. That's Mr. Cope. Out for the land of the Astons and the Tracys and their blood. And so an end. It is the end, Giles."

Giles put a hand to his eyes. "Sorry," he gulped. After a moment he turned to Reggie. "There's my mother. She keeps asking where he is, why he doesn't come. What am I going to say? Shall I tell her?"

"She'll have to know," said Reggie. "I'll come with you."

In the great chamber of Elstow Manor the curtains were drawn, and the old tapestry on its walls showed only vague, pitted shapes of horses and people through a drab uniformity of color.

The expanse of the huge four-poster bed was in tumbled disorder. Over it stooped the old womanservant fussing with the clothes and muttering endearments.

"Don't, don't, let me be." A faint, fretful voice spoke to her. "Where's Mr. Giles? Why did he go away? Go and fetch him. Where—"

At the sound of footsteps in the room Mrs. Aston raised herself and sat up, a wraith of a woman in the dim light, and cried out, "Giles! Oh, you—you—" She saw Reggie.

"Nothing to fear from me, Mrs. Aston." Reggie came to her. "No more fear for any of you here. That's all over."

"What do you say?" she gasped. "Where's my husband?"

"There's nothing against him now, nor you, nor Giles. The police have caught the man who murdered Charles Tracy's father. It was Cope. That's proved; that's certain; and he did more than one murder. All of you are cleared."

"Cleared?" She broke out in shrill, miserable laughter. "More than one murder? Cope— What do you mean? Where is my husband?"

"The police have no doubt Cope contrived Charles Tracy's death. Cope didn't leave them any doubt. When he was caught he shot your husband. Your husband didn't live a moment. There was no chance to save him."

She gave a long, moaning cry. Then, as if she were talking to herself, she whispered, "He's dead, he's dead," and fell back on her pillow and lay in the whimpering, sobbing laughter of a woman delivered from her pains.

"Mother." Giles bent down, held her to him and kissed her.

"Oh—it's you," she said, putting her head back to look at him. "Dear." A thin hand came in a tremble to touch his face. "Giles!" The sobs died away in her laughter. "You poor dear. It's all gone now. There's nothing, nothing. Isn't that good? Yes, dear." She went on laughing softly.

"Let her rest," Reggie murmured.

Giles laid her down in the bed, and she turned her face to the shadow and was still.

CHAPTER XL *Evidence of a Tracy*

BY A WINDOW which gave a view of the military precision of General Duddon's garden Alison sat in an easy chair.

Reggie had finished telling her the story of Cope and Aston. She sat silent. She looked out at the array of the general's espalier trees. Her bosom rose and fell in deep waves. Her pale face was drawn with distress and self-reproach, and tears glistened on it.

"Do you remember?" said Reggie. "I told you there would be tomorrow. Here it is. Lots of tomorrows. Good days."

"When did you know?" She spoke in a whisper, not looking at him.

"Difficult question. There isn't an answer. What I know isn't evidence. Proof required."

"Why did it have to happen like this?"

"Not a question for me. I didn't make the world. I've done the best I could with it. Not too bad." He smiled. "Nobody helped me much. You didn't, did you?"

"Oh." She turned with a cry. "I'm sorry. I was afraid—"

"Afraid it was Giles—or his father. Yes, I understood that."

"Don't tell him," she whispered. "Don't."

"My dear girl! Oh, my dear girl," Reggie sighed. "I also understood that you love him."

A dark blush came up from her bosom. "How *could* I believe it!" she said fiercely.

"Nasty thing, fear. You've all been living in fear. That's gone. You have it beat, you two. Not a bad thing, love. For the right people. You'll do, Alison."

"Me!" She was still blushing; she laughed contempt of a worthless woman.

"Oh yes. He'll do too."

She was silent. She looked down at her breast. "Where is he?" she asked.

"I left him with his mother."

"Oh, it's terrible for her!"

"It has been, yes. Fear's gone from her too. Their name's clear."

"But she has nothing left."

"Giles," said Reggie. "And a clean name for him. I don't think his mother's going to be unhappy. She also loves him."

He sat, legs up, on one of the ruthless seats which were all the means of idleness provided by the general's garden. He was smoking with his eyes shut when he heard the fuss of a neurotic car. As it stopped in a scream he reached it and met Giles.

"Yes. You have been asked for," he smiled.

"I came over as soon as I could. Mother's asleep now, quite quiet and peaceful. How's Alison?"

"I wouldn't say peaceful," Reggie murmured. "Come and see."

Giles trod on his heels upstairs.

Reggie knocked at the door of Alison's room. An eager cry answered. Giles rushed in, and Alison came running from the window—bare arms, white out of the flow of her wrapper, open for him, eyes aglow, giving, asking. They met and clung together.

"Yes. That's all right," Reggie murmured and shut the door upon them.

CHAPTER XLI *Judgment*

IT IS among Reggie's most painful memories of the case that General Duddon's cook disappointed rational expectation. At other tables than his own the general had revealed a perverse ignorance of the possibilities of eating. The man did not even want to know. But he had one virtue as an eater which atoned for all his deadly sins of omission and commission. There is hope of salvation for any creature who has a true and wise love of sweets. This the general revealed even in the discouraging conditions of clubs, and when he dined at Reggie's house it expanded beautifully. But for that claim to fellowship he would never have secured Mr. Fortune's attention to the bones of his giant and these murders in Durshire. Such are the forces which direct the course of justice and control the life and happiness of man.

Reggie was prepared for dull, plain meat in the general's house, but he maintains that the coldest rational calculation justified the hope of some comfortable sweets. Whether from servility to his rigorous cook or a horrid pride in abstinence from what he enjoyed, the general provided never a sweet which rose above the level of stodgy nutriment.

There is ground for the opinion that the most resplendent example of Reggie's success with elderly women is the ultimate softening of the heart of the general's cook. He records with pride her telling the general Mr. Fortune did look that pulled down, her asking whether there was anything he would like for dinner. The consummation came in a strange, nameless confection which was something between an omelette and a pudding, which had in it apricot jam and cream, studded with bits of crystallized fruit and ginger, perfumed with port.

Though it was not subtle it was very earnest, and Reggie worked upon it earnestly, and that dinner lasted longer than any he ever ate in General Duddon's house.

After it his routine refusal of port was a trifle emphatic, but he needed sherry. He was still drinking when Inspector Underwood arrived.

The general sprang up with a chatter of hospitable offers. "No, thank you, sir, nothing for me," said Underwood gloomily. "Sorry to disturb you. I had to come out for a talk with Mr. Fortune."

"By all means—leave you to it. Have a glass of wine, or the whiskey's there—" The general pattered out.

"Oh, my Underwood!" Reggie reproached him. "Why this face of woe? What's worrying you?"

"I'd like to know if you're satisfied, Mr. Fortune." Underwood took the general's chair and leaned across the table with a solemn, searching gaze.

"My dear chap! Absolutely. Replete. All according to plan. Perfect case!"

"You said plan." Underwood spoke in a tone of horror. "Do you mean to say you thought it would go like it did? You didn't expect Cope to shoot him?"

"Oh. That." Reggie's eyelids drooped. "Who could expect that? Not part of the case. Our job to prove who did the Tracy murder. And we did. Any doubt about it?"

"No, of course I haven't. There can't be. We've found Cope's watch locked up in his private safe. It was dented. It was stopped two minutes past eight."

"Stout fellow. I thought you'd get it. Cope wouldn't throw property away. That kind of man. Who found it? You or the blameless Bubb?"

"We did the search together, not to take chances. I let him find it, having seen it was there."

"Quite good, yes. That would please Bubb."

"He's as pleased as a cat with two tails," said Underwood with contempt. "He'll believe he made the whole case, tomorrow."

"He will, yes. He does already. He explained to me how it all happened. A kind heart, our Bubb. Have you told Mr. Lomas?"

"I reported to headquarters," Underwood answered slowly. "Just how it worked out. A message was passed to me from Mr. Lomas—'Good work' and to tell you, sir, he was pleased to find you really helping the police for once."

"Another grateful soul," Reggie murmured. "However. Everybody's happy." He offered his cigar case to Underwood who refused. "Oh, except you." He lit a cigar. "What is your trouble?"

"I think you know, sir." Underwood lowered his voice. "We ought to have saved the old gentleman. We never ought to have let that devil murder him too."

Reggie blew smoke rings. "Sorry," he said. "Not your blame, Underwood. No chance to save him."

"You said according to plan," Underwood repeated. "I knew you were going to work up Cope till you caught him. Did you think he'd get mad and take to shooting?"

Reggie went on blowing smoke rings, and between them he said slowly, "I thought he'd give himself away. And he did. You remember, two Tracys have been murdered—the son as well as the father. And old Aston was living with the guilt of the boy's death on him. No suspicion of him or his people any more."

"I know. That's what Bubb says. That's all right. Cope killed the boy, too, of course. Cope killed Mr. Aston for spite that he was cleared. Everybody can see that. But it don't let us out. We ought to have saved the old man."

"Sorry, Underwood. You're a good chap. I was in charge. Not you. My responsibility. I'll carry it."

Underwood looked at him with something of fear.

"Oh no. No," Reggie smiled. "Only human, Underwood. Same like you. I can only work on the stuff that's handed me. I don't make the stuff."

Behold him again on a mellow afternoon of autumn. A few people still lingered, gaping and gossiping, about the mean classic portico of the assize court of Colsbury—remnants of the crowd which had come to hear that Cope was really sentenced to death according to their desire. By one of the minor ironies of fate the court is in the same style of architecture as Coke's bank.

Reggie came out to the steps with a man who had, above his thin frame, a rubicund face in the likeness of a kindly and intelligent pig. The gossipers told the gapers that was the great lawyer from London, what was sent down to make sure Cope was hanged—and he done it proper cunning. Cope hadn't never no chance with him. Their rural experience discussed shrewdly what breed and condition of hog he most resembled.

Unconscious of these tributes, the Solicitor General, Sir Samuel Hale, remarked to Reggie that he wanted some air after that frowst. "You were going to show me this happy land, weren't you?" His little eyes twinkled, but his voice was in no way pig-like—a deep, husky voice charged with assurance that he was a man and a brother.

"Oh yes. If you've time. Quite worth a run round."

"I believe you." The solicitor general chuckled. "Don't run too fast. I have nerves, in the plural; yours is singular, Fortune."

"Me?" Reggie was pained. "My dear chap! Safety first with me, always."

"As in this case," said the solicitor general.

"Oh yes. Maximum of safety in the conditions." Reggie led the way to his car, and they drove off in a slow, serpentine course through the wayward and halting traffic. "Do you mind my humble congratulations, Hale? Neat work."

"You handed me the case on a plate," said Hale. "I only passed it on."

"I wouldn't say that, no," Reggie remonstrated. "Style is all."

"Why the butter?" Hale cocked an eyebrow at him.

"It isn't butter. One workman's appreciation of another. 'And each for the joy of the working.' This job wanted to be done."

"Accepted. I am free to say I was pleased to assist."

"Yes. Cope makes one feel like that, doesn't he? Not a nice man."

" 'A clever chiel—nane the waur of a hanging,' " Hale quoted. "I agree.

He does rouse one's best ferocity. I never had more satisfaction in a capital sentence."

"Not often. No." Reggie let the car out on the open road.

"He took it hard," said Hale. "I liked that. It is gratifying to hear a condemned man curse the court when the evidence is beyond challenge. He strengthens confidence in the rectitude of justice."

"A felt want?" Reggie asked.

"Sometimes." Hale's eyes twinkled. "Why did you praise my style, Fortune?"

"Clarity," Reggie murmured, "simplicity, economy of means, not a stroke too much."

"So glad you think so. You're a judge of tact." Hale gave him a keen, satiric glance.

Reggie slowed down and changed the subject. "Look at this. This is the first cause. Peaceful, fat and friendly." He pointed to the expanse of flat fields on either side the road. Their furrows, fresh from the plow, glistened with a dark, oily sheen in the soft sunlight. "The black land, you see. Old alluvial. Primeval marsh and forest. Rich stuff, all down the simple ages. Gold mine. The holy love of gold—there's the immemorial motive. This was Tracy's land till Cope shot him. In the old time before, it belonged to fellows just like our Cope—short, solid, dark people. Lots of 'em about still. You'll see 'em in all the villages. Strong stock. But they don't own it any more. Only work on it. Big blond beggars—Saxon or Celt or whatever they are— like the Astons came along and took it from them, pushed 'em off to the white land up there." He pointed to the hills, to the glimmer of a chalk pit. " 'Black land, white land, always at strife.' The old general told me that was a proverb in the county when I came here first to look at his giant's bones. Said it was the eternal truth of the place. I didn't know he was giving me the clue to everything. My error. I have no imagination, Hale. Well. The Tracys came along. Out of Normandy, I should say. Red French folk. Lots of drive. Lots of grip. Drove the Astons out and grabbed more as the centuries evolved and held what they grabbed. Till the family of Cope rose out of the earth again, and Cope started to get his ancestral own back from Aston and Tracy, using their old family feud to smash 'em both. There you are. First cause, geological. The way the earth's made. Working out of the case—by an inheritance of greed and hate."

"Thank you for the exposition," said Hale. "Quite scientific, Fortune, and profoundly immoral. I find it very comforting. They are all helpless victims of the past. An inevitable curse was on them to suffer and kill and die violently. Your friend Cope murdered because it was his fate to murder. He could not choose; he was irresponsible. And so we have a clear right to hang him. That is our modest fate. We also bear no responsibility. I quite understand your feeling that you had a free hand."

"My dear chap!" Reggie was hurt. "Oh, my dear chap! Not me, no. Far otherwise. I haven't been free. Never less. I was called in to deal with the long result of time. No responsibility for the mess. But ordered to be responsible for clearin' it up into some decent order. Exactin' master, providence. Expects a lot for the money. However. In a way it's a compliment."

"What humility!" said Hale. "I thought you were providence. But we seem to dally. The facts are more significant than the philosophy." His tone was sarcastic and sharpened as he asked, "Aren't you going to show me where the boy Tracy was killed?"

"If you like, yes," Reggie murmured and let the car out again. "That 'll take you on to the white land. You see?" They rushed up the long hill of the chalk ridge.

Hale looked across the treeless turf to the gracious shape of Elstow Manor. "Omitting the geology, what's that place?" he asked.

"Can't omit the geology. It's the dominant factor—from Cope's primeval ancestors to Alison and me down in the flint mines at Giants' Graves. The house is Aston's. Lovely, isn't it? Poor beggar!"

"Your sympathy is affecting," said Hale as Reggie stopped the car. "Ah, I see the point of the geology. The site which provided facilities for the boy's murder is quite close to the Aston home."

He spoke with mordant precision. He was answered casually: "Oh yes." Reggie got out. "No strain on the legal legs. Only just across here." He strolled on over the rough turf and again lectured. "Observe the sea fretting in yellow foam under the gap. That tumble of stuff is the landslip which brought the bones out. Notice how the cliffs split all along the edge. Gravel underneath bein' perpetually washed out. The boy went down into a crack like one of these. And that was that. Poor child!"

"A tear for him too?" Hale asked. "Your impartiality is exquisite. Who put the poor child underground?"

Reggie turned to face him with a look of plaintive surprise. "My dear chap! No evidence. You know that. I admired the way you kept the boy's death out of your case against Cope."

"I'm sure you did. I quite understood your praise of my style, Fortune. I was not flattered. You presented me with proof Cope murdered two men. I had to act upon that and exclude any other issue. Don't assume that I am satisfied. Who murdered the boy?"

"First time you've asked me," Reggie murmured. "Very discreet. You didn't want to know. Quite right. Might have embarrassed you."

"I could have no embarrassment in obtaining Cope's conviction," said Hale sharply. "There is no doubt that he murdered the father. Do you dare to suggest that he murdered the son?"

"Oh no. No. If you want my opinion I have no doubt old Aston killed the boy. But there never could be proof."

"Unless Aston had confessed," said Hale. "It is probable he might have done if you hadn't let Cope shoot him."

"My dear Hale!" Reggie was shocked. "You mustn't say things like that. Most unprofessional. Cope wasn't let. Ask our Bubb."

Hale gave him a bleak smile. "I should have said, if you hadn't driven Cope mad."

"No, you shouldn't. Quite inaccurate. Cope was mad because he'd been caught and knew he couldn't escape."

"Because he knew you meant to hang him, and Aston wouldn't be hanged," Hale corrected.

"If you like," said Reggie. "Doesn't matter."

"So you drove him on to kill Aston. That was calculated, Fortune."

"You think so? What the solicitor general says isn't evidence."

"The facts are clear. You arranged for Aston's murder in order that the truth of the boy's death should never be known."

Over Reggie's face came a slow, benign smile. "Clarity, simplicity, economy of means." He purred again his former praise. "But a lawyer. Evadin' the real issue. No doubt Aston killed the boy. He's paid. Publishin' the truth of that death would only keep the old misery alive to torture the innocent. The problem was to make an end of it all and save 'em. They've been saved, Hale. Any objection?"

"You're without a conscience, Fortune," Hale answered.

"Oh, my dear chap!" Reggie laughed gently. "If I hadn't a conscience nobody would have done anything about the boy when the cliff gave up its dead. The bits of him would have been shelved like the bits of extinct elephant. Inconvenient force, conscience. You don't feel that. However. I also have a mind." He walked back to the car, and Hale followed slowly and got in without a word. Reggie drove straight on along the chalk ridge above the sea.

Hale looked at it and protested. "Where are you taking me? This isn't the way we came."

"You have noticed it!" Reggie murmured mild surprise. "No, we're not going the same way. Not any more." He crooned the Greek verse: "Tis an palin agkalesait epaeidon."

"What?" Hale asked sharply. "What's the jingle?"

"Don't you recognize? I thought you had a classical education. Our Cope's message to Alison on her marriage. 'Blood of death that once has fallen dark before a man's feet, who can call it back by his charms?' Grim old question. Your answer's the old answer. Blood for blood. Death for death. Well, you have it. Not adequate answer. Only punishment, only vengeance. There's another. Save the victims. Heal their wounds. Give 'em peace. My answer. I've done it."

Hale sat silent while the car turned away from the sea, down from the high, bare, white land to the shining, winding stream of the river and the black land in the valley.

Reggie slowed and swung round into the valley road. He checked again as they came to the village, touched Hale's arm and pointed to the green where children were playing. "Look. There's Aston's widow."

She was alone; she was not near the children. She paced to and fro, bent and stooping often to pick something from the grass. As they passed they saw a smile on the pale, fragile face; her lips moved in talk; she was making a daisy chain.

"Like that," said Reggie. "She goes there every day to see the children. To think of children. Not so bad."

When they had left the village behind he held the car still to the same slow pace. Hale looked a silent question.

"One moment," he murmured. "Oh yes. Here they are." Giles and Alison came out of the gate of their white house. "Going to fetch her home. They have to. At present." The two came arm in arm and very close. "There you are." He set the car going again as they passed, waving to him, and he took off his hat. "That's the future. Judgment for me, Hale."

"Your case goes to the last assize," said the solicitor general. His little eyes twinkled. "I shan't appear against you."

THE END

About the Rue Morgue Press

"Rue Morgue Press is the old-mystery lover's best friend, reprinting high quality books from the 1930s and '40s."
—*Ellery Queen's Mystery Magazine*

Since 1997, the Rue Morgue Press has reprinted scores of traditional mysteries, the kind of books that were the hallmark of the Golden Age of detective fiction. Authors reprinted or to be reprinted by the Rue Morgue include Catherine Aird, Delano Ames, H.C. Bailey, Morris Bishop, Nicholas Blake, Dorothy Bowers, Pamela Branch, Joanna Cannan, John Dickson Carr, Glyn Carr, Torrey Chanslor, Clyde B. Clason, Joan Coggin, Manning Coles, Lucy Cores, Frances Crane, Norbert Davis, Elizabeth Dean, Carter Dickson, Michael Gilbert, Constance & Gwenyth Little, Marlys Millhiser, Gladys Mitchell, James Norman, Stuart Palmer, Craig Rice, Kelley Roos, Charlotte Murray Russell, Maureen Sarsfield, Margaret Scherf, Juanita Sheridan and Colin Watson..

To suggest titles or to receive a catalog of Rue Morgue Press books write 87 Lone Tree Lane, Lyons, Colorado 80540, telephone 800-699-6214, or check out our website, www.ruemorguepress.com, which lists complete descriptions of all of our titles, along with lengthy biographies of our writers.